Cooking Up Trouble

Lisa R. Schoolcraft

i

Lisa R. Schoolcraft

Cooking Up Trouble

Lisa R. Schoolcraft

Printed in the United States of America

First Printing, 2020

ISBN-13: 978-1-7339709-1-4

Publisher: Schoolcraft Ink LLC

Visit the author's website at www.schoolcraftink.com

Dedication

To my family and friends, for always believing in me.

Lisa R. Schoolcraft

Table of Contents

Chapter 1

Ravyn Shaw leaned back in her economy seat and tried to relax, trying to flatten her neck pillow to make it more comfortable. It was a long flight to Rome and she was hoping she'd catch a little shut-eye before she landed at Leonardo da Vinci International Airport.

The cabin lights had already been dimmed. Ravyn had enjoyed her evening meal: Southwest Sirloin Steak with tomato risotto. It was as close to Italian food as she was going to get on an Air France flight to Rome, but it helped to put her in the mood for the cooking school she was about to attend.

Ravyn was the managing editor for *Cleopatra* magazine in Atlanta, Georgia. The cooking school, or rather the destination vacation/cooking school, was the featured cover story for the upcoming March issue. She could have assigned the story out to a freelancer, but Ravyn decided she deserved a working vacation and opted to write the story and take the accompanying photos herself.

Gavin Owens, the magazine's photographer, had given her a crash course in F-Stops and lighting before giving her his second-best camera to use on the assignment. He also gave her the ramifications of what would happen to her if she lost the camera.

"This is the second camera I ever bought and it still works great. Don't lose it!" Gavin admonished her. Ravyn almost wanted to give the camera back and just wing it with her iPhone camera, but Gavin assured her the Nikon he was handing her would work much better for the food photos she was going to have to take for the cover and inside pages.

Chase Riley, the magazine's art director, also gave her tips on what photographs he wanted her to take — lots of food shots, including some up close.

"Just remember, take lots of photos, like you are an Instagram junkie. I can usually find something I can work with, even if they aren't so good, but if you don't take that many, I'll be stuck," Chase warned her. "And be sure to get some photos of Rome, even if they are kind of touristy photos. Maybe I can do a collage page of the city."

"I promise I'll take lots of photos," she said, suddenly wishing Gavin was going with her.

Gavin would have liked to have gone on the assignment, but with a new baby at home, that prevented long-term travel at the moment. Quite frankly, Ravyn was happy she was traveling solo. It would give her a chance to immerse herself in Rome and go where she wanted to go without having to check in with a traveling companion.

Ravyn closed her eyes again, trying to get comfortable, or as comfortable as one can get trying to sleep sitting up. Then she reached into her backpack and pulled out her sleep mask, hoping that might help. She envied the folks in first and business class, with the nearly flat seats.

Even though this was a work trip, she couldn't justify a first-class or business-class ticket. She was just happy the magazine was paying for the flight, hotel and cooking school. It was the first real vacation she'd had in years, even if she would have to take food photos and write about her experience. That was a fair trade for essentially an all-expense-paid trip to Italy.

Cooking Up Trouble

Ravyn had only been in her new job for a few months, so she wasn't quite sure her pitch about destination cooking school vacations would fly with the publisher and the higher-ups at the magazine, but they had all signed off on it.

Ravyn researched various cooking schools and schedules, settling on Dolores Reed's Italian Kitchen program in Rome in early November. In the school, she'd meet with other like-minded travelers and interview them about why they attend cooking schools. She'd get recipes of the dishes they were to prepare, take photos and have a nice cover story.

If Ravyn were being honest, the trip was also a way to soothe her broken heart.

She'd recently ended a relationship with the CEO of an Atlanta startup that had blossomed last year when she interviewed him for a profile story. That was back in her freelance days. She'd begun working for Marc Linder on some marketing materials and their relationship had heated up, only to come to a crashing end earlier this year when he accused her of being careless and inputting incorrect figures in a fourth-quarter report to investors.

Turns out, Marc's ex-girlfriend had hacked into his laptop and changed the numbers, hoping to break up Ravyn and Marc. It had worked. Well, sort of.

Marc eventually figured out what had happened, and Ravyn and Marc had tried to rekindle their relationship. It worked for a while, then fizzled out. Too much damage had been done leading up to their breakup.

Now Ravyn was single again. "Hmm," she thought as she drifted off to sleep. "Maybe there will be an Italian man on the menu this week."

Ravyn awoke when the cabin lights came up for the breakfast service and the gentleman seated next to her needed to get out to use the restroom. While she was grateful for the aisle seat so she could stretch out her legs, she knew she might have to get up a few times to let her seatmates out. Actually, it hadn't been so bad. She'd slept for a few hours of the flight uninterrupted.

Ravyn let her seatmate out and stood in the aisle for a moment, attempting to stretch, but felt a crick in her neck from sleeping awkwardly on her travel pillow. She also realized she'd need the restroom as well, and could see a queue of people in the back of the plane. "Well, no time like the present," Ravyn thought as she made her way down the aisle.

Returning to her seat just as breakfast was served, Ravyn watched the flight monitor in front of her with interest. She was going to be cutting it close on her connection in Charles de Gaulle Airport in Paris. She had hoped for a direct flight into Rome, but those were too expensive for the budget she was given for the trip, so a connecting flight to Paris was required on this Air France flight. She'd never been to this airport and wasn't sure what to expect.

Ravyn hadn't traveled much internationally. Oh, she'd done the girls' trip to Cancun shortly after college and a trip to London for a friend's destination wedding back when she was working at the daily newspaper in Atlanta. Before the recession. Before the layoff. Before the freelance struggle.

Ravyn sighed deeply. She hoped that was behind her now that she was the managing editor of the lifestyle magazine *Cleopatra* and could shore up her very thin savings. Then she could take more trips like this one. She was excited to get a new stamp in her recently renewed passport. "A blank passport is a sad tale," she thought to herself.

The flight landed in rain and fog. Upon deplaning, Ravyn quickly realized how confusing Charles de Gaulle Airport was laid out. Years of traveling through Atlanta's Hartsfield airport meant she wasn't intimidated by big, bustling airports. She sprinted down de Gaulle's terminal hallways toward what she hoped was her connecting flight's gate. She arrived with just minutes to spare.

Settled back in for her shorter flight to Rome, Ravyn breathed just a bit easier. "Won't be long now," she thought, "and the great adventure begins."

If Ravyn thought Charles de Gaulle was bustling, Rome's Leonardo da Vinci airport was twice that. She loved listening to the babble of different languages as she made her way to the train station. She knew she could take the train into the heart of Rome and take a taxi from there to her hotel, which was not too far from the Colosseum. On the train, she reached in and opened her passport, showing the Italian stamp and date, and smiled.

Ravyn queued up for the taxi stand outside Termini Station under a bright morning sky. She was quickly hustled into a cab. Her driver, an older man, pulled out from the curb and put New York City taxi drivers to shame. At one point, Ravyn had to close her eyes. The man was driving like a maniac!

"You are here for vacation?" the driver asked, turning to look at Ravyn, instead of the traffic ahead of him.

"Yes, yes, a cooking school," she replied.

"Ah, cooking. My mother is the best cook. You should take lessons from her," the driver replied, still not looking at the road.

Cars, trucks and Vespa scooters whizzed by, weaving in and out of travel lanes. Ravyn felt faint. "I'm going to be killed before I even start my vacation!" she thought.

Suddenly her driver slammed on the brakes and began shouting in angry Italian, fist-waving out the window. Another driver was shouting back. The sound of fenders being bent could be heard behind her. Horns blared as traffic was at a standstill. Then, almost as suddenly, horns stopped, the shouting stopped, and traffic began moving again.

"Is it always like this?" Ravyn asked tentatively, trying not to show how scared she was.

"Oh yes, this is the busy time of morning. And these people don't know how to drive. Don't worry, *signora*. I do," the driver responded, seriously.

Ravyn got out of the taxi on wobbly legs and stood before the Il Giardino hotel. Her driver had placed her luggage on the sidewalk and sped off.

Ravyn looked at the front door, which was locked. Did she have the right address? She could see the sign above her head. An immaculately dressed elderly man walking down the sidewalk looked at her, understanding her distress.

"*Buon giorno, signora.* You have to ring the bell," he said pleasantly and pushed the call button on the side of the door. There, in small letters were the words "IL GIARDINO" next to a small call button.

"Oh, thank you. *Grazie*, I mean."

He smiled at her. "*Prego. Benvenuti a Roma!* Welcome to Rome!"

Ravyn blushed a little, knowing she looked very much like a tourist.

"*Pronto*," the voice sounded from the call button.

"Yes, I'm Ravyn Shaw, staying at the hotel."

A loud buzz sounded as the door unlocked. The elderly gentleman held the door for her as she pulled her luggage through and saw the sign for the hotel, up a steep flight of stairs. "So much for Americans with Disabilities Act requirements," Ravyn thought.

"Please, allow me," the gentleman said, as he took her bag and began up the stairs.

"Oh, no. I couldn't…" Ravyn trailed off as the gentleman began climbing. For an older man, he sure was spry. Ravyn followed up the steps to the small lobby, where the man set her bag down, tipped his hat and began back down toward the door.

"Thank you! *Grazie!*" Ravyn called after the stranger as he disappeared down the stairs.

"*Buon giorno, signora*," said the well-dressed woman behind the hotel lobby's counter. "How may I help you?"

"Ravyn Shaw. Checking in."

"Yes, Mrs. Shaw. You are staying with us for seven nights, I see."

"Yes. And it's Miss. Miss Shaw."

"Very good, Miss Shaw. I have you in room No. 4, just down the hall and to your left," the desk clerk said, pointing down the corridor before handing Ravyn the largest key she had ever seen. She took the key, feeling its heft in her hand.

Ravyn had chosen Il Giardino because it was not far from the cooking school, which had recommended some hotels near the Pantheon. But this hotel better suited the budget Ravyn was given. The hotel was small, didn't have all the luxuries of more modern, up-to-date ones. The giant key in her hand was proof of that. She was used to opening hotel doors with a keycard.

But Il Giardino was clean and close to the cooking school. Ravyn smiled thinking she would certainly be getting her exercise with that flight of stairs every day.

"Continental breakfast is down the hall to the right," the desk clerk said, pointing in the same direction as Ravyn's room. "If you hurry you can just make it. It closes at 10."

"I'm fine, thank you," Ravyn said. "*Grazie.*"

Ravyn rolled her bag down the narrow hall and found her room. She opened the door to a small L-shaped room with a small double bed, a small nightstand and even smaller bathroom with just a shower stall.

At first, Ravyn frowned, thinking that she had chosen poorly with her hotel. Then she saw the small balcony and opened the doors to a tiny, plant-filled space that overlooked the street. To the left, she could see a church. To the right, she could see how the road rose up a hill to shops and buildings beyond. In an instant, Ravyn knew she had chosen well. This would be her little slice of Italian heaven for the next week.

Ravyn left the balcony doors open as she began to unpack her suitcase. The November air was cool, but not cold. She'd packed sweaters and a leather jacket for the trip and hoped she would be warm enough. She could hear street noises below, even a smattering of Italian conversation that drifted up.

She'd listened to an Italian language app in the weeks leading up to the trip, trying to familiarize herself with food names, basic directions, numbers, and greetings. She was by no means fluent, but she hoped she wouldn't come off as a rude American tourist. "But first, a power nap," she thought, and laid down on the small bed and fell fast asleep.

An hour and a half later, Ravyn awoke to the sounds of traffic noise and conversation in the hallway of the hotel. "This is going to be a bit noisier than I expected," she thought. She closed the balcony doors, washed her face, looked in the mirror and smiled. "Time to check out the neighborhood," Ravyn thought and set out onto the streets of Rome.

Ravyn turned to the left as she exited the hotel, a small map in her hand. The front desk attendant had marked out for her where the cooking class was to be held. It was several streets over, somewhere beyond Palazzo Venezia and the Vittorio Emanuele Monument, or what the Italians called "the wedding cake," the large white marble building that did look like tiers of a huge cake.

The clerk had also marked out a few places of interest not far from the hotel and had called out *"Buona fortuna!"* as Ravyn descended the lobby stairs. Ravyn hoped she would not need much luck finding her way around the city.

Ravyn found a steep flight of stairs leading down to a lower street level. The street where her hotel stood was clearly built into a hill. A turn to the right and Ravyn came out near Trajan's Forum. She looked up at the tall marble Trajan's Column, with the incongruous St. Peter statue at the top. She checked her map again and turned right toward Piazza Venezia, not quite to Vittorio Emanuele Monument, where a street festival was well underway.

Ravyn stopped for a moment to take it all in. Food, music, and people were all around. After a short while, she continued down the sidewalk until she realized she had to cross the busy street. But there were no streetlights, just a marked crosswalk. Ravyn stood for a moment, wondering what to do as vehicles and Vespas sped past.

Ravyn noticed Romans simply walked out into the crosswalk without a backward glance. Screwing up her courage, she marched out into the street, grateful there were a few people around her doing the same thing. "If I get run over, I won't be the only one," she thought. She held her breath almost all the way across the street.

To her surprise, the cars, trucks, motorcycles and Vespas just whizzed around her. She got to the other side with a sigh of relief and continued toward Via del Plebiscito and found the non-descript door of the cooking school. Once again it would require ringing a nearly hidden bell along the door panel. She was glad she already knew to look for that thanks to the earlier hotel experience.

Ravyn looked at the shops along the street by the cooking school. A leather shop with some lovely handbags hanging in the window, a jewelry shop with all kinds of expensive-looking earrings, necklaces, rings and bracelets, and a clothing boutique were nearby. She stood and looked at the leather handbags in the window longingly. She hoped they weren't too expensive. She might be able to buy one as a keepsake of her trip.

Ravyn then doubled back toward Trajan's Forum, sure she could find the cooking school tonight for the introductory meeting.

At Trajan's Forum, she looked east and could see the Colosseum in the distance. Not far, just a short walk. And Rome, she had been assured, was all about walking. She was glad more than one friend had warned her to bring comfortable walking shoes. She wandered down Via del Fori Imperiali toward the Colosseum, window shopping and stopping for a first taste of gelato. The selection in the gelateria was overwhelming.

She was used to gelato from Paolo's Gelato Italiano in Atlanta's Virginia-Highland neighborhood, but in Rome there were dozens of flavors to choose from. Rows and rows of gelato were behind the glass counter, some colorful, some shades of cream.

The flavors were listed in Italian but had pictures of fruit, nuts, chocolate or flowers to help guide her to a selection. She opted for *pesca*, peach, since she was just arrived from Georgia, the Peach State. Ravyn was not disappointed as the first bite landed on her tongue. She knew she would be back in the shop many times this week to try other flavors.

Ravyn spent the rest of the afternoon wandering the streets near her hotel, doing more window shopping and getting a feel for the area. She was supposed to meet Dolores Reed and the other cooking school attendees that evening for an introductory meal, and she'd begin working in earnest, letting her fellow classmates know she was writing a feature story for *Cleopatra* magazine and getting the release forms signed.

Dolores Reed had already let all five of the others know of the story and had gotten preliminary confirmation that they agreed to be part of the article, but she'd formalize everything tonight.

Ravyn looked at her iPhone for the time. It was almost 5 p.m. The festival was winding down as she passed by. Tents, tables, and musical instruments were being packed up. She decided to head back to the hotel to freshen up. She had plenty of time before she needed to arrive back at Dolores Reed's apartment and cooking school.

Ravyn turned toward the steep steps leading up to the street where her hotel was located when she was approached by a young man with short curly hair and a small mustache.

"*Ciao, bella,*" he said. "I'm Massimo, what is your name?"

Ravyn was taken aback. Was he speaking to her? "Me?" she asked, looking behind her to see if he was talking to someone else.

"Yes, *bella*. What is your name?"

"I'm Ravyn," she answered, still a little perplexed. Ravyn had heard Italian men could be very forward, but she wasn't quite prepared for it.

"Raven? Like the bird?" He made a little gesture with his hands, imitating a bird flying.

"Yes."

"You have such beautiful eyes, Ravyn. Prettier than a bird," Massimo said, reaching over and taking Ravyn's left hand. Ravyn pulled back, unsure what he was after. Was this an elaborate purse snatching? She clutched her shoulder bag tightly on her right shoulder and pulled her hand away.

"Thank you, Massimo, was it?"

"Yes. You are staying here?"

"Not far."

"Then I will take you to your home."

"No. No thank you. No *grazie*." Ravyn was now feeling a little panicked. She was feeling vulnerable, alone near the deserted steps with a man of whom she was unsure. "I'm on my way to meet my boyfriend," Ravyn lied.

"Your boyfriend? Is he as handsome as me?" Massimo stuck his thumb to his chest.

Ravyn smiled. "You could be twins."

Massimo looked disappointed. "*Che peccato!*" He reached over again, took Ravyn's hand and kissed it, before turning on his heel and walking away.

Ravyn rang the bell at Dolores's business at 7 p.m., as her instructions suggested. She heard a buzz as the door unlocked and pushed on the heavy wooden door, stepping into a dark foyer.

"Up here!" an older woman with a slight British accent called from the top of a flight of stairs.

"I'm Ravyn Shaw. Are you Dolores Reed?"

"Yes, please come up. Some of the others have arrived. We're waiting on two more."

Ravyn climbed the stairs, feeling her legs and calves beginning to burn. Climbing all the stairs in Rome would be better than any stair climbing machine at the gym. She could see now why all the Italian women in business suits she'd seen today on her wanderings looked so trim.

Dolores Reed had a fleshy, round face with bright hazel eyes and an easy smile. The woman, with soft silvery blonde curls, led Ravyn into her apartment and then into a dining room with a long wooden table that appeared to be able to seat 12. It was set tonight for seven.

"Welcome, welcome. Please introduce yourself," Dolores said to Ravyn.

Ravyn looked around the room at a young blonde woman and an older couple. "Hi. I'm Ravyn Shaw. I'm the magazine editor who is doing a feature story on destination cooking schools. I think you got an email that I will be writing about you and the class this week for my magazine back in America."

"Yes, sounds exciting," said the young woman with short blonde hair and a distinctive Australian accent. "I'm Amy. Amy Foster," she said. "I'm from Australia, as if you couldn't guess. I'm backpacking my way across Europe before I start my new job in London next month."

"Hi, Amy," Ravyn said, shaking the young woman's hand. "Your travels sound exciting. I can't wait to hear more."

"We're Carl and Clare Richards, from Chicago," the man of the couple said, raising a hand in greeting. "We're retired and do this sort of thing for our vacations."

"Wonderful!" Ravyn said. "You'll all be excellent for the story."

Just then another set of voices could be heard, loud and argumentative, at the bottom of the stairs.

"Indie, I told you we were at the right door, but you don't want to listen to me. Just because I had the directions and you didn't," a British man said, sounding annoyed.

"Piss off, Stevie. You are going to ruin my evening," a young woman responded, sounding just as annoyed.

The couple then appeared at the top of the stairs, both seeming to realize they'd been overheard by the group.

"Welcome!" Dolores said, with a somewhat frozen smile on her face. "Come in and introduce yourselves."

"Sorry, sorry. I'm Steve and this is my wife, India. We're the Prescotts. We're newlyweds, here on holiday. From England."

Steve Prescott seemed to keep talking to overcome his embarrassment. "It's quite alright, darling," India said, placing a hand on her husband's arm and he quieted. "We got a little lost on our way over from our hotel. Stevie's not really good with a map."

"Yes, well, welcome, everyone. We'll get started with an *aperitivo*," Dolores said, as an older woman in an apron came out with a tray of olives, nuts, and cheese as the guests began to sip fluted glasses filled with prosecco.

"I thought the ladies might enjoy the prosecco more, but here are some Negroni cocktails as well," Dolores said, pointing to a tray.

"Right-o!" Steve exclaimed, reaching over to take two glasses of the Negroni. "India and I will take the ones with the gin."

Steve took a big gulp and turned to look for his wife, who was across the room. He then quickly downed her cocktail as well before putting down both glasses and reaching for another full one.

Having never had a Negroni, Ravyn wanted to try the cocktail, but one small sip made her realize it wasn't the drink for her. She swallowed the bitter drink, made with gin and Campari, and even though she could taste some hints of citrus, she shuddered. It was too bitter.

"Don't like it?" Steve asked. "I'll take it off your hands. Just pour it into this one." He held out a half-empty glass.

Ravyn was only too happy to oblige. She then picked up a glass of prosecco and took a sip, was glad to rinse the bitter Negroni cocktail off her palate and walked over to her other classmates.

Ravyn, with some of the buttery cheese on a small plate, made small talk with Amy and India. Dolores went around the dining room talking with the guests and periodically disappearing down the hall toward what appeared to be a kitchen.

The dining room had a large wooden table, with a delicate lace tablecloth. Tea lights gave a soft glow and fresh flowers adorned the table's center. Faded rose-print wallpaper covered the walls, but the entire room gave off a homey feel, Ravyn thought. It reminded her a bit of her Aunt Miriam's dining room: a bit dark, a bit old, but always inviting and cozy.

Near where the cocktails sat on a sideboard, larger jarred candles gave off a slight fragrance of lemons.

Dolores popped back into the room, shooing everyone toward the table, two bottles of white wine in her hands. "*A tavola, tutti!* Everyone to the table! Please be seated. We'll make introductions all around again as we get started with our meal. Francesca, my assistant, will be serving us." Dolores nodded toward the older woman who had served them the tray of appetizers and cocktails. Francesca showed no emotion on her face.

Dolores quickly walked around the table, pouring a glass of white wine at each setting.

The guests sorted themselves, with Carl, Clare, and Amy on one side of the table, Dolores at the head, and Ravyn, India, and Steve on the other side. Inwardly, Ravyn groaned. She didn't necessarily want to be seated next to what appeared to be a bickering newlywed couple. But she smiled and took her seat. The heavy wooden dining room chair creaked as she sat down. Ravyn could feel little to no padding in the seat cushion.

Francesca came out with a large pasta bowl with two serving utensils sticking out. She placed the bowl near Amy and began spooning a serving into a smaller pasta bowl in front of her.

"What is this?" Amy asked in her Australian twang.

"This is our first course," Dolores explained. "The *primo*. Italians eat their formal meals in courses, with a pasta or risotto dish first. This is pasta with green cauliflower."

Francesca continued around the table, dishing out portions of the pasta. When she came to Steve, he quickly put up a hand. "No, no. None for me. I am on a low-carbohydrate diet."

Ravyn turned to stare at him. "Why on earth would he come to an Italian cooking class if he was on a low-carbohydrate diet?" she wondered. Ravyn glanced at her fellow students, who also had looks of surprise on their faces. Dolores seemed to have a frozen smile plastered on her face.

"Fine, fine," Dolores said with a hint of exasperation in her voice. "But you should have let me know about special diets before the beginning of class. It was in the email."

"No worries," Steve said, waving a hand. "I'm sure you can work around my needs."

Dolores shot Steve a withering look and Ravyn tried hard not to snort out a laugh. "What a clueless jerk!" Ravyn thought. Now she really regretted sitting next to Steve and India.

Francesca moved to Ravyn's plate and Ravyn nodded. The dish smelled heavenly and she could see flecks of Parmesan cheese mixed throughout.

"*Mangiate!*" Dolores said. "Let's eat."

Ravyn put the first forkful in her mouth and felt her taste buds come alive. She closed her eyes and inhaled, making sure to enjoy the bite.

"This is delicious," Clare said. "Will this be one of the dishes we will be making?"

"Not this one, but I have several that are like it," Dolores explained. "Clare, why don't you begin and introduce yourself."

Clare smiled and put her fork down. "I'm Clare Richards. This is my husband, Carl. I'll let him introduce himself. We're both retired teachers from the Chicago area and this is what we like to do. We travel to different cooking schools, mostly in Italy, but we've done a few in France and one in Spain."

"That sounds lovely," Dolores said.

Clare smiled at her husband, who then began. "I'm Carl. I was a professor of English at a community college in a suburb of Chicago for 30 years. My wife is really the cook. If you don't mind, I'd prefer just to observe this week. But I love these adventures. To new friends," he finished, raising his glass of white wine.

"To new friends," the rest chimed in, everyone taking a sip of wine.

Amy, caught with a bite of food in her mouth, put down her fork and grinned.

"I guess I'm next. I'm Amy Foster. I'm from Australia. I bet you couldn't guess," she said, her accent a dead giveaway to her nationality. "I'm backpacking my way across Europe on my way to London. I start my new job there in about a month. From here I head to Paris for a week or so and then to London."

"What will you be doing in London, Amy?" Clare asked.

"I'll be working in the finance department of a bank," she answered.

"You are quite the adventuress to backpack on your own," Clare said, a little afraid for the young blonde woman.

"Oh no," said Amy, pushing the sleeves of her soft green sweater up so she didn't get pasta on it. "I'm traveling with two other girls. They're staying in Paris. They are going to be au pairs there. I'm only on my own from there."

Clare nodded, but only looked slightly less worried for Amy.

Dolores turned toward India. "And you, my dear?"

"I'm India Prescott, and my husband, Steve," she said, putting her hand on his upper arm. "We were married six months ago and are on a bit of an extended honeymoon holiday. We weren't able to take much time off from work for a proper honeymoon, so this is part of it. From here we will go to Florence and then Venice. I'm very excited to be here."

"What do you do?" Dolores asked India.

India glanced at her husband before answering, "Oh, I'm taking a short leave from work right now. A little bit of a mini-break. I wanted to really enjoy myself on this trip."

"Very understandable," Dolores smiled at her. "Weddings are a lot of work. You deserve to enjoy yourself."

"Oh, I will."

India had jet black hair and brown almond-shaped eyes. She was stylishly dressed in a cream-colored cardigan and brown leggings which tapered off into calf-length brown leather boots. Her husband gave off a rather rumpled look, but he was equally well dressed in jeans and a sports coat, which he wore through dinner. All eyes turned to Steve when India stopped speaking.

"I'm Steve. I'm an account executive in sales for a big pharmaceutical firm in London. No, sorry. I can't get you any free samples," Steve tried to joke. He smiled a toothy grin, but no one laughed. No one even smiled.

"Well, right," he said, looking serious again. "We're on a delayed honeymoon and this was my wife's idea, so here I am."

The room went silent. Ravyn looked up from her notepad, where she had been jotting down the details of her student companions.

"Sorry, I guess I'm next. Last, but not least. I'm Ravyn Shaw. Yes, raven like the bird, but it's spelled with a Y. R-A-V-Y-N," she spelled out her name. "I'm the managing editor of a lifestyle magazine in Atlanta, Georgia, in the United States. I'm here on a working holiday."

Ravyn went on to explain how she'd be writing a story about destination cooking schools and why people do them. "I'll be interviewing all of you as we are together this week," she said. "I'll be taking photographs of you as you prepare the food and of the food itself. I'll need to get release forms signed by all of you."

She reached into her handbag and pulled out several pieces of paper and dug out three ink pens as well. She placed all of them beside her table setting.

Ravyn realized she was talking too much about the work ahead for her. "But I get to enjoy myself while I'm here, too," she said with a smile. "This is my first real vacation in a long time, and my first time in Italy, so I plan on having fun."

"Wonderful!" Dolores said as the guests scraped the last of the pasta off their plates. All except Steve, who sat stiff and upright, but emptied his wine glass. "Are we ready for the next course? Francesca!"

Francesca appeared and whisked away the dirty plates, returning from the kitchen with a platter of meat with vegetables that smelled so good, Ravyn thought her eyes might water. Steve reached over and refilled his wine glass, then topped off his wife's glass as well.

"This is roast pork with orange sauce and fennel," Dolores explained as Francesca began filling their plates. "No one indicated they could not eat pork, correct?"

"Actually," Steve began. India swatted him not so playfully on the arm. "Stevie, don't be rude!" she hissed.

Dolores looked rather panicked. "No, no, just kidding. I love pork," Steve said. Now Dolores looked like she might hit him with something sharp. India gave Steve an angry glance.

"Very well," Dolores said with a tight smile. "Let's begin. This is *secondo*. It's usually heavier than the *primo*, usually meat, but it could be fish."

"It's delicious," Amy said. Heads around the table nodded in agreement, including Steve Prescott, who was almost shoveling the food into his mouth.

"Dolores, tell us a bit about yourself. How did you start your cooking school?" Clare asked.

Dolores sighed and took a sip of her wine, motioning to Francesca to bring another bottle to the table.

"I followed a man." Then she smiled wanly. "I fell in love with an Italian man and followed him here. We were married. I have a son and a daughter, both grown and married. I loved cooking Italian food and would try new recipes all the time. I taught school at the British academy for ex-pats and when I retired all my friends said, 'You should teach cooking,' so I started my cooking school."

Ravyn was sure there was a bit more to it than that but admired that Dolores had re-invented herself for her second career in life.

Francesca arrived with another bottle of white wine and began clearing the dinner plates. She returned with fresh fruit tartlets and whipped cream. Coffee arrived next in a silver coffee pot. Ravyn looked down at her watch. It was already 9:15 p.m. It seemed like they had just started. "No coffee for me unless it is decaf," she said. "I arrived today and I've got to sleep to get on track with the time zone."

"Ah, very good," Dolores said. "Class will begin at 10:30 a.m. every morning except Wednesday and Friday when we will meet at 6 p.m. for dinner. That will give you a chance to visit the Vatican on Wednesday and see the pope if you want. He is in Rome this week."

Ravyn knew that when the pontiff was in Rome, he offered a public mass on Wednesday and Sunday mornings. Even though she was a lapsed Protestant, she would plan to visit the Vatican on Wednesday to see what she had only ever seen on television.

"On Tuesday morning we will meet here, but walk over to Campo de Fiori to the open market to do some shopping, so you can see how a true Roman shops and prepares the meals," Dolores said. "Any questions?"

Dolores eyed Steve, sure he would ask something that would annoy her. He was busy pouring the last of the white wine into his glass.

"What time will class end each day?" Amy asked. "I just need to let my friends know when to pick me up."

"We should be finished by 2 o'clock each day. You will have the afternoons to enjoy the sights of Rome. Just be wary of pickpockets around some of the tourist areas, especially the Colosseum. They are everywhere," Dolores chided. "And Ravyn, you are by yourself?"

"Yes," she responded.

"Well, you should be fine, but don't stay out by yourself past midnight. This area is very safe, but don't take chances."

"I'm quite certain I'll be back at the hotel long before then. Sounds like we will have a very full week," Ravyn said.

"You will. We will eat what we prepare, so come hungry every day!" Dolores said as she got up to see her guests to the door. As she walked past the sideboard, she blew out the lemon-scented candles.

"Oh, you shouldn't do that," Steve Prescott said, a little wobbly on his feet.

Dolores turned to him, puzzled. "Why not?"

"To get the candles to burn evenly, you should really let them burn for three hours at a time," Steve said, completely serious. "That's the maximum burn rate, you know. We never burn our candles unless we know we'll be in the house for three hours."

Ravyn could barely suppress a giggle, seeing the shocked look on Dolores's face.

"Mate, you must never go out of the house then!" Amy said with a snort of laughter. "I've never heard such arsetalk."

Steve looked hurt and India pursed her lips, glaring at Amy. "Well, we just want our candles to have the correct burn rate," he said stiffly.

"Well, yes," Dolores said, moving everyone out the door. "I'll try to remember that for next time. I had no idea there was a maximum burn rate. Thank you for letting me know, Mr. Prescott."

Ravyn said goodbye to her companions on the sidewalk outside, still smiling at Steve's comment about "maximum burn rate" for candles, and began the short walk back to her hotel. Rome had a different feel at night, she realized.

A Sunday night, the streets were still busy. Thankfully, the traffic wasn't as busy as before, although she did have some trepidation as she stepped into the crosswalk. She kept a steady pace as she walked across the street by the Monument of Vittorio Emanuele II, dramatically lit up at night.

The air was crisp that night. She walked toward Trajan's Column and glanced down the street toward the rest of Trajan's Forum and beyond to the Colosseum. Ravyn turned left to find the steep steps leading up to the street of Il Giardino hotel. She buzzed to be let in and climbed another flight of steps to the hotel's lobby.

"*Buona sera, signora,*" the desk clerk, a young man this time, greeted her.

"*Buona sera,*" Ravyn replied, noticing how good looking he was. Were all the Italian men so handsome? she wondered.

She slipped into her room, removed her shoes and sat on the bed, rubbing her feet. She could suddenly feel just how tired she was. But she wanted one last look from her balcony, so stepped out, feeling the cool air and listening to the street noises below. "Such a beautiful city," she thought. "And it's all mine for almost a week!"

Classic Negroni Cocktail

1 oz (1 part) Gin
1 oz (1 part) Campari
1 oz (1 part) Sweet red Vermouth
Slice of orange
Ice

Stir or shake the gin, Campari, and vermouth in a cocktail shaker. Fill a small cocktail glass with ice. Run part of the orange peel around the rim of the glass for extra flavor. Pour the cocktail into the glass and garnish with the orange slice.

Buon appetito!

Chapter 2

ANTIPASTO

Ravyn heard her smartphone's alarm trilling and rolled over, bumping her head against the wall. Then she remembered where she was: Rome! She sat up in the double bed and stretched, trying to lift the fog in her head. It wasn't from the wine she'd had last night, although she'd had several glasses during the course of the introductory meal.

She knew most of her cottony head was from jet lag. She wished she could curl back up in bed, but she had to get up to get ready for her first day of cooking school.

Ravyn opted to shower and dress first before finding the hotel's continental breakfast dining area. It took a few seconds to figure out how to work the shower, which seemed to be the size of a postage stamp. In fact, the entire bathroom was small.

She got into the shower and realized she could barely turn around without hitting her elbows on either the wall or hitting the lightweight plastic shower curtain, causing it to billow out, allowing water to spray out on the bathroom floor. She'd heard European bathrooms were smaller than those in America. Now she knew!

Ravyn toweled off in the main bedroom, rather than trying to contort herself in the bath. She opened the bathroom door to allow the steam to dissipate as well.

She opened her balcony's glass-paned doors to see what the weather would be like. A slight chill in the air helped her decide her wardrobe for the day. She quickly dressed in some skinny denim jeans and a light blue sweater, one that would complement her blue-gray eyes, and pulled on her leather boots last.

Her light brown hair was still slightly damp when she left her room to find breakfast, so she pulled it up into a ponytail. She put just a bit of makeup on and lip gloss before leaving her room.

The dining room was small and L-shaped, but one wall was filled with windows that overlooked a courtyard below at the back of the hotel. She could see some hotel patrons sitting out on a small terrace with their breakfast, but no tables were available outside. Since it was a little chilly to sit outside anyway, Ravyn took a small empty table near the windows.

A dark-haired, dark-eyed young woman with an East European accent approached. "*Prego. Caffe?*" she asked.

"*Si,*" Ravyn responded, pleased she had learned a little Italian from her language app. She had listened via Bluetooth through her car speakers in her Honda Civic as she commuted from her rented condo in Atlanta's Midtown neighborhood to *Cleopatra*'s offices in downtown Atlanta, only a five-mile distance.

But in Atlanta, five miles could mean an hour in the car, or more. If Atlanta drivers saw a raindrop or, God forbid, a snowflake, the entire city would come to a grinding halt.

Earlier that year, in late January, a snowstorm had caused Atlanta's roads to glaze over in ice, paralyzing the city for nearly a week. On the first night of the snowfall, school children had been stuck in school buses overnight or forced to camp out in their schools.

Motorists had to sleep in their cars overnight or abandon them on icy highways altogether. Employees unlucky enough not to leave work early that day spent the nights sleeping on cots or the floors of their office buildings.

City and state transportation and government officials were roundly criticized for not having the wherewithal to deal with the inclement weather. It later came to light that, of the city's four snowplows, two were inoperable. Atlanta became something of a national joke. Even "Saturday Night Live" spoofed the event. It had been a citywide nightmare and national embarrassment.

Ravyn had been housebound for a few days during what came to be known as "Snowmageddon." She smiled at that thought as she sipped her rich Italian coffee. She'd been a freelance writer then, and worked from home as a rule, but she had ended up housebound with her then-boyfriend Marc Linder. It was a rather pleasant way to be caught indoors.

Sadly, about a week later, they had broken up after Marc accused her of falsifying some fourth-quarter numbers on his company's financial documents. Ravyn had been falsely accused, but it didn't matter. The relationship hadn't worked out.

Now here she was in Rome, about to work and play in the Eternal City. Ravyn reached into her blue canvas backpack and pulled out her journal. The waitress came by and refilled her coffee cup as Ravyn pulled out her pen.

She looked down at her leather-bound journal and smiled. Her best friend, Julie Montgomery, had given it to her right before the trip to Rome. The two friends had met up at their favorite lunch spot, Twist, in Atlanta's Phipps Plaza.

Julie had slid into her seat with several shopping bags on her elbow.

"God, I love to shop here!" she exclaimed.

Phipps Plaza was one of Atlanta's luxe shopping centers in the Buckhead area. Julie had been a fellow journalist with Ravyn back in the day but had met and married a wealthy "source" and left the daily newspaper years ago to raise two daughters.

Ravyn had loved being a reporter at Atlanta's daily newspaper, the Atlanta Daily Tribune, but had gotten laid off during the downturn in 2010. After that, she'd gone into business for herself as a freelance writer and editor, but it was a tough go.

Ravyn was constantly on the edge, barely paying her bills on time in the nearly three years before she got hired on at *Cleopatra* magazine.

Julie's face was flushed. "I have a surprise for you," she said to Ravyn.

Ravyn's eyes grew wide. "What are you talking about?"

"Well, I know you are headed to Italy for some fun and adventure, and I wanted you to have this," Julie said, as she thrust a wrapped package toward Ravyn.

Just then, the waitress at Twist walked up.

"Are you two ladies ready to order?"

Twist was a sushi bar, mostly, but had lots of other offerings. Julie and Ravyn often met here for lunch and split sushi rolls, or sometimes hand rolls. They rarely ordered the specials.

"We'll just take our regular order," Julie said, being very authoritative. "We'll have the dragon roll, the volcano roll, and the spicy tuna roll. If we are still hungry after that, we'll order more. Oh, and we'll split the seaweed salad."

Julie snapped the brown leather menu closed and handed it back to the waitress, who had a disinterested look in her eyes. "What is going on with her?" Julie wondered.

But she turned back to Ravyn with a gleam in her eye. "Open your present," Julie pressed.

Ravyn picked up the package with its silver wrapping paper and blue ribbon. "Julie, what did you do? Whatever you got me, you shouldn't have."

As Ravyn spoke the words, she smiled, and Julie knew she was lying. Her friend was delighted at the surprise gift.

Ravyn tore into the wrapping and uncovered a leather-bound journal. She turned it over in her hands, the leather cover feeling soft and buttery.

"What's this?" She asked Julie.

"A gift for your upcoming travels," was the reply.

Ravyn's blue-grey eyes looked up at Julie, tears forming.

"What do you mean?

"I want you to write about your adventures in this journal. I want you to remember everything years from now."

Ravyn looked at the cover. It was a picture of Trevi Fountain in Rome. It was perfect for her upcoming trip.

"Oh Julie," she said, a tear slipping down her cheek.

"No, no!" Julie admonished. "If you start crying, I'll start crying. Just say thank you and be done with it."

Cooking Up Trouble

"Oh! Thank you! Or should I say *Grazie*! This is perfect!"

Ravyn ran her hand over the soft leather cover of the journal Julie had given her as she sat in the hotel's dining room. She swept away a few crumbs from the table before she opened it to the first page, fresh and clean, and began writing.

"I am here in Rome. The trip over was long and I'm still a bit jet-lagged, but I'm sitting here having my first Italian coffee. That should help. It sure is strong. I'm in the cutest hotel. I had some trouble finding the place, but now that I have, I'm so glad I found it online. It's inexpensive and really a better value than I expected. My goodness! I get a lovely breakfast every morning and I have an ensuite bathroom! (I'll describe the bathroom, later, but in a word, minuscule).

Navigating the Roman roads are a challenge, but I think I've got it. It really is an act of faith, and if it hadn't been for the elderly Roman man who marched across the crosswalk yesterday morning without fear, I might still be standing on the side of the street waiting to cross. It is unnerving to have cars and scooters whizzing by you as you cross, though.

My fellow cooking school students are an interesting lot. There are just six of us in the class, two couples and two single women.

Amy Foster is from Australia. She's young, blonde, blue-eyed and gorgeous. She's stopping over before she starts work in London. I must say I'm a little jealous of her. She seems to be far more put together than I was at her age. She's in her early 20s I'm guessing.

Clare and Carl Richards seem nice. They are older, from Chicago, both retired, and very friendly. They said they had traveled extensively throughout Italy and it was fun to hear some of their stories at dinner last night. Carl Richards was a college professor, so I bet I'll have a lot to chat about with him since Dad teaches at Clemson University. She was a teacher, too, but I don't remember if she said where she taught.

The kind of weird pair are Steve and India Prescott from England. They just seem like they are trying too hard. I like her more than I like him. She looks as though she could have been a model. Thin with luxurious black hair and almond-shaped brown eyes. He's really a bit of a weirdo. He kept going on last night about how he's a top salesman in London. Trying a bit too hard to be liked, if you ask me. And then he says he's on a low-carb diet! Who comes to Italy, the land of risotto and pasta, on a low-carb diet? I thought our teacher was going to brain him when he said that.

I really like our teacher, Dolores Reed. From the little she shared about her past and how she came to be a cooking school instructor, I bet she'd make a great article all by herself. Maybe I'll do a little sidebar on her, but I'm not sure it will fly with the magazine since she's not from Atlanta. She's British, very warm and generous. You can tell she enjoys what she does. And you should see her apartment! It's in an old palazzo, or palace. She said she's renting parts of two floors. Her private quarters, where we had dinner last night, are below the commercial kitchen she had installed. I can't wait to see it today.

Well, I've got to get moving or I'll be late for my first day of class. Ciao!"

Ravyn closed her journal and finished up her continental breakfast. She couldn't wait to start class. Rushing back to her hotel room, she quickly put the finishing touches on her makeup, pulled her soft brown hair from its ponytail and gave it a good brush, then brushed her teeth before dashing back out the door.

Ravyn dropped the heavy room key at the front desk, waving to the day-time front desk clerk, the woman who had checked her in the day before. *"Ciao!"* she said as she took the stairs down to the front door.

Ravyn met Clare and Carl Richards at the door of the cooking school and pushed the doorbell to be let up. They took an elevator up to the third floor and then up a short flight of stairs to the commercial kitchen, where the classes would begin.

The kitchen was painted in a light teal color and included a long white tiled L-shaped countertop with a double butcher's block toward the middle. Two sets of range tops were at each end of the L. Just around from the kitchen area was a square wooden table with eight chairs around it. A small round window in the dining room had a view facing the Monument of Vittorio Emanuele and Ravyn was mesmerized by the buses, trucks, cars and motor scooters that buzzed around the square.

"Are we ready to begin?" Dolores asked brightly. She was dressed this morning in a purple sweater and a blue and purple skirt. Ravyn noticed she was wearing good sturdy flat shoes. Ravyn looked down at her cute boots and wondered if she'd made the right choice in footwear that day.

Dolores Reed ushered all six participants around the dining room table, where six bright green folders were laid out on top. The folders, with "Cooking With Dolores Reed" stamped on the cover, would be where the participants placed their recipes from each dish prepared during the week.

Ravyn picked hers up and looked inside. A single sheet of paper outlined the different courses of an Italian meal.

Dolores began with basic safety instructions. "There are only seven of us here today, but we will be working with sharp knives. Please handle the knives with the blade down, and please announce your use of the knife with 'Sharp knife! Sharp knife!' to your fellow students," she admonished. Clare and Carl Richards both nodded.

"We've said that at our other cooking classes," Clare said. "We'll be mindful."

"We'll also be working with the stove and boiling water, so please be careful as you remove pots from the stovetop," Dolores went on. "Please use the oven mitts and remember there may be someone behind you."

Ravyn and Amy Foster looked at each other and nodded in agreement. India and Steve Prescott looked tired, or maybe bored. Ravyn wondered if they were even paying attention.

Ravyn took out Gavin's Nikon camera and began shooting a few tentative photos. She wasn't quite familiar with it yet, even though she'd tried to practice with it in the few days leading up to the trip to Italy. She smiled thinking that she'd taken a lot of photos of her cat Felix just before she left.

She felt a sudden pang of loneliness. She missed her big gray tomcat. Ravyn's neighbor, Jack Parker, was feeding and watering Felix while she was on the trip. She was lucky to have a neighbor that was willing to do all that and clean out a dirty litter box.

But she'd watched over Jack's condo when he and his girlfriend Liz were on vacation too. The fact that they only had houseplants was not lost on Ravyn. She'd have to remember to bring them something nice from Italy as a thank you gift.

Ravyn snapped out of her reverie as Dolores was explaining how they would make an appetizer and a main dish at each class. Some classes would include a dessert and some would include a side dish or other items, such as an olive oil tasting or the making of limoncello.

Ravyn had never had limoncello and was excited to try the aperitif. Clare and Carl seemed excited about that too. India and Steve still looked bored. Ravyn wondered why in the world they were here at the class if they weren't going to pay attention or be excited.

"Now tomorrow morning will be a little different," Dolores said. "We'll meet here at 9:30 a.m. and then walk over to Campo di Fiori to the open-air market and gather some ingredients. I want to show you how a traditional Roman housewife would prepare her meal, beginning with the freshest ingredients. Be sure to wear good walking shoes. It's not too far, but it will be a bit of a walk."

Dolores stood up from the table. "Now, let's begin with an appetizer."

Dolores pulled four large eggplants from a wicker basket, wiping each one with a dishtowel. Ravyn pulled up the Nikon camera and got a few shots.

"We'll be making eggplant rolls," Dolores said. "Or for you Brits, aubergine rolls. In Italian, aubergines are called *melanzana*."

"*Melanzana*," Ravyn said, as a few other classmates echoed the word.

Dolores placed the deep purple vegetables on the counter and drew a long, sharp knife. She cut off the bottom end of the eggplant, then pulled at the cap at its neck before cutting off the top. "I want you to cut the eggplant just like that to start. Amy and Ravyn, why don't you pair up. Clare and Carl, you can do one and Steve and India you do the third one."

Amy went to the knife stand and took a sharp knife, announcing "Sharp knife! Sharp knife!" as she walked back to the counter. Clare and India did the same, although India mumbled her words, practically stifling a yawn.

Amy sliced the top and bottom off of the eggplant as Dolores had demonstrated, as did the others.

"Now, I want you to thinly slice the eggplant lengthwise," Dolores instructed. "You can take turns slicing. It's not easy. You don't want your slices to be too thick. Just a half-centimeter or so."

Amy looked at Ravyn, who was trying to figure out centimeters to inches. As if reading her mind, Dolores said, "That's a quarter-inch for you Yanks."

Ravyn grinned.

"Do you want to try first?" Amy asked, trying to hand Ravyn the knife.

"Oh no. I'll let you. I'll get some photos of everyone else before it's my turn," Ravyn said.

"Oh, right. Let me mess up first," Amy joked and smiled. Ravyn smiled back.

"I'm sure I'll mess up plenty of times this week," she replied, taking a few quick photos of Amy cutting two thin slices from the eggplant.

Dolores walked around the kitchen as her students not so deftly began slicing up the eggplant. Amy did far better than Ravyn, who was admonished for making her slices too thick.

"Now we salt down the eggplant to remove the bitter juices," Dolores said. She went on to explain that many people don't properly prepare eggplant, so it can taste bitter. By salting the eggplant for a half-hour, the bitterness is removed.

Dolores generously salted the thin strips, then covered them with some wax paper and put a heavy pot on top. "That will help get the juices out. While we are waiting on that, let's start to make our sauce."

Dolores pulled out several large ripe tomatoes, some garlic, basil and onion. She had the class dice the onion and garlic and place them in a pot with some olive oil to gently cook. She then had the students dice the tomatoes and put those in the pot on a low flame. Dolores tore some basil leaves into the pot and added salt and pepper.

"Now just stir the sauce until it is well heated," Dolores said. "Once you make your own sauce, you will never buy a jar of pasta sauce again."

Ravyn wasn't so sure. Although the contents of the saucepan smelled great, it looked more like chunky tomato lumps, not a smooth sauce.

Dolores came over to give the pot another glance and declared it done. She then pulled out a large food mill, clamping it over the top of a clean pot. Ravyn had never seen such a contraption.

"Now we put the sauce through the mill," Dolores explained. She motioned for Steve to begin slowly pouring the sauce into the mill, while India turned the crank. "Be careful, Steve. That sauce is still hot. Do it slowly. Don't splatter."

"Ouch!" India cried out, as she pulled her left hand away from the food mill. "You did let it splatter! I'm burned, you bloody ass! And look at my pants!"

Dolores rushed to India's side, trying to salvage the pasta sauce slopping over the saucepan and to render aid. "Quick, run your hand under some cool tap water. Amy, there should be some club soda right over there," Dolores said, gesturing toward the pantry. "That should keep the stain from setting."

India, glaring at Steve, stepped over to the kitchen sink and began to run her left hand under the water.

Dolores took over the cranking of the food mill and noticed not too many of the larger bits of tomato, garlic and onion had fallen into the saucepan below. "There, I think the sauce is done. India, how is your hand?"

India pouted. "I'll live, no thanks to my husband."

Amy handed India a bottle of Pellegrino.

"I'm sorry, Indie. Really I am. I didn't mean to," Steve said, looking apologetic. "Here, let me see your hand. Did it leave a mark?"

Steve tried to hold India's hand, but she pulled it away. "It's fine."

Steve sighed and the other classmates looked uncomfortable. "Nothing like a lover's spat in class," Ravyn thought.

"Well, yes, let's continue then," Dolores said. She turned the flame off the pasta saucepan and turned back to the eggplant slices, which were now swimming in dark juices. "See here. The bitter juices have come out. Now we just drain off the juices and give the slices a little rinse to get the rest of the salt off."

Clare, Amy, and Ravyn began rinsing and patting dry the slices, while India sat on a chair and scowled, her legs and arms crossed. A wet mark on India's pants showed where she had tried to use the club soda to dab out the pasta sauce stains. Ravyn knew India wouldn't be participating in cooking class for the rest of the day. Steve and Carl looked on.

"Now we'll gently sauté the eggplant in some olive oil, just to make them slightly soft," Dolores said. "Steve and Carl, why don't you cut some mozzarella cheese into rectangles?"

"I don't know if you should trust Steve with a sharp knife," India said.

"Now, now, Indie," Steve answered over his shoulder.

India just glared at Steve and the rest of her classmates.

Carl and Steve began cutting a soft round of mozzarella cheese into the rectangles as Amy and Ravyn placed the cooked eggplant slices on paper towels to drain. Clare gently patted each one. As Ravyn finished her task, she got the camera and got some photos of Clare and Amy doing their tasks and Steve and Carl cutting the cheese. She dared not take any photos of India, who was still pouting on her chair.

Dolores then reached for a large bunch of basil, breaking off leaves and placing them on the counter.

"Now we'll start making our eggplant rolls," she said. "Each of you take a slice of the cooked eggplant and place a bit of the mozzarella cheese and a basil leaf on one end and then roll it up, like this."

She demonstrated and showed a tight roll of eggplant surrounding the cheese and basil. "Place these seams side down in a pan."

The class began rolling and placing the appetizers in two small glass pans. When they were done, Dolores took the pasta sauce and spooned just a slight amount over the top of the dish. "Just a little bit. You don't want to drown them. That will make them too wet when they come out of the oven. Oh! The oven! I forgot to turn it on!"

She quickly turned the oven on and smiled sheepishly. "Even the best cook can forget the oven, so always check that first," she chided, almost to herself.

"One last step is to grate a little Parmesan cheese over the top of the sauce," Dolores said, pulling out a grater and a small wedge of Parmesan. "Don't use that awful stuff from a can. Buy the best ingredients you possibly can and real Parmesan cheese is the best."

She grated some of the cheese over the first pan and handed the grater and cheese to Clare. "Finish off the second pan, Clare," she instructed. Clare gave the cheese a quick grate and Dolores took both pans and placed them in the oven. "These will need to cook for 20 minutes, so we can start our next dish."

Dolores pulled out two bunches of asparagus and announced the class would next make asparagus risotto. About 15 minutes into the preparation, Dolores said the eggplant rolls were ready to come out of the oven.

The class oohed and aahed as the bubbling dishes came out of the oven and were placed on the table. Ravyn quickly took some photos of the finished dish as Dolores opened a bottle of white wine and poured small glasses for everyone. They then dug into the appetizer.

Gooey mozzarella cheese came out in strings as Ravyn dug her fork into the eggplant roll and scooped a bite. She blew on it, knowing it would be hot. It was, but it was also so delicious.

The rest of the cooking session seemed to fly by as they finished making the asparagus risotto and then ate that. Dolores opened two more bottles of white wine and as the class cleaned up, Ravyn felt full and a little tipsy. She wasn't used to drinking a few glasses of wine in the middle of the day.

Ravyn and Clare were wiping down the kitchen counters when Clare asked if Ravyn had dinner plans for the evening.

"No, I don't," she said. "Do you and Carl have something in mind?"

"We're meeting some friends who happen to be in town for dinner tonight," Clare said, as Carl came around and stood by his wife. "We'd love for you to join us if you'd like."

"I'd love that!" Ravyn exclaimed. She was excited that she'd get to know Clare and Carl a little better and ask them about their teaching careers.

"Wonderful," Clare said. "Why don't you meet us at our hotel around 6 p.m. tonight? Our hotel is right at the Piazza della Minerva. Walk over with us after class so you can find it later tonight."

Ravyn's classmates departed with Dolores reminding them they would meet at 9:30 a.m. the next day and walk over to the Campo de Fiori, so to wear good walking shoes.

Ravyn, Carl and Clare then walked over to the older couple's hotel and Ravyn, noting where it was, walked back to her hotel so she'd be sure to know where to return that evening.

As she wandered back to her hotel, Ravyn stepped into Santa Maria sopra Minerva, a church that houses most of the remains of Saint Catherine. Ravyn pulled out her guidebook on Rome and learned the head of Saint Catherine of Siena was in another church in Siena. She also found the floor tomb of Fra Angelico at the church and a small marble cross carved by Michelangelo.

Ravyn then walked the short distance to the Pantheon and the bustling Piazza della Rotonda. The square was teeming with tourists, street performers and what looked like native Romans using the square as a cut through to wherever they were going.

Ravyn entered the Pantheon and waited a minute for her eyes to adjust to the dimmer light. Outside it was bright sunshine, but inside was cool and dimmer light. She walked the circular walls, noting the tombs of Vittorio Emanuele II and his successor Umberto I, and the artist Raphael. She looked up at the niches where Roman gods once were housed, and then up further still to the oculus, the hole in the dome where a small circle of sunshine came through.

Ravyn then wandered over to the Piazza Navona, where the Fountain of the Four Rivers sits in the center. She sat down on a concrete bench and pulled out her guidebook, reading about the fountain, which represents the four greatest rivers in the world: the Ganges, Danube, della Plata and Nile. She then pulled out three postcards she had bought at a corner shop near the Pantheon, addressing the postcards to her best friend Julie, her parents and her sister Jane.

Ravyn was glad to be sitting down. Her feet felt swollen in her cute boots she'd put on that morning. Standing during the cooking school all morning and now walking around Rome was making her feet ache.

Ravyn got up to take some photos of the piazza and the fountain, then searched for a postal box for her postcards. She was glad she'd thought to ask Dolores where to buy stamps earlier that day.

Around 4 p.m., Ravyn decided to make her way back to her hotel for a short rest. She stopped at a side shop to buy some bottled water before trudging her way up the long flight of steps that led to the street to her hotel. She felt winded as she got to the top.

She was happy when she finally sat on the end of her bed and pulled off her boots. She rubbed her feet. "How am I going to put these back on and walk back to Carl and Clare's hotel?" she wondered. Ravyn laid down on the bed for some quiet time, thinking she could honestly fall asleep right then and there and not wake up until the next morning.

Ravyn stood in the lobby of the Hotel Albergo Santa Chiara, waiting for Carl and Clare. She was only a few minutes late and she hoped they hadn't left without her. She looked around the lobby, which looked modern, compared to the outside. "Then again," she thought, "this is Rome. Everything is more modern on the inside."

Ravyn was just about to sit down to rest her aching feet when she saw Clare and called out.

"There you are!" Clare said. "We were down earlier but didn't see you."

"Yes, I'm sorry I'm a little late," Ravyn replied. "I wandered around the city after the class and then got back to the hotel and laid down on my bed. That was a mistake! I dozed for just an hour, and I'm lucky I woke up at all. A truck's horn from the street below my room woke me up, thank goodness."

"Don't worry, we're meeting our friends at the restaurant at seven, so we have some time to walk over," Clare said.

Clare and Carl had changed clothes since the morning's class. Clare was dressed in a loose white blouse with a black skirt and a light brown jacket. Carl wore a polo shirt and khaki pants and a sports jacket. Ravyn hadn't changed out of her clothes and wondered if she was underdressed. "Am I too casual for dinner?" she asked, uncertain.

"No, you're fine," Clare responded. "We both took a nap this afternoon. Still trying to get over jet lag. So that's why we changed clothes. I thought we looked too rumpled."

Ravyn was relieved, although she probably looked rumpled as well. "Too late now!" she thought to herself.

They began walking and met Clare and Carl's friends Sandy and Dennis Johns and Luca Ricci outside a restaurant that was clearly closed. Ravyn was surprised. She thought it would just be the two couples and herself.

"Carl! Clare!" Dennis said. "So glad to see you! We've run into a bit of trouble. The place we wanted to try is closed. Our friend Luca here says some of the better Italian restaurants are closed on Monday nights. We'll have to find something else."

Dennis went on to make introductions and Ravyn tried not to stare at Luca. He was gorgeous. Tall, with wavy brown hair that came down just to the top of his collar, Luca wore a black leather jacket, black pants, and a cream-colored V-neck sweater. She could see a slight tuft of dark chest hair under the sweater.

"Hi," Ravyn said, shyly. "I'm Ravyn Shaw from Atlanta, Georgia. I'm taking the cooking classes with Clare and Carl."

"Well, let's walk a bit and find somewhere to eat," Sandy said. "I don't know about you, but I worked up an appetite walking all over Rome today."

"We ate quite a bit in our class today, but I still want to sit down at a restaurant," Carl said. "We were on our feet more than I thought we'd be. My knees don't really like that."

The three couples walked on, stopping at a couple of restaurants before selecting one, Myositis, just a few blocks from where they had met up.

They were seated at a big round table in a corner of the restaurant and Luca pulled the chair out for Ravyn before sitting down next to her. Bread, water, and menus were brought to the table and although Ravyn thought she wasn't that hungry, the smells of the food in the restaurant made her realize otherwise.

Clare sat next to Ravyn on her left as Luca sat to her right. Ravyn was glad. Luca was so handsome it was distracting. With Clare to her left, Ravyn thought she would be able to carry on a conversation without drooling.

"Listen to me," Ravyn admonished herself. "What am I, a 12-year-old middle school girl? He's a man I just met. It's not like I'll see him after tonight."

Although with his good looks, Luca was definitely someone Ravyn wouldn't mind seeing after the evening was over.

Ravyn was looking over her menu when Luca bumped her right arm. She jumped slightly when she felt his slightly hairy forearm brush hers.

"*Mi scusi*, Ravyn," he said. Ravyn realized he was left-handed. She was right-handed. They were going to bump each other throughout the meal, she realized.

"Do you know what you will order?" Luca asked.

"I'm not sure. What would you recommend? Have you been here before?"

"No. This is my first time, too."

Ravyn began studying the menu again before the waiter appeared at their table.

"Are you ready to order?" the waiter asked.

Murmurs from around the table indicated most were ready to order. Ravyn decided on the saltimbocca alla Romana and a glass of house red wine. She figured any house wine in Italy would be great. She was not wrong.

Ravyn chatted a bit with Clare, but she kept glancing at Luca to her right. She could hear his low voice and his sexy Italian accent as he talked to Dennis.

Finally, she gave him her full attention.

"You are here for a cooking school?" he asked.

"Yes. I'm here for the week."

"Don't you already know how to cook?" he asked, teasing her.

"Well, I know some things to cook, but I'm also here to write an article for the magazine I work for, all about the cooking school."

"You are a journalist?" he asked.

"I was, at one time."

Luca raised an eyebrow. "Was? But you said you work for a magazine."

"Oh, yes. I do work for a magazine. But I used to work for a newspaper. I got laid off when the economy got bad in the United States."

Ravyn winced inwardly. She had loved working at the Atlanta daily paper, but in 2010 she got laid off, along with dozens of other reporters and editors. Friends. They were all friends and they all suddenly found themselves without work.

Earlier this year she had landed the job as managing editor at *Cleopatra*, a lifestyle magazine, and she'd been able to breathe again. She had health insurance again. She was able to pay her bills and put a little away in savings. Life was getting better, much better. But she hadn't forgotten the hard times when bills went unpaid and she had barely scraped by.

"Ravyn," Luca said, breaking Ravyn from her reverie. "What did you do after you had no work?"

"Oh, I was my own boss. I wrote stories and did marketing for clients. But it wasn't always steady work. Then I got the job I have now and here I am in Italy, going to cooking school for a story!"

She smiled. Luca smiled. She wasn't sure he completely understood her, but that was OK. He was just a man she would talk to for one night. What did it matter if he understood her and her life?

The evening continued with laughter, conversation, and wine. Three bottles came and went. Ravyn savored her saltimbocca, its salty meat over sautéed spinach.

Ravyn learned Luca knew Dennis through work. They both worked in financial services. Ravyn wasn't quite sure how Sandy and Dennis knew Clare and Carl, although they said they had been to a cooking school in Spain together. The evening was light and breezy. Conversation flowed along with the wine and final coffee.

The bill came and Luca put his hand over Ravyn's hand. "Please, allow me," he said, picking up her bill.

"Oh no, Luca, I couldn't," she began to protest.

"You would do me an honor," he said and gave the waiter several 20 euro bills.

Ravyn was flattered. It had been a long time since a man had treated her to dinner and in Italy no less!

The three couples then decided to walk to a gelateria Sandy had read about on a travel blog. Ravyn was astonished at the selection.

"What will you have?" Luca asked.

"I'm not sure. There is so much to choose from," she said.

Ravyn decided on three scoops, even though she was full from dinner. This was Italy after all, and what was a night in Italy if not a decadent dessert?

She decided on tiramisu and champagne gelato but was undecided on her third flavor.

"Try the *ciliegia*," Luca said.

Ravyn turned to Luca, puzzled. That wasn't a word she remembered from her Italian for Beginners language app.

"Cherry," Luca said, smiling. "It's cherry."

Ravyn took Luca's advice and was soon scooping up flavor upon flavor. "This is so good," she said. "I'm going to gain 10 pounds on this trip!"

"Oh, you are so skinny. You should eat more," Luca said.

Ravyn blushed. She didn't mean to fish for a compliment from him. "Thank you," she said. "*Mille grazie.*"

"*Prego*," he replied, flashing his warm smile again.

Gelato finished, the six new friends began to say goodbye.

"It was wonderful to meet you," Ravyn said to Sandy and Dennis, who were headed back to their hotel by the Spanish Steps.

"We're off to Florence tomorrow," Sandy said with a wave of her hand. "I'm glad we could meet tonight for dinner."

Ravyn turned to Luca, putting out her hand to shake his. "It was very nice to meet you. too, Luca. Thank you so much for dinner and the gelato tonight. You were too kind."

"Please," he said, taking her hand in his. "Let me walk you back to your hotel. It's late. I wouldn't want anything to happen to you."

Ravyn wasn't sure anything would happen without Luca walking her to her hotel, but she agreed since the company would be nice.

"See you tomorrow in class," she said to Clare and Carl, waving goodbye.

"Good night and take care," Clare admonished, giving Luca a glance of misgiving.

Luca then offered his arm to Ravyn and he walked back toward her hotel, passing the Colosseum, which was dramatically lit at night. The night had turned a bit cooler and Ravyn leaned into Luca for warmth. He took off his leather jacket and draped it around her shoulders.

"But you will be cold," Ravyn protested.

"How can I be cold next to you?" he asked.

Ravyn was sorry when they got to Trajan's Forum and wound around to the steep steps that lead to Via XXIV Maggio. "My hotel is up that way," she pointed.

Luca and Ravyn climbed the steps and she turned right toward her hotel. She got to the heavy door and stopped, lifting Luca's jacket off her shoulders.

"Thank you," she said. "I had a lovely evening, thanks to you."

Luca bent down and kissed Ravyn deeply. She felt her entire body strum with electricity.

"The pleasure is all mine," he said. "May I see you again tomorrow? After your class?"

"I'd love that," Ravyn said, surprising herself. "I get out around 2 p.m. What time do you get off work?"

"I'll meet you here at your hotel at 2:30 p.m. *Buona sera,* Ravyn." Luca placed his hand on her cheek, cupping her chin, and kissed her again. His hand then brushed down her neck.

In a daze, Ravyn buzzed to be let into the hotel. She heard the click of the lock and pushed the heavy wooden door, climbing the marble steps up to the hotel's lobby.

She nearly fell onto the bed, but sat up and removed her shoes. She had a large blister on her right big toe, thanks to her cute boots that she'd worn earlier that day.

She rubbed her foot, then touched her lips where Luca had kissed her and brushed her neck where his fingertips had stroked her. "Luca," she whispered. "Luca."

As tired as she felt that evening, Ravyn reached over to the bedside table for her travel journal and opened to a new page:

"It has been a very full first day of class. We made some amazing dishes, and I even think I like eggplant more than I did before the trip. We made these eggplant roll appetizers that roll up over mozzarella and basil. Of course, what doesn't taste good with melty, gooey mozzarella cheese?

There was a bit of drama in class, however, courtesy of Steve and India. They are an odd pair. I can't quite tell if they are the happy couple they try to portray. Steve accidentally splattered some homemade pasta sauce on India and she got a slight burn. At least I think it was an accident. I hope it was! She was really mad at him. He's probably sleeping on the floor of their hotel room tonight.

After class I roamed around Rome, visiting the Pantheon, my old school paperback guidebook has been invaluable. I'm glad I thought to bring it and not rely on my iPhone for information. It does sort of mark me as a tourist, though.

Carl and Clare invited me to join them for dinner and I'm so glad I went. We were to meet a couple they knew, but their friends brought along a hot Italian dish for me. His name is Luca Ricci. He is stunning. Like a Roman god made human. I'm exaggerating, but he really is handsome and has a sexy Italian accent, of course! He walked me back to my hotel tonight and kissed me. That was an unexpected surprise, and very pleasant, too. He has full, soft lips and soft brown eyes.

Good heavens, I'm sounding like a lovesick girl. Really, he was just a nice distraction.

Dinner was amazing at Myositis. I had the saltimbocca. Then we found a gelateria and I had three scoops, even though I was more than full after dinner.

The only undelightful part was wearing those cute boots I bought before the trip. I knew I shouldn't have let Julie talk me into buying them, no matter how good they looked on my feet. I have a blister on the top of my right toe and it hurts. I'm glad I have a few bandages and more comfortable walking shoes. I'll need them for tomorrow as we will visit the Campo de Fiori market first. Dolores Reed said she'd also take us through the Jewish Ghetto here in Rome.

It's 10:30 p.m. and I can now hear church bells outside. That makes me think of noon here in Rome. A cannon is sounded and then all the church bells are sounded. We heard it today in class. Gave me a little start. Well, to bed. It will be busy tomorrow, too."

Eggplant Rolls

Italian eggplant(s), approximately 1 pound
5 oz. fresh mozzarella cheese
Fresh basil leaves
Olive oil, for frying
2 Tbsp. freshly grated Parmesan cheese
Salt and black pepper
1 cup fresh tomato sauce*

Heat oven to 350°F. Cut off the rounded tip of the eggplant(s) and the bottom. Cut the eggplant lengthwise into thin slices, approximately ¼ inch.

Discard the rounded bottom and top skins, which will not roll easily. Sprinkle the slices with coarse salt and leave for 30 minutes to purge the bitterness.

Cut the mozzarella cheese into thick slices and divide each slice into batons, allowing one baton for each eggplant slice.

Rinse the salt off the eggplant and pat each slice dry thoroughly. Heat the oil and fry the slices in batches until they are golden brown on each side. Allow excess oil to drain off on paper towels.

Lightly oil an oven-proof serving dish that will contain all the rolls in one layer.

Place a mozzarella baton and a basil leaf at one end of an eggplant slice and roll it up.

Place each roll, seam side down, in the oven dish. Spoon a little tomato sauce atop the rolls. Sprinkle a little Parmesan cheese atop the sauced rolls.

Bake in the oven for 15 minutes.

*Fresh Tomato Sauce
1 small onion, finely chopped
2 cloves garlic, finely chopped
3 pounds ripe tomatoes, chopped
2 Tbsp. extra virgin olive oil
2 Tbsp. basil leaves, roughly torn
Salt and black pepper

In a shallow pan, heat the oil and gently cook the onion and garlic until soft. Add the tomatoes and roughly torn basil and cook quickly on a high heat until most of the juice has evaporated. Put the sauce through a food mill, season to taste.

Buon Appetito!

Chapter 3

PRIMO

Ravyn awoke with a start. Her cell phone was trilling. She looked over to check the time.

"Oh my God! I'm late!" she nearly shouted.

Ravyn didn't realize she had hit the snooze on her phone's alarm and now at almost 9 a.m., she was likely going to be late getting to cooking class and the trip to Campo de Fiori. "Shit!"

Ravyn decided against a full shower since that would require drying her straight brown hair with a less-than-powerful travel hairdryer. She quickly dressed, washed her face, applied the slightest bit of makeup, tied her hair up into a ponytail and raced out the door.

She walked quickly to the hotel's dining area and asked the young waitress from Monday if she could get a *caffe* to go.

"*No, signora*," the waitress shook her head. "*Mi dispiace.* I'm sorry. I can bring a cup right now for you."

"*Si, per favore*," Ravyn replied. She wasn't sure how she would manage this morning without at least one cup of the rich Italian coffee.

The woman returned with a white mug filled with coffee and Ravyn quickly poured in a bit of cream and drank as quickly as the hot liquid would allow. She left her empty mug and a few coins as a tip on the waitress's stand.

Ravyn struck out toward the cooking school still feeling slightly unnerved that she had slept through her alarm. But as she walked toward the Monument to Vittorio Emanuele II she began to remember the dream she'd been having.

She had dreamed of Luca. She had dreamed she'd made love to Luca. She could almost feel the wetness between her legs as she began to remember the dream. It had felt so real.

Ravyn could almost feel Luca caressing her body, the warmth of his kiss, his fingertips lingering on her neck and collarbone. She wondered why a dream of good sex could almost feel like the real thing.

Ravyn felt her face flush and shook her head to banish her thoughts of Luca as she neared the crosswalk. But it did make her heart race thinking she would see him later that afternoon. At least, she hoped she would. She hoped he would keep his promise to meet up with her after class.

Ravyn walked out into traffic at the crosswalk almost like a native Italian now. She walked a few more steps before seeing Dolores, Carl, Clare, and Amy standing at the front door of the cooking school. "I'm glad I'm not the last one," Ravyn thought. But she noticed who was still missing, the honeymooners, Steve and India.

Amy stood with a cup of coffee and Ravyn walked over to stand next to her. "Lucky you," Ravyn said, inhaling the coffee's aroma. "My hotel didn't have travel coffee cups."

"Yeah, I made my friends stop at a coffee shop before they dropped me off today," she replied, smiling. "I needed it today. We went out to the nightclubs last night."

"I slept through my alarm this morning," Ravyn admitted. "I think I've got a bit of jet lag."

"Oh, that's rough," Amy said. "Maybe we can stop for more coffee on the way over to the market."

Dolores smiled. "Of course. Then I can show you how real Romans have their morning coffee. We'll wait just a few more minutes for Steve and India."

The Prescotts ambled up 10 minutes later, linked arm in arm, India holding her own cup of to-go coffee.

"Sorry we're late," Steve said. "India is not a morning person."

India scowled at her husband.

"Yes, well, let's get started," Dolores said brightly, starting off toward Campo de Fiori, passing by Largo di Torre Argentina, Roman ruins and also a cat sanctuary. Ravyn could see tins of cat food left out along a crumbling wall. Dolores gave a sound of disgust and waved her hand at the tins. "People are overfeeding these cats. They are becoming a real nuisance."

Ravyn, a cat person, was secretly glad someone was taking care of them and peered over the wall to see if she could see any cats. She saw a few sunning themselves in a far corner.

They stopped briefly at a little Roman coffee shop, where true Romans stood at little bars drinking their coffee. "This is the way Italians do it," Dolores explained. "If you sit down at a table, there is an extra charge."

With Dolores's help, Ravyn and Amy ordered coffees to go and they continued on to Campo de Fiori. Ravyn could almost feel the strong Italian coffee energizing her. She looked over at Amy, who held up her own cup. "Cheers, mate."

Ravyn wasn't sure what to expect, but Campo de Fiori market was a very large square, teeming with stalls and shops. The proper shops were along the walls of the square, with tents and stalls making up nearly every square inch of the interior of the square.

Dolores walked into and out of several shops, with the class trailing behind. After two stops, India and Steve stopped following and found a corner to sit.

"We'll be right here when you are done," Steve said. Dolores frowned, then shepherded the remaining class members like a mother hen to her chicks.

Dolores bought some veal, more basil, and shrimp, or prawns as she called them, all from different shop vendors.

"This is the way it used to be," she said. "Roman housewives would come to the market every day to get their fresh bread, meat, and cheese for the day's meal. You got the fish from the fishmonger, the veal from the butcher, the bread from the baker. It's getting all modern today. Now it's mostly tourists who come here, but I still have my favorite shops. They know not to overcharge me."

Next, they began walking up and down the interior of the square where fresh fruits and vegetables were laid out. There were also tents and stalls that catered more to the tourists, with leather handbags, belts, T-shirts and other non-food items. Ravyn could tell Dolores didn't care for that either. She frowned at the T-shirt vendor.

Dolores stopped at one stall, looking over bright yellow flowers. They were zucchini flowers and Dolores said they looked so good and fresh she was going to get them and change our menu for the day. The class would be making some appetizers with them when they got back to class.

Dolores collected Steve and India and the group, loaded down with several bags of herbs, vegetables, and meats, started toward the Tiber River and a walk through the Jewish Ghetto.

Dolores pointed out where the ancient gate once stood, used to shut in the Jews at night after curfew, and more modern restaurants that still served all Kosher meals. They passed by the Fountain of Turtles before walking by the cat sanctuary again. At last, they turned on Via del Plebiscito and came to the door of the cooking school.

Ravyn opted for the stairs as others waited to get into the small elevator and was glad to sit down when the group was gathered in the kitchen. She was even happier when Dolores got glasses of water for everyone.

Dolores began unpacking this morning's produce and meats, putting away some things and keeping others on the counter.

"Today we'll make fried zucchini flowers," she said.

Dolores had the class make a yeast batter, then clean the zucchini flowers, carefully removing the stalks, stamens, and pistils from the inside of the blossoms. Next, the class stuffed a baton of mozzarella cheese and a bit of anchovy fillet in the zucchini flower before dipping them in batter and then into hot oil for a quick fry.

Clare was in charge of removing them from the oil with a slotted spoon and carefully placed them on some paper towels.

"These will be hot on the inside, so do be careful as you bite into them," Dolores said. "You can eat them with your fingers. That's how Romans eat them."

Ravyn picked up a deep-fried blossom, blew on it, and bit in. It was hot, and she nearly burned her lip on the melted mozzarella cheese. The salty anchovy and creamy cheese were a flavorful balance, she thought.

The rest of the class went smoothly, with the group making pasta with green beans, tomatoes and cheese, a shrimp appetizer and finally a lamb stew. Ravyn felt like she might burst at the kitchen table she felt so full.

As they cleaned the kitchen, Dolores reminded the class they would meet the next evening at 6 p.m. for class, rather than during the day. "The pope is in Rome, so if you want to hear his morning mass, you'll have a chance."

"Oh, I'm just going to look forward to sleeping in," India said. "And then I want to do a little shopping. Ravyn, did you see the jewelry store right next door?"

"I did, but I also want to look at the handbags in the leather shop," she said.

"Oh no!" Steve said. "India, you know we are on a budget. No more jewelry!"

India pouted at her husband, then narrowed her eyes. "I'll spend my money as I see fit," she said.

Ravyn could tell an argument was brewing between the couple.

Steve sighed. "Very well," he said, as they all started down the stairs at the end of class.

Ravyn had forgotten that Luca had promised to meet her at the end of class until she saw him leaning against a parked BMW motorcycle a few steps down from the cooking school and holding two helmets.

"Luca!" she exclaimed. "You're here!"

A wide smile broke over Luca's face. *"Ciao, bella,"* he said, as he kissed Ravyn.

Amy's eyes grew wide as she saw the kiss. "Well, hello, mate. Ravyn, who is your handsome friend?"

"Amy, this is Luca," Ravyn flushed. "We met at dinner last night. I think he means to be my tour guide this afternoon."

Luca put the helmets down and shook Amy's hand. *"Piacere di conoscerti,"* Luca said. "Pleased to meet you."

"Very nice to meet you, too," she replied, giving Ravyn a grin. "You two behave now. My cooking buddy better not be late for class tomorrow."

India grabbed Ravyn's arm. "Before you run off, let's look in the jewelry store," she said, pulling Ravyn into the small shop, a bell jangling above the blue wooden door.

Ravyn looked around at earrings, rings, and necklaces set with colorful gemstones. Ravyn was partial to sapphires and looked into the glass jewelry cases. Clare, Amy, and Carl followed them in, then Steve and Luca, who was still holding the motorcycle helmets. Luca stood by the door as Steve slouched nearby.

"What can I show you?" the young woman behind the counter asked. "Are you shopping for something special?

"I'm just looking," Ravyn said.

"I'm not," India replied. "May I see that emerald necklace?"

"Not another emerald necklace," Steve whined, walking over to stand by his wife. "India, you have four already."

"Well, I don't have *this* one!" she hissed.

The shopkeeper's eyes widened, clearly flustered by the pair. But she took a key off her wrist and unlocked the case, pulling the necklace out and onto a velvet pad.

"May I?" India asked, reaching for the necklace to try it on.

"Of course," the woman replied. Steve turned away from the counter.

India, donning the necklace, looked at her reflection in a small mirror the shopkeeper tilted toward her.

"Oh, it looks lovely on you, India," Clare said. "It looks lovely with your eyes and coloring."

"It does, doesn't it?" India agreed, turning her head one way, then the other, watching the light catch the gold necklace and the deep green of the emerald. "I'll take it."

"Indie!" Steve exclaimed, stomping back over to the counter. "You didn't even ask the price, or haggle!"

"I don't want to haggle and I don't care what the price is," she shot back.

"Please, darling, it's very beautiful, but let's wait one day before you buy it," Steve said, placing a hand on her arm.

"Will you please place the necklace aside? We'll be back tomorrow."

Ravyn was sure India was going to cause a scene and was surprised when she acquiesced. "OK, but I'm getting it tomorrow," she said, reaching for the clasp.

"Very well," the shopkeeper said, as India reluctantly handed the necklace back. Only then did India look at the price tag: 500 euros. "I'll put the necklace behind the counter, but I'll only keep it aside for one day."

As they left the jewelry store, Ravyn asked if Luca minded if she looked into the leather shop right next door. "Oh, I'd like to go there, too," Clare said.

"Please, I'll wait outside," Luca said. "I'm not one much for shopping."

Ravyn, Clare, and Carl went into the leather shop, and Ravyn immediately saw a beautiful black handbag for 50 euros hanging on the wall. She pointed at it and the clerk reached for a pole with a hook. The clerk deftly removed the bag from its wall hook and handed it to Ravyn.

She loved the buttery feel of the Italian leather. "May I also see the one over there?" she asked, pointing to another black leather handbag with some tooling patterns on the front. She knew she could only afford one of the bags, and couldn't decide which one to purchase.

"I like the second one you picked better," Clare said. "Look at that lovely pattern on the front."

"You're right," Ravyn agreed, as she turned to the clerk, handing over the second bag. "I'll take this one."

Steve and India wandered in, with India looking at wallets and handbags, before turning her attention to some thin leather belts along a wall.

"Where's the door lead?" Steve asked, pointing to a door covered with hanging leather belts.

"Oh, that leads into the other store," the clerk said. "But it's sealed shut. You can't cut through."

"Oh no, I was just in the jewelry store," Steve said with a short bark of a laugh. "I don't want to go back in there. Too expensive for me."

India glared at her husband. "It's not too rich for me," she announced and slapped two handbags on the counter. "I'll take both of these."

Ravyn and Clare looked at each other and moved toward the front door. Ravyn was pleased with her purchase.

"I bought a handbag," she said, excitedly showing Luca.

"It is lovely."

Ravyn began to put it into her blue canvas backpack, mindful of Gavin's camera already in it.

"If you want, that should fit back here," Luca said, opening the rear compartment box. He took Ravyn's backpack and carefully placed it inside before shutting it and handing Ravyn a helmet. She looked at it and thought her ponytail might be uncomfortable, so pulled the band free. She shook her hair out but knew her brown hair would have that odd hairband bump for a while.

"*Che bella*," Luca said, reaching for her hair and stroking it. "I like you with your hair down." He brushed a lock of hair from her face.

"It's very messy today."

"No, you are wrong. You are very beautiful."

Ravyn felt bashful. It was a long time since a man had complimented her.

"Have you been on a motorcycle?" Luca asked.

"Years ago," she said, fumbling with the helmet's strap.

"Here, let me do it for you," Luca said, unbuckling the strap, putting the helmet on her head and then adjusting the strap under her chin. "Is it too tight?"

"No, I think it's just right."

"Good."

"Where are we going?"

"Where do you want to go?"

"I wanted to see Piazza Barberini and the Spanish Steps today," Ravyn replied.

"Very good, we'll go to Piazza Barberini first," Luca said, putting on his own helmet before getting on his bike and signaling for Ravyn to sit behind him. "Hold on."

Luca roared off and into the swarm of traffic. Ravyn, her arms tight around Luca's waist, closed her eyes, afraid for a moment as she felt the bike weave in and out of other vehicles. Eventually, she opened her eyes and gave a little yelp as they entered a roundabout and cars, buses and trucks buzzed by. She tightened her grip on Luca. She couldn't see the wide smile on Luca's face.

Luca found a place to park his motorcycle along Via delle Quattro Fontane, just a short walk from Piazza Barberini. Ravyn attempted to fluff her hair after wearing the helmet, knowing she was likely going to sport helmet head for the rest of the day.

As if reading her mind, Luca said, "Don't worry, you look beautiful."

Ravyn flushed. Luca took her by the hand as they walked north toward Triton Fountain, built by Bernini. Then Luca led her to a corner of the square where one of Bernini's smaller fountains, The Fountain of Bees, stood.

"There is a really interesting church just up this way," Luca said, pointing toward Via Vittorio Veneto. "Are you scared of bones?"

"Bones?" Ravyn asked as they proceeded along the sidewalk.

"Ah, skeletons? Are you afraid of skeletons?"

"You mean a real skeleton?"

"Yes," Luca said, as they arrived at Santa Maria della Concezione dei Cappuccini, they turned right and walked toward the Monumental Cemetery of the Capuchin Brothers. Luca paid the few euros for their tickets and they entered.

Ravyn didn't know what to expect, but she wasn't expecting elaborate works of art made out of the bones of the dearly departed Capuchin monks.

Chandeliers of bones hung from the ceiling in the dim light of the crypt. Walls were covered in long bones and small bones. Ravyn gave an involuntary shudder. Luca wrapped his arm around Ravyn's waist and pulled her close. "*Non aver paura*," he whispered. "Don't be afraid. I am here."

Ravyn leaned into Luca, enjoying the warmth of his closeness, but shuddered again when she saw the plaque: "What you are now, we once were; what we are now, you shall be."

Luca and Ravyn spent about an hour in the macabre crypt before climbing the stairs outside and into the sunshine.

"That was different," Ravyn said. "I appreciate the artwork that they made out of bones. But they made artwork out of bones. That creeped me out a bit."

"It is one of the more unusual places here in Rome. Not as many tourists come here," Luca said, as they walked back to his motorcycle. "Now I'll take you to the Spanish Steps."

Luca unlocked the motorcycle and handed Ravyn her helmet. She frowned slightly as she thought of what her hair would look like at the end of the day. She brushed her hair back and put the helmet back on. Luca tightened her strap again before climbing on his bike and starting the engine. Ravyn got behind him and held on tight, leaning into his strong, muscular back. Luca smiled once again behind his helmet's visor.

Luca's parking spot wasn't as close to the Spanish Steps as it had been to Piazza Bernini, but Ravyn didn't mind as they walked hand in hand down the narrow streets before emerging into Piazza di Spagna.

The crowds were incredible. Even in the offseason, the Spanish Steps were crowded with tourists, trinket vendors and residents alike. Luca and Ravyn slowly climbed the steps to the top before turning and looking out over the street below.

"It's beautiful," Ravyn said.

"It is," Luca agreed, sitting on one of the steps and pulling Ravyn down to sit next to him.

"And you get to see it all the time," Ravyn said. "Do you live near here?"

Ravyn realized she really knew nothing about Luca — where he lived, where he worked.

"Down at the bottom is the boat fountain," he replied.

Ravyn realized he didn't answer her question, but Luca stood and pulled her up, leading her back down the steps. They got to the bottom and found a place to sit near the boat fountain.

"I live just outside of Rome," Luca said.

"And you came all the way in to see me?"

"Of course. I wanted to spend more time with you. You are a beautiful woman. Why would I not want to spend time with a beautiful woman?"

"You are making me blush."

"Ah," Luca said, brushing Ravyn's hair from her face. "You don't even realize how beautiful you are."

Luca leaned in and gave Ravyn a long, deep kiss. Ravyn leaned in. It has been so long since she'd been kissed that way. His tongue flicked against hers, teasing.

Luca's fingers brushed against Ravyn's breast. She felt a rush of desire.

They pulled apart but remained touching as they sat, looking over the boat fountain and street beyond. Ravyn reached for Luca's hand, lacing her fingers into his. He squeezed her hand, then brought it to his mouth, kissing its back.

They remained like that, sitting silently, holding hands. Ravyn felt so content. But as content as she was, her butt was starting to hurt from sitting on a cold stone step.

"I still want to see Trevi Fountain," Ravyn said. "Is it far?"

"No, it's close. We can walk there. Is that OK?"

"Yes. I'd love to walk. I feel like I'm eating so much on this trip I need to walk off some of the calories."

"You American women. You always think you eat too much. Men like women with some, what do you say? Meat on the bones."

Ravyn laughed, slapping her thigh. "Well, I have some meat on these bones, but I'd still like to walk anyway." She stood up, offering Luca her hand.

He stood, taking Ravyn's hand and pulling her to him. He kissed her deeply again, running his hand down her back and stopping at her ass, which he gave a little squeeze. "I like this meat," he whispered in her ear.

Ravyn reached down and removed Luca's hand from her behind. She didn't want to give him the wrong idea. And what idea was that, she wondered. Does he think all American women are easy?

If Luca was offended that she'd removed his hand, he didn't show it. They walked hand in hand again to Trevi Fountain, where again they were met with crowds of people, most of them near the front of the fountain, craning with their phones to take selfies with the massive fountain behind them.

Ravyn's eyes widened as she took in how big Trevi Fountain was, the water gushing out in several spots like a waterfall.

"Wow! This is amazing," she said.

"You know you have to throw a coin in the fountain," Luca said.

"I do?"

"Yes. It means you will come back to Roma," Luca said as he kissed the top of her head.

"Well, I'd better throw one in, then." She reached in her handbag and tossed a coin in underhanded.

"No, no. Not like that," Luca said, taking Ravyn's hand. "That's not the way you do it."

"There's a way to do it?"

"Yes. You must do it the right way."

"Show me."

Luca took Ravyn by her shoulders and turned her so her back was to Trevi Fountain. Ravyn could hear the babble of various languages around her, mixed with the rush of the water of the fountain.

"You need to throw a coin over your left shoulder," Luca said.

"What? You are serious? There is really a way to do this?"

"Yes. It means you will come back to Roma. You want to come back to Roma, yes?"

"Yes," Ravyn breathed. For at that moment, she knew she wanted to come back to the Eternal City. She closed her eyes, took her euro coin in her right hand and tossed it over her left shoulder. She didn't hear it splash into the fountain's basin, but she knew it was there. She was ensured of her return to Rome. She opened her eyes and looked at Luca, who was smiling at her.

He walked toward her and kissed her deeply again. They held each other at the fountain, kissing and caressing.

"Get a room!" a tourist shouted. Ravyn flushed again as they pulled away. Luca turned and made a gesture that she was sure was offensive to Romans. But she smiled inwardly and grabbed Luca's arm and laughed as she pulled him away from Trevi.

As they turned, Ravyn spied a gelateria on the corner. "Oh! Gelato!" She pulled Luca toward the corner store.

"You want more gelato?"

"I love gelato! I want to eat as much as I can on this trip. You said you wanted a woman with meat on her bones. Gelato will definitely put meat on my bones," Ravyn laughed.

Luca pulled her along as they reached Cuba Café. The place was packed and they wrestled their way to the counter. Ravyn ordered cantaloupe and apricot flavors, or *cantalupo* and *albicocca*. Ravyn was glad the glass counters included pictures of the fruit. She hadn't studied fruit in her Italian language app.

Luca got mint and chocolate. *Menta* and *cioccolato* in Italian. Ravyn delighted at how everything sounded fancy in Italian.

They walked out licking their treats. "Let's walk back to the motorcycle, but slowly," Ravyn said. "*Mio Dio*, this is so creamy and sweet."

"Just like you," Luca said, lowly.

"You are such a flirt!"

"Why am I a flirt when I say the truth? Why do you American women say this?"

"Oh, you have said this to other American women?" Ravyn teased back.

Luca stopped on the sidewalk, looking serious. "I only want to know you." He pulled Ravyn in close again and kissed her. She dropped the rest of her gelato on the sidewalk and pulled him closer. She could feel him getting aroused against her. She was feeling aroused as well.

"What is happening?" Ravyn wondered, feeling a little uneasy.

Luca walked them back to his motorcycle. "What should we do now? Is there somewhere else you want to see?"

"I really would like to go back to my hotel for a short rest. Is that OK?"

"Of course. I'll take you there."

They rode back to Ravyn's hotel, Ravyn holding on tightly to Luca. She was still amazed at and a little afraid of the busy Roman traffic.

They arrived at Il Giardino. "Do you mind if I go up by myself? I really need a shower. My hair," she started to say, reaching up to her hair, all matted from the motorcycle ride and greasy from the day.

"Let's meet later for dinner," Luca said. "Do you have your class tomorrow?"

"Not in the morning," Ravyn replied, out in front of the hotel, hearing the traffic buzz by. Luca was locking Ravyn's helmet to the motorcycle's side. "We are meeting in the evening. I want to go to the Vatican in the morning. I want to hear the pope speak. Il Papa."

"We can do that. I will come to the hotel tonight at eight tonight for dinner," Luca said, awkwardly holding up eight fingers, his black helmet tucked under his arm. "You will be ready, yes?"

"Yes," Ravyn said, retrieving her shopping from earlier in the day from the motorcycle and leaning into Luca for a quick kiss. "I will be ready."

Ravyn felt the warm water of the shower running down her body, melting away the grime and stickiness she felt cling to her. She was grateful for clean hair and skin as she toweled off.

She sat on the end of the bed, a towel wrapped around her and rubbed her aching feet and ankles. She laid back on the bed and stretched. She could easily close her eyes and sleep for the rest of the night.

But then Ravyn would miss dinner with Luca. She looked at her cell phone to see the time. Did she have enough time for a power nap? Maybe.

Ravyn dried her hair before laying back on top of the fresh-smelling sheets and pulling out her travel journal. She rolled onto her stomach and began to write:

Jet lag must have claimed me this morning as I woke up late for cooking class. I got there just in time for our outing to Campo de Fiori, however. It was a fun walk through the market and we also saw the Jewish Ghetto. And what a nice surprise at the end of class when I Luca met me on his motorcycle! He took me to several tourist attractions, including a crypt of Capuchin monks. The 'artwork' along the walls and ceilings is all made from the bones of the deceased monks. It was interesting and macabre at the same time. I wouldn't want to visit on a ghost tour at night. Creepy! I was glad he was there with me.

Luca also took me to the Spanish Steps and Trevi Fountain and we found a gelateria where I had cantaloupe and apricot flavors. Luca got mint and chocolate. I got to try some of his. I got to try some of him, too. We had a bit of a PDA moment at Trevi Fountain. My God, he's a good kisser. And I love his accented English. He's sexy. I'll need to tell Julie all about him.

He's picking me up for dinner tonight, and since I don't have class until tomorrow evening, I think we'll spend tomorrow together visiting the Vatican. He told me he'd take me. I really like him. He's funny and kind. A real gentleman. It's nice to have a man pay that much attention to me. I haven't had that happen since Marc and I broke up.

I know nothing will happen with Luca, but it does feel nice to feel a man's body next to mine, feel his strength. He has long fingers. How do I know? He wanted to hold my hand almost all day as we walked around. That is, when we weren't on his motorcycle and I was holding on to him for dear life. But, that was kind of nice, too. Holding onto him, leaning against his nice strong back. He has broad shoulders, too.

Good God, I sound like a teenager. I just miss the weight of a man on me. I miss a man in my life. So, I'll enjoy my time with Luca, even though it will be short.

I have no idea what I'll wear tonight. I didn't pack a dress or anything. I guess that's just as well since I think Luca will come get me on his motorcycle. I wonder where we're going for dinner. I don't care, as long as I can sit across from him and gaze into those soft brown eyes.

Closing the journal, Ravyn smiled, closed her eyes and rolled onto her right side. She could hear the traffic below through her balcony door, but it was muffled, almost soothing. She was asleep within minutes.

Ravyn awoke with a start as the phone in her hotel room rang.

"Hello?" she asked sleepily.

"*Buona sera, Signora* Shaw," said a female voice on the other end. "There is a gentleman in the lobby to see you."

Ravyn sat bolt upright and looked at her cell phone. It was 8:15 p.m. She had fallen asleep! Luca!

"I'll be right there. Please ask the gentleman to wait."

"Very good."

"Shit, shit, shit, shit!" Ravyn cursed as she ran to the bathroom and tried desperately to erase the sleep from her eyes and the bed head from her hair. She changed into a burgundy blouse and her black jeans. It was the nicest outfit she had in her luggage. Ravyn winced as she put her black boots back on. Her feet rebelled, but she knew they were the nicest footwear she had for the outfit as well.

Ravyn looked at herself in the mirror as she grabbed her jacket and handbag. For the second time today, Ravyn raced out the door, late for an appointment.

Luca turned to see Ravyn rush toward him. He wore dark denim jeans, a dark gray knit shirt, and a black leather coat. He also wore a look of worry on his face.

"I'm sorry I'm late," Ravyn said, reaching Luca and touching him on the arm, trying to reassure him. "I fell asleep. I'm so glad you came up to get me. I might have slept all night."

Luca reached down and gave her a kiss on the lips. "I was worried you did not want to come."

"Oh no. I am looking forward to dinner tonight," she said, trying to get her arm through her jacket. "I was just a bit tired after all of the places we went today. It was a busy day."

Luca stopped her, took her jacket and helped her into it. "Do you still want to go out?" he asked, as they began down the steps to the front door and street level.

"Yes, I do. You want a girl with meat on her bones, right?" She smiled up at him. "Where are we going? Are we driving there?"

"I parked my bike down the street. I thought we'd walk over to a restaurant by the Pantheon. It's very nice there."

"Wonderful," Ravyn said, as inwardly she cringed at thinking about walking in her cute boots. She took his arm as he began to lead her toward the steps that lead down to Trajan's Forum and along the streets to the Pantheon.

Luca led Ravyn to a restaurant right in Piazza della Rotonda and got a table outside so they could enjoy the hustle and bustle of the square, as well as look at the

Pantheon, dramatically lit at night. She was glad there were some overhead heaters to help stave off the chill.

"This is lovely," Ravyn said, shrugging out of her jacket as Luca held out her chair for her. When was the last time a gentleman had held her chair for her? she wondered. European men seem so much more sophisticated.

Luca removed his coat and draped it over an empty chair. A waiter came to the table and looked at Luca, who was just about to sit. "*Ciao*, Luca!" he said, grabbing Luca by the arm and giving him a friendly pull.

"Antonio!" Luca replied. "Are you working at my cousin's restaurant now?"

"*Si, si*," he said, then looked at Ravyn, and made a little bow. "*Signora.*"

"Antonio, this is my friend Ravyn. Why don't we start with some *vino rosso della casa*, eh? Is red wine OK, Ravyn?"

"That would be lovely," she replied. Sitting al fresco at the restaurant was lovely, but there was a slight chill in the air. Red wine would warm her up, she knew.

Antonio bustled away and Luca sat, smiling.

"He's my friend from *calcio*, ah, football," Luca said. "What do you Americans say, soccer?"

"Oh, you play soccer? I mean football?"

"*Si*, with my friends. I am very good."

"And your cousin owns this restaurant?"

"*Si*. I have many cousins. There is always a cousin who runs this or has that."

"That's wonderful to have a big family like that. I don't have many cousins, and they don't live close to me."

"That's too bad. Does your family live close to you?"

"No," Ravyn shook her head. "My parents and sister live in South Carolina, about two and a half hours from where I live in Atlanta. It's not too far to drive, so I try to see them when I can. But I'm pretty busy these days with my magazine work, which keeps me in Atlanta."

"Just one sister?"

"Yes, Jane," Ravyn replied. "Do you have a sister?"

"I have three! And two brothers."

"A big family then."

"Ah, in Italy it might be more of a small family. My mother has four sisters and four brothers. My father has five brothers and two sisters. That's how I have so many cousins."

"I'll say! I can't imagine having that many brothers and sisters. Have you always lived in Rome?"

"I grew up just outside of the city, but most of my brothers and cousins now live in Rome. My sisters are still outside the city, raising babies."

Ravyn smiled. Luca was animated when he talked about his family. He clearly loved them.

"Are you a middle child, the oldest or the baby?" she asked.

"I'm second to last. I have a younger sister. I had another sister who was the youngest, but she died at birth."

"I'm so sorry, Luca. Your poor mother."

"Yes, it was hard on her. I was too young to know anything about it. I don't even remember her. I was just three."

Antonio returned to the table with a basket of bread, two wine glasses and a bottle of red wine. "Matteo says dinner is on him, so order the specials. They are good tonight." Antonio showed Luca the wine's label and Luca nodded before Antonio opened the bottle, poured a small portion in the glass and handed it to Luca.

Luca took a sip and nodded and Antonio continued pouring out wine for the both of them.

"What are the specials?" Ravyn asked, reaching for her glass and smelling the rich, earthy aroma of the red wine.

"Tonight, it is *Cacio e Pepe*," he said.

Ravyn tilted her head, perplexed. She recognized the word pepe, pepper. But what in the hell is cacio? "Sounds good, I'll take that," Ravyn told Antonio.

"Due," Luca said, holding up two fingers.

"*Prego*," Antonio said, walking away.

"OK, what does *cacio* mean? I don't know that word. I know *pepe*, but not *cacio*," Ravyn asked, turning toward Luca as she took a long sip of the wine.

"Cheese," he said.

"I thought *formaggio* was cheese."

"It is. We have another word for cheese, too. Cacio."

"So I'm getting a dish with cheese and pepper?"

"One of the best dishes in Roma."

"OK. Sounds good," Ravyn said, sipping more wine. The dark red wine was starting to course through her veins. She could feel how it warmed her body.

Ravyn and Luca walked back to her hotel hand in hand. Ravyn felt the glow of a great meal, great wine, and a great man at dinner. It had been such a long time since she felt this good.

Luca walked beside her with a bottle of the house red wine his cousin Matteo had given them on the way out of the gate of the outside patio. No check came for dinner, which included a wonderful chocolate dessert. Matteo and Luca hugged, spoke rapid Italian and then hugged some more. The Pantheon looked beautiful bathed in lights and Ravyn enjoyed watching street performers work the crowd of tourists in the square.

Luca had started to wave off some gypsy children who came through the patio with roses, but then reached into his pocket and put a couple of euros in a small hand and took the red rose and handed it to Ravyn. Ravyn held it to her nose as they walked through the street, which was still teeming with tourists.

They walked along and Ravyn looked to her right toward the Colosseum and gasped. The Colosseum was bathed in lights as the nearly full moon hung above it.

Luca stopped as he heard Ravyn gasp.

"It is beautiful, no?" he asked.

"It is. This is magical."

"You are beautiful and magical."

Ravyn turned to face him. He put his free hand behind her back, pulling her to him. They kissed a long, deep kiss.

As they pulled away, Luca took her hand again as they walked again toward the Il Giardino hotel.

Ravyn asked for two glasses at the front desk after she and Luca climbed the stairs to the lobby of the hotel.

Glasses in hand, Ravyn opened her hotel door as she and Luca almost fell in, her back against the door and Luca's hand on her shoulder. Ravyn caught the stink eye of the evening front desk clerk as she looked at Luca. "Yes, bitch. He's hot, and he's mine," a slightly tipsy Ravyn thought.

They stumbled through the door and Luca kicked it shut. He put the wine down on the small nightstand near the bed and pulled off his leather coat, laying it across the chair where Ravyn liked to sit to write in her journal. Luca began to pull at her jacket.

Ravyn suddenly felt panicked. She was in her hotel room with an almost perfect stranger. A hot Italian stranger, but still. Was this wrong? Was this safe?

Luca kissed her deeply. *"Cara mia,"* he murmured.

Ravyn understood that. She pulled away. "Should we open the wine?"

Ravyn suddenly felt hot and opened one of the balcony doors, letting the cool night air into her suddenly small hotel room.

"Si, I'll open it."

Luca reached into his coat pocket and pulled out a wine key.

"Where did you get that?"

"Matteo gave it to me when he gave me the wine," Luca responded. He smiled as he twisted it into the bottle, then deftly pulled out the cork.

Ravyn heard the slight pop and sat on the end of the bed, pulling off her boots one at a time.

"Ugh," she moaned, rubbing her feet. "These have been killing my feet all night."

Luca handed her a glass of wine, knelt down and reached for her right foot. He began rubbing her arches, then her toes. Then he began rubbing her left foot.

Ravyn took a sip of her wine, then moaned. She felt herself getting wet as he rubbed her ankles, too. This was bliss, she thought, and all he's doing is rubbing my aching feet.

Luca began moving up her legs, then pushed her flat against the bed. Ravyn almost spilled her wine. She put it down and pulled Luca closer to her. His breath slightly smelled of cheese and wine.

He kissed her, his body pressing into hers. Ravyn could feel the weight of him on her and sighed deeply. Luca moved his hand to her right breast, giving it a small squeeze through her clothing. She gasped again. "Luca," she moaned.

"*Bella, bella,*" he breathed.

Ravyn tried to sit up, thinking this was going too far.

"I think you should leave," Rayvn said, trying to push Luca off of her. "I don't know you, really."

"But I don't want to leave," Luca said, stroking Ravyn's hair and pushing her back down on the double bed. "And what do you want to know about me? I'll tell you anything. Anything."

Before Ravyn could ask a question, he covered her mouth with his, his tongue exploring. They continued making out, their kisses getting longer, deeper.

"Do you really want me to leave?" he asked huskily.

"No," Ravyn responded.

He kissed her deeply again and Ravyn could feel the tightness in her body ease.

It had been so long, perhaps too long, since Ravyn had been intimate with a man. Not since she had broken up with Marc earlier that year. Luca was awakening a yearning Ravyn had not realized she'd had for warmth, intimacy.

Her whole body felt hot with desire. Suddenly Ravyn was rushing to pull off her jeans, her top, her bra. She could feel Luca's skin next to hers. He moved down her body, his facial stubble rubbing against her soft skin.

She parted her legs, feeling Luca's stubble between her thighs. She moaned loudly, not caring that the thin hotel walls might not hide her pleasure.

Luca's fingers began toying with her panties, then within her. Ravyn gasped again. Luca slowly pulled her panties off her.

"Luca," she moaned.

"*Bella, bella,*" he replied into her inner thigh.

Ravyn could feel his hot breath on her. She wanted him. She began to scrabble for him, pulling him up toward her.

He moved upward, landing on her body. He was still fully dressed, but she could feel his fullness against her. She began pulling at the front of his jeans.

Luca pulled back from Ravyn, easing his jeans off and quickly pulling his shirt over his head. A single gold chain remained around his neck.

Ravyn put her hand on his hairy chest before wrapping her arms around him and pulling him back on top of her.

"Do you have a condom?" she whispered. Ravyn's muddled brain realized she didn't have one. She didn't think she'd need one on this trip.

Luca moved onto his right elbow. "*Goldone? Sì,*" he said, stretching over Ravyn to grab a foil packet from his coat pocket. Ravyn sigh deeply. "*Goldone,*" she mimicked. It was the last word she spoke as Luca moved his body onto hers and passion ignited within her.

Asparagus Risotto

2.5 pounds of asparagus
1 ⅔ cup of risotto rice
4 Tsp. butter
1 yellow onion, finely chopped
4 Tsp. fresh grated Parmesan cheese
Salt and pepper

Break the tough ends off the asparagus and discard. Break off the tops and set aside.

Roughly chop the rest of the asparagus spears and in a medium-sized pot cook in lightly salted boiling water. When cooked, puree with the water to make a thick stock and keep simmering on low heat. I use an immersion blender to do it, but you can also use a food processor. Just be sure to do it in small batches and be careful of the hot liquid.

In a second medium-sized pot, heat half of the butter and cook the onion until soft. Stir in the rice and let it begin to absorb the butter before adding a ladle of the asparagus stock. When absorbed, add the asparagus tips and another ladle of stock.

Keep adding the stock a ladle at a time until the rice is cooked, about 20 minutes.

When cooked, stir in the remaining butter and Parmesan cheese. Beat with a wooden spoon to release starches. Risotto will look silky after the beating.

Cover and let stand for 5 minutes.

Spoon into bowls and salt and pepper to taste. Add extra Parmesan cheese, if desired.

Cooking Up Trouble

Buon appetito!

Chapter 4

Secondo

Ravyn rolled over and leaned into Luca, feeling his warm body and smelling his musky scent, the scent of sex.

⹀s flew open. "What happened?" she wondered. "Where am I?"

Then she slowly remembered the night before. The peeling off of their clothes, the fumbling with the condom. The uncircumcised penis. Ravyn, who had had a few lovers, had never seen an uncircumcised penis and was surprised by Luca's. That hadn't ruined the lovemaking, which had been erotic, sensual, satisfying.

Ravyn leaned back into Luca, who was sleeping soundly. Still asleep, he wrapped his arm around her and pulled Ravyn closer. Now she was a bit sorry since she had to pee. She eased out of his arm and went to the tiny bathroom.

When she returned to the bed, she tried to slide in quietly, but Luca stirred. "*Cara*, you're awake?" he asked.

"Sort of," she said, moving back into his strong arms. She could feel his morning erection. She hoped he had another condom. They'd made love twice last night, all legs, arms and intimate parts.

"Mmmmm," Luca groaned with a throaty moan. He pulled Ravyn closer before moving on top of her.

"You have another condom? *Goldone?"* she whispered.

"Of course."

Cooking Up Trouble

Ravyn didn't need to hear any more. She felt herself float into Luca's intimacy.

When they awoke a couple of hours later, Ravyn blinked into the morning light. They had left the balcony door open the night before and now Ravyn felt cold in the hotel room. She shivered, feeling the goose flesh prickle on her arms as she pulled the duvet cover over her.

Luca stirred beside her. He opened one brown eye, then closed it.

Ravyn turned so she was facing him in bed, taking in his wavy brown hair, his dark eyebrows, the overnight stubble on his face. "He'd be handsome with a slight beard," she thought. "Hell, he'd be handsome just about any way you could imagine."

She rubbed her leg up and down his hairy one, her toes curling to stroke his leg.

"What are you thinking, *cara*?" Luca asked, now looking back at Ravyn, pulling her close.

"Just that you are very handsome, *bello*. Is that right?" she said as she smiled, running her finger down his stubbly chin.

"*Sì*, but it is you who are more beautiful, *bella*," he replied, leaning in to nibble her neck.

Ravyn giggled. His stubble tickled her neck. She pulled the duvet up to her chin. She wasn't sure why she suddenly felt shy around Luca. There had been no shyness the night before, or earlier this morning.

She felt herself blushing thinking about what they had done on that small double bed. She'd almost fallen off at one point. Luca certainly wasn't timid in bed.

"What time is it?" Ravyn asked, rolling over and reaching for her phone. Luca stopped her, pulling her close again.

"What does it matter?" he whispered, his voice husky. With his free hand, he parted her hair and began kissing the nape of her neck.

"I wanted to go to the Vatican today, to see Il Papa, the pope," she replied. Ravyn broke from Luca's arms and reached over, fumbling for her phone on the side table. The phone screen read a little after nine o'clock.

"Shit, we won't make it to hear the blessing," she said, disappointed. She laid back down, frowning.

"Don't make that face, *cara*. You are too beautiful to make that face. I will bless you," he teased, running a finger down her cheek.

"I think you've blessed me plenty," she giggled. "I'm going to be very sore today."

Luca smiled at her. "Come, I have my motorcycle. We can get there in time."

"I need to shower and I want to get something to eat. I worked up an appetite last night, and this morning." Ravyn gave Luca a knowing grin, then got up from the bed, shut the balcony door and hurried to the bathroom to start the shower. She hoped the hotel had lots of hot water this morning. It would feel good over her cool skin.

She stepped in, feeling the warmth cover her. She heard the bathroom door open and close. Luca lifted the thin white shower curtain, peering in at her. "Is there room for me?"

Ravyn turned, catching sight of Luca, naked. It took her breath away. He was lean, muscular and clearly turned on.

"Luca, we'll slip and break a leg in here."

"I will be careful," he said, stepping in behind her, lifting her wet hair to kiss her on the nape of her neck. He began soaping her back, running his hand down to her butt and her thighs.

Somehow, Ravyn knew she would not be seeing Pope Francis later that morning.

Luca deftly maneuvered his motorcycle through the Roman streets, finding a small parking space on a side street not far from the Vatican. At least Ravyn thought it was a parking space.

Roman drivers seemed to park in places that weren't meant for parking. Then again the cars tended to be on the small side, all the Smart cars, tiny trucks, motorcycles, and Vespa scooters. Perhaps drivers just learned to take advantage of small empty spots wherever they could find them. Ravyn eyed one parking job along the side street, the car angled half in, half out of the travel lane. "They even take advantage of not so empty spots," she thought.

Cooking Up Trouble

Ravyn pulled her helmet off, handing it to Luca, who locked it with his helmet under the motorcycle's seat. Then she shook out her brown hair, wondering if the helmet had matted it down.

As they walked away from the motorcycle, Ravyn asked, "Don't you worry your bike will be stolen?"

"Oh, it's been stolen twice," Luca casually replied.

Ravyn was suddenly alarmed. She'd left her backpack, with her new leather handbag and Gavin's camera locked in the motorcycle's box compartment all day yesterday. She hadn't even worried that they might have been unsafe there.

"You got your bike back, though."

"Oh yes, one of my cousins stole it, well, borrowed it, for a little while each time."

Ravyn sighed with relief. "Well, that's good, I guess. At least you know who took it."

"*Si, che stronzo*, that Raffaele. He put marks on it there and there," Luca said with disgust, pointing to missing black paint on the side of the motorcycle.

"*Stronzo?*" Ravyn asked.

"Asshole. He's an asshole, my cousin," Luca said, truly angry.

Ravyn nodded. That was probably the kindest thing she would have called a cousin who damaged her vehicle.

"But it's an old bike," Luca said. "I really want a Ducati, a racing bike."

Ravyn could see his eyes light up when he talked about the Ducati.

"A racing bike? Do you race?"

"No, but I'd like to."

"Why don't you get one then?"

"They are expensive and then I'd have two bikes and nowhere to put them. Raffaele would steal my Ducati for sure. If he put scratches on that bike, I'd have to kill him."

"Why would you need two bikes? You could sell the BMW."

"No! I can't sell my BMW. That's my work bike. The Ducati would be my racing bike." Luca looked wistful.

"I see," Ravyn said, not really understanding his logic.

Luca had taken Ravyn's hand as they walked down Via Leone IV, coming up along the outer wall of Vatican City.

They turned down Via di Porta Angelica, eventually turning right into Saint Peter's Square, with its colonnade arms embracing those who walked toward the basilica.

Ravyn gasped at its enormity. Even though it was November and the offseason, she could see a long line forming at security to get into the church, which wouldn't open until noon since there had been a papal blessing that morning. Luca and Ravyn had missed the blessing, but crowds now lingered.

"Let's not wait now," Luca said. "Let's go over to the museum. You want to see the Sistine Chapel, yes?"

"Yes, I do."

"Let's come back after we go to the museum. The church will be open."

They began to retrace their steps back to the sidewalk and make their way to the Vatican Museum, where a line also formed, but it seemed to move quickly.

Ravyn saw the signs indicating appropriate dress for the museum. No shorts, no bare shoulders, no midriffs. It was cool enough that she needn't worry. She wore her black jeans, a cream-colored knit sweater, and a jacket. Luca was wearing what he'd worn yesterday.

Ravyn blushed when they had left her hotel just an hour before, feeling like she was doing the walk of shame, as if she were the one in the same clothing as the day before, even though she was showered and had on fresh clothes.

It was Luca who was unshaven in slightly rumpled clothes. If anything, he looked even more handsome. Still, she felt like she got a second stink eye from the day clerk at the front desk as they walked down the stairs of the lobby hand in hand.

They had stopped at a local coffee bar for a caffe latte, which they drank *al banco* at one of the small banisters around the shop, in true Italian fashion. Ravyn felt like she was getting an authentic cultural experience with Luca at her side.

Now standing in line at the Vatican Museum, Luca held her hand, circling his thumb over the back of it. She smiled up at him. Luca was over six feet tall, to her five-foot six-inch frame. He bent down and gave her a kiss. She could taste the strong espresso on his tongue.

Cooking Up Trouble

"*Muovetevi, avanti!*" came a voice from behind them.

Luca turned and fired off rapid Italian, but Ravyn could see the line had moved up without them. She quickly pulled on his coat sleeve, pointing toward the entrance door. They paid their fee and stepped inside, with Luca giving a final glare to the man who had shouted for them to move along.

Luca and Ravyn strolled through the museum, with Ravyn stopping once or twice to gape at the Egyptian or Etruscan art or even the colorful marble floors beneath her feet, some with mosaics embedded in them. Luca always gave a small smile as she oohed and aahed at the artwork.

They passed marble statues, gold works in the shape of hawks, masks of mummies. Much of what Ravyn looked at through the glass cases or along the walls were items she had only seen in art books or on educational TV shows. In reality, the artworks looked larger or smaller than she'd imagined.

She remembered seeing Salvador Dali's "The Persistence of Memory" in real life at the Museum of Modern Art in New York City the year before and being struck at how small it was. At the University of Missouri, in an art appreciation class she'd taken, she had only seen it on a large projected screen at the front of the class. As she had gazed at it in reality, it was small, with the tiny details jumping out at her.

At the Vatican Museum, the vast expanse of some of the work took her breath away, yet it was some of the tiny detail of beads, bronze or gold filigrees that also gave her pause.

Finally, Luca and Ravyn walked through the Gallery of Statues and the Octagonal Court. At every turn, Ravyn gazed upon large marble statues, including the Laocoon group, snakes entangling the limbs of distressed figures. She gave a little shudder.

"*Che cos'hai?*" Luca asked, concerned.

Ravyn looked at him, uncertain.

"What? What did you say?"

"What's wrong?" he asked.

"Oh, it's just that the statue looks so... It almost looks real. You can see they are...distressed, upset. They are in trouble," Ravyn said, pointing at the Laocoon group.

71

"Yes, they are."

They reached the Raphael room. From every angle, Ravyn could see beautiful frescoes in bright colors on each of the four walls. Her eyes widened as she saw Raphael's School of Athens, which she had studied in that same art appreciation class in college.

And yet there was more to come. Caravaggio's Deposition, Federico Barocci's Rest on the Flight to Egypt, and Leonardo da Vinci's St. Jerome.

"How could she see anything better?" she wondered. Ravyn was awed by all the art she saw around her.

Luca and Ravyn began their walk through the Gallery of Maps as they moved toward the Sistine Chapel. Interpretive guides and panels showed how the chapel had been renovated, removing centuries of dirt and grime from Michelangelo's frescoes. Ravyn stopped to read several panels before Luca pulled her along.

Ravyn stepped into the Sistine Chapel and felt her breath escape. "Ah!"

She felt tears come to her eyes as she looked up, surrounded by bright colors and a press of people, all gazing up.

Thin benches lined the walls, the benches filled with people, who sat and gazed toward the colorful ceiling.

"*Silenzio! Silenzio!*" the guards admonished if the murmur of the crowd grew beyond a venerated whisper.

Ravyn squeezed Luca's hand as she craned her neck to see more. On the ceiling, almost in the middle, was the iconic Creation of Adam by Michelangelo. She had to look hard to find it, with so many colorful frescoes covering the ceiling. She wished she'd thought to bring binoculars or opera glasses. Some tourists around her had them.

Suddenly Ravyn giggled, remembering an old "Cheers" TV episode, where Sam the bartender referred to the Creation of Adam fresco as "two muscular guys touching fingers."

"*Silenzio!*" a guard said, walking by Ravyn. She immediately returned to her reverent, and quiet, state.

Luca and Ravyn had lunch at a restaurant near Vatican City, ordering *quattro stagioni* pizza, which had ingredients from the four seasons: artichokes, mushrooms, prosciutto, and olives.

Ravyn looked at the pizza, which was so different from American pizza. It was not loaded with cheese and wasn't overly bready. It reminded her of Antico Pizza not far from Georgia Tech's campus in Midtown Atlanta. She'd been there a few times and the pizza she and Luca shared reminded her of that.

Ravyn bit into a slice of the pizza, the grease running down her chin. She wiped her face with her thin white napkin, then swallowed a gulp of the house white wine she had ordered with lunch. She loved that Italians celebrated lunch with wine. It was no big deal. In America, wine with lunch was considered more of a celebratory event, or brunch.

Luca grinned at her as he bit into his slice of pizza, loaded with artichokes. Since Luca hadn't shaved that morning, he was now showing a nice bit of stubble. It made him look rakish. Especially since she saw the barbed wire tattoo on his upper arm peak through his short-sleeved gray knit shirt that showed off his muscular arms. She hadn't noticed he had tattoos until last night. She'd found another one, a small dragon, on his hip.

As she saw the glint in his eye as he smiled at her, Ravyn's heart melted a bit more.

Ravyn and Luca cleared security at Saint Peter's Basilica and crossed the threshold. Ravyn looked right, noticing the cement that guarded the Holy Door. It was sealed until its next opening. They moved right and Ravyn saw Michelangelo's marble sculpture Pieta straight ahead. Tears sprang to her eyes as she looked at the serene face of the Madonna holding Christ in her arms.

Despite having to view the statue through bulletproof glass, Ravyn marveled at how lifelike the stone looked. The folds of the Madonna's drape and her dress seemed real. Christ's leg and arm seemed like flesh.

Ravyn wiped her eyes with her hand, then reached in her handbag for some tissues, dabbing her eyes once again.

"*Bella*, you are sad?" Luca asked.

"My God, it's so beautiful. It's so lifelike. It's a mother grieving for her dead son."

"*Sì*," was all Luca could say.

They stood together, holding hands, for a few more minutes. Finally, they moved throughout the basilica, gazing on tall marble statues, smaller cherubim, the bronze Saint Peter, the central nave and the Baldachin, a large Baroque sculpted bronze canopy over the high altar. She marveled at the four twisted columns that rose skyward.

Ravyn and Luca walked down to the grottoes, viewing the popes buried there, then paid a small fee to climb up Michelangelo's cupola. Ravyn's already complaining calves rebelled on the narrow stairs. She wasn't claustrophobic by nature, but as the passage and stairs narrowed even more, she began to worry. She was also out of breath. She and Luca took a small break at one landing before the final ascent.

They walked out onto the landing, feeling the crisp breeze on their faces, and saw the breathtaking view of Rome. Luca gave Ravyn a deep kiss on what felt like the top of the world in Rome. Ravyn kissed Luca back, pressing into his body. She felt his strong arms around her. His kisses tasted like pizza and wine.

Ravyn and Luca moved down from the cupola, coming upon a gift shop. Ravyn bought several postcards and Vatican postal stamps. She quickly filled out the postcards to her best friend Julie, her parents, and her sister and then dropped them into the blue Vatican mailbox.

She also bought a book on the Vatican artwork and a rosary for her co-worker Chase Riley, the art director at *Cleopatra* magazine. She looked for a nice gift for her friend Julie, but nothing at the Vatican gift shop seemed appropriate. Julie was not an overly religious woman. She'd find something else for her in Rome.

Back at the hotel, Ravyn once again rubbed her aching feet. Luca had dropped her off, promising to see her later that evening after the cooking class ended. Ravyn was dying for a shower and a nap. She looked over and saw the nearly full bottle of red wine from the previous before on the nightstand. They had barely touched it.

Cooking Up Trouble

She smiled to think about what they did touch the night before: the tangled limbs of hers and Luca's. She remembered his warm breath on her breast, on her inner thigh. She felt flush.

Ravyn sighed. Maybe she should go buy some more condoms. She didn't want to rely totally on Luca. She really didn't want to leave the hotel, since her feet hurt. But going to a pharmacy would mean she could get some ibuprofen for her sore feet and body.

Ravyn stood up, winced, grabbed her jacket and new Italian leather handbag and headed back out to the streets of Rome.

Ravyn arrived at cooking school promptly at 6 p.m., greeting Amy and Clare with hugs.

"I had such a great day today," Ravyn said. "I saw so much of the Vatican and its museums."

"Did you have a handsome tour guide?" Amy asked with a grin.

Ravyn flushed. "Yes, I did. It does help to have an Italian to show me the city."

"I bet," Amy said. "Is that all he showed you?"

Ravyn felt her whole face go red.

"Good on ya, girl," Amy said, giving Ravyn's arm a little slug. "I want to know if he has a twin brother."

"He's got brothers and lots of cousins."

"Sweet as! I want to meet one!"

Ravyn laughed. "I'll see what I can do." She turned to Clare and Carl. "Did you do some sightseeing today?"

"We did a little shopping, went to the Capitoline Museums and walked around the Forum," Clare said. "But we came back in the early afternoon. We did a lot of walking. Carl's knee has been bothering him, so we didn't want to overdo it."

"I know what you mean about all the walking. My feet are killing me. I stopped at the pharmacy for some ibuprofen. Thank goodness that word is the same in English. I don't know what I would have gotten if I'd had to pantomime medicine for my aching feet. I might have gotten athlete's foot cream."

Clare and Carl both laughed.

Dolores waited patiently as the conversation began to die out. Steve and India still had not arrived, but the instructor was ready to begin.

"I know we aren't all here yet, but let's go ahead," she said. "Tonight, we will make two pasta dishes and veal scallopini. Amy and Ravyn, why don't you get started by mincing some onion and garlic."

Ravyn saw garlic, onions, tomatoes, celery, and parsley on top of the counter. She moved into the kitchen, removing two knives, one for her and one for Amy. "Sharp knife! Sharp knife!" she called out.

"Clare, help me rinse the lentils we'll be putting in the pasta and lentils dish," Dolores said. "Carl, do you want to help?"

"No, thank you. If it's all the same, I'll sit and rest my knee," he said, rubbing his right one.

Dolores gave Carl a "poor man" look before turning her attention back to her pupils.

Ravyn took her chef's knife and began crushing the garlic under the blade to get off the papery skin. "Don't crush too hard," Dolores admonished. "You don't want the oils releasing too much."

"Oh, sorry," Ravyn said. She put her left hand on the tip of the knife and began to mince the garlic in a semicircle, lifting just the handle of the blade, a trick she had learned on her first day of class.

"I'm glad you are doing the garlic tonight," Amy said. "My hands still smell of it from yesterday. At least no vampires will get us."

"Oh! Team Edward!" Ravyn grinned, referencing the Twilight series that pitted angst-ridden vampires versus angst-ridden werewolves."

Amy laughed. "Oh, I was always a Team Jacob gal myself," she said, meaning she was hot for the werewolf main squeeze. "I have a thing for hairy, beastly men who howl in the night."

Now it was Ravyn's turn to laugh.

"Well, I know what you mean about the garlic," Ravyn said, giving her fingers a quick sniff. "All day today as Luca and I were walking around I was afraid the garlic was coming out of my pores."

"I'm sure your Romeo didn't mind. Those Italian men are probably used to it." Amy teased. "It was probably in their mother's milk."

"Maybe. What I can't get over is all the Italian women walking on the cobblestone streets in those stiletto heels. Have you seen them? I'd break an ankle! And they all are so smartly dressed. But why is everyone always in black? You'd think with all the Italian fashion there would be more color in their outfits. Everyone looks like they are on their way to a funeral."

Amy laughed. "Yeah, and you can tell the blokes and sheilas on holiday, can't you? They're the ones who dress casual and have the selfie sticks."

"Yeah, there were a lot of tourists in Saint Peter's Square with them. But there were notices in the Vatican Museums and the basilica that selfie sticks are banned. It didn't stop a few of them, I noticed."

"I'm hoping to get over to the Vatican tomorrow," Amy said. "I meant to try to get there today, but my mates and I went out clubbing again last night and so we slept in pretty late. I never even got a proper brekky."

"Brekky?" Ravyn asked.

"You know, eggs, coffee, toast?"

"Oh, breakfast! I didn't know what you meant."

"Oh, you Yanks!"

The sound of loud voices came from the bottom of the small landing near the elevator. Ravyn and Amy turned toward the door, knowing who was coming up the stairs.

"We're late! Hurry up, Stevie," came India's irritated voice.

Ravyn thought she was a pleasant enough woman, but wondered why in the world she'd married Steve Prescott. They did not seem suited temperamentally. "But then," Ravyn thought, thinking of her recent relationship fails, "What the hell do I know?"

"It's not my fault," came Steve's sharp reply. "You were supposed to wake me up from my nap."

"Well, I can't help it if I fell asleep, too. Just come on!"

Steve and India Prescott arrived at the door, neither one looking particularly happy. "Sorry we're late," India called out, cutting her husband a dark look as she slipped out of her jacket and hung it by the door.

Dolores Reed frowned, then showed her bright British face as she turned toward the late-comers. Ravyn thought she would never be able to give the British "stiff upper lip" to that pair.

It's not that she disliked the Prescotts. She could tolerate India in a one-on-one conversation. And Steve seemed harmless. A little befuddled, but not a bad man. But she could not understand how the two had managed to find each other and fall in love and marry. They just didn't seem that well suited. Always bickering and not really showing much affection toward one another.

Ravyn thought that might be the key to a good relationship: affection. She felt like two people had to genuinely like each other. She wondered suddenly if she'd ever genuinely liked any of her former boyfriends, or if they had genuinely liked her.

"Ravyn, are you done with the garlic?" Amy asked, pulling Ravyn out of her thoughts.

"Oh, yes. But my fingertips won't be done with it for a while."

Ravyn scraped the minced garlic into a small pile with her knife. Ravyn quickly washed her hands and grabbed Gavin's camera, getting a few photos of Amy chopping her onions. Amy laughed as she tried to wipe her watering eyes on a dishtowel.

Ravyn then got some shots of Clare with the pasta and lentils before swinging the camera around to get a couple of photos of Carl sitting in his chair, his arms folded over his chest. Carl grimaced rather than smiled, Ravyn noticed. "Maybe he just doesn't like his photo taken," she thought.

Dolores then waved her hands, gathering everyone together to compile the ingredients for the pasta and lentil dish.

The evening continued, with the class making another pasta dish and then a meat dish. As each dish was ready, they gathered around the wooden table, drinking wine and chatting.

Cooking Up Trouble

Ravyn enjoyed talking with Clare and Carl about their years as educators in the Chicago area. Carl regaled her with stories of co-ed shenanigans and professorial misbehavior. She wondered if her father, a professor at Clemson University in South Carolina, ever did such things.

Well, considering they had named her Ravyn, thanks to their love of J.R.R. Tolkien's Lord of the Rings series, she thought it likely there were some parental shenanigans. She smiled. She was missing her parents on this trip.

She usually chatted with her parents once a week and with the run-up to the trip, she hadn't been able to talk to them. She'd be sure to call them when she got home later this week.

"I wish I could introduce you to my parents, Carl," Ravyn said. "My father still teaches. You'd have some good stories to tell each other. What courses do you teach?"

"Oh, business," Carl said, a little flustered. "I teach general business."

Ravyn was confused. Hadn't he said he taught English? She'd have to check what she had put in her notes. She didn't want to get that wrong.

"And you've always taught at DePaul? Is that the community college you teach at?"

"No, DePaul is bigger than that," he said. "University of Chicago is bigger. But I like smaller campuses. Why did you think I worked at a community college?"

"Oh, I thought Clare said you worked at a community college, and taught English. I must have misunderstood her."

Carl gave a warning glance to Clare.

The class began clearing the table of the supper dishes and India caught Ravyn's arm.

"I love your new handbag," she said, pointing to Ravyn's leather purse sitting on a chair in the corner.

"Oh, I love it, too," Ravyn replied. "I'm glad you dragged me into the leather shop. What did you end up getting in the jewelry store? Did you get that emerald necklace you wanted?"

"No, not the emerald one, but another necklace. It has a small bit of amber in it. We should go back there tomorrow. They have lovely things, and they really have good prices for what is there. You can't get that in America, I'm sure. Meet me there tomorrow, please?"

"Oh, sure. What time do they open tomorrow? I know our class starts at 10:30 in the morning."

"They open at 10. Let's meet then."

"OK. See you tomorrow morning before class."

Ravyn wondered why India was so excited to meet her back at the jewelry store. Maybe she just liked a shopping buddy.

Ravyn's best friend Julie Montgomery was like that. Julie loved to shop, but she loved to shop more when she had Ravyn at her side. Ravyn didn't mind. Julie had great taste and it was fun to watch someone else spend money.

When she was laid off, there were no shopping splurges for Ravyn. She'd follow Julie around Atlanta's luxury malls, helping Julie select shoes, handbags and clothing, but could only "oh" and "ah" at a distance and with a closed wallet.

Now that she had a steady paycheck again, Ravyn had been able to breathe a little easier when it came to shopping. She didn't have to question every purchase. Maybe she'd find a nice bauble for Julie at the jewelry store tomorrow morning to thank her for all of her support over the lean years.

As Ravyn cleared the last of the plates from the table, she turned to look out the small round window that looked out onto Piazza Venezia. The Monument to Vittorio Emanuele II was lit up in the distance.

It was getting close to 9 o'clock as they finished wiping down the countertops. Ravyn had started to run water in the large kitchen sink, but Dolores stopped her.

"Leave that for Francesca, my woman," she said, waving at the dirty dishes. "She comes in early to do those things when I have my night classes. I've had her for years, but she does help herself to my good wine."

Ravyn smiled. She felt full and a little tipsy. She'd had more than a couple of glasses of white wine tonight. She moved around the kitchen, occasionally bumping into Amy and Clare. India was nowhere near them as they stacked the dirty dishes and wiped down the countertops.

"Do you have plans tonight?" Ravyn asked Amy. "Headed back to the clubs?"

"Maybe. I need to see what my mates want to do. I can't stay out as late as last night. I had a terrible hangover today. What about you? Seeing Romeo tonight?"

"I think he'll meet me tonight to walk me home, but we don't have any plans."

"Are you sure?" Amy looked at Ravyn slyly.

Ravyn shook her head.

"Too bad," Amy said with a knowing look.

They gathered at the front door of the cooking school saying goodbye. Amy Foster's friends were there to pick her up and she gave an animated waved from the Smart car as it pulled away from the curb.

India and Steve Prescott stopped to look briefly through the window of the jewelry shop, then walked arm and arm down the street, looking happy and content. Ravyn shook her head in amazement.

Ravyn chatted with Carl and Clare Richards for just a few minutes. Carl stood looking in the leather shop, while Clare looked around, worried that Ravyn would have to walk back to her hotel alone.

"Where is your gentleman friend?" Clare asked.

"I don't know. He said he'd try to meet me, but I guess he couldn't."

"Will you be OK walking back to your hotel?" Clare asked, looking even more worried. "We'd offer to walk you back, but Carl's knee is bad."

"I'll be fine," Ravyn said, leaning in to hug the older woman, smelling her slight rose-scented perfume. "Really. It's not that late. I'll be fine. Look at all the people about."

"OK. If you're sure."

"I'm sure," she said, as she turned to walk toward Piazza Venezia and then on toward Trajan's Forum and her hotel. She turned back and waved at Clare and Carl, who waved back. "I'll see you in the morning!" she called out. "*Buona notte!*"

Ravyn briskly walked toward the Monument to Vittorio Emanuele II. The "wedding cake" as the Italians called it, was beautiful all lit up at night. She breathed in the cool night air. She was glad she had her jacket with her and she pulled it tighter around her.

She waited to cross the busy street, knowing she just had to walk out into traffic like the real Romans. But she hesitated for just a moment. Finally, she took a deep breath and strode out into the crosswalk.

Even at this time of night, shortly after 9 p.m. on a Wednesday, the Roman streets were alive. Cars, trucks, and Vespas roared by her as she traversed the street. When she was safely across, Ravyn let go of her breath. She didn't even realize she had been holding her breath as she crossed the road.

Rayvn walked along, a hedge to her left side with a retaining wall in front. She saw couples sitting on the wall, snuggling and kissing. One young man of a couple looked at her, jutted his chin, then called out in Italian she couldn't understand. Ravyn was sure whatever he said, it wasn't what his girlfriend, or whoever she was, wanted to hear. Ravyn hurried along.

She got to the edge of Trajan's Forum and turned left, quickly climbing the steps up to Via XXIV Maggio. She stopped at the top of the steps, caught her breath and turned right toward Hotel Il Giardino.

"Ravyn," a low male voice called out.

Ravyn started, whirling toward the voice as her hands went up in defense.

Luca stepped out of the shadows. "*Bella*, I've been waiting for you."

"You scared me!" she exclaimed, trying to calm her racing heartbeat. "I thought I'd see you at the cooking school."

"*Mi dispiace*, I came here instead, so I could park my motorcycle nearby," Luca said.

"It's OK," she said, looking up at him, wearing his shorter black leather jacket tonight, a dark shirt and pants. Ravyn caught her breath. Luca was so handsome. But he certainly was a typical Italian, dressed as if he were headed to a funeral.

"Are you hungry?" he asked.

"Good God, no. I'm stuffed from all the food at the cooking school."

Cooking Up Trouble

"Oh, *si*," Luca said, looking around, embarrassed. "*Ho fame*. I am hungry. Will you join me for a drink, some wine maybe, while I eat?"

"Of course," she replied. "I'd love that."

"There is a trattoria up the street. We can go there."

Luca extended his right hand to Ravyn. She took it, feeling the warmth of his touch as they walked up the street.

Pasta and Lentils

10 ounces dried green or brown lentils, washed and soaked for several hours

1 small stalk of celery, chopped

2 Tbsp. extra virgin olive oil, plus a little extra for garnish (optional)

1 slice pancetta or bacon, chopped

1 small onion, finely chopped

2 cloves garlic, finely chopped

1 small dried chili pepper, crushed

2 red tomatoes, peeled and chopped

Salt to taste

7 ounces tubetti pasta, or spaghetti, broken into short pieces

1 Tbsp. chopped fresh parsley (optional)

Drain the lentils and cook with the celery in 2 ½ pints of boiling water. The exact time needed will depend on the quality of the lentils and will take from 30 to 90 minutes.

In a large pan, heat the olive oil and gently melt the fat from the pancetta or bacon before adding the onion, garlic, and chili peppers. Stir in the tomatoes and simmer for a few minutes.

When the lentils are cooked, discard the celery, add salt and throw in the pasta. When the pasta is nearly cooked, stir in the onion mixture and cook together for a few minutes. Stir in the optional parsley, check the seasoning and serve. Grated pecorino or Parmesan cheese can be added separately if desired, but a fine thread of excellent extra virgin olive oil drizzled on top is also preferred. Be sure to then stir it in.

Buon appetito!

Lisa R. Schoolcraft

Chapter 5

CARNE

Ravyn stirred, reaching over to touch Luca in the hotel bed. He wasn't there.

She sat up in the darkened room. "Luca?"

he whispered. "I have to go."

"What time is it?" Ravyn asked sleepily, swiping her brown hair out of her face.

"Very late. I must go. I have to work in the morning," he responded, pulling on his shirt as he sat on the end of the bed. Ravyn watched in the dim light as his arm tattoo disappeared under his shirt.

"Oh."

"*Non ti preoccupare*," Luca said, reaching over and putting his hand on her leg under the bed covers. "I'll see you after class. What time should I be there tomorrow night?"

"I should be done by two or two-thirty tomorrow afternoon," she answered, leaning on her elbow and pulling the duvet across her naked breasts. "Can you meet me then? Will you be free?"

Luca frowned, moving up to the edge of the bed next to her. "I will be at work. I have a big meeting. I will meet you here at the hotel for dinner, *sì?*"

"*Sì*," Ravyn said, nodding.

Luca bent over and kissed Ravyn deeply. "*Dormi bene, bella*. Lock the door after I leave. I want you to be safe."

"Is this hotel not safe?" Ravyn asked, suddenly alarmed.

85

"No, it is safe. But you should lock the door. Otherwise, I might be tempted to come back in and not go home."

Luca stood. Ravyn smiled, got out of the bed, wrapping the duvet around her and padded toward the door, following Luca, who was shrugging on his leather jacket as he turned to leave.

"Do you have to leave?" she asked.

"Yes," he said. "But I don't want to. I'd rather stay with you." Luca kissed Ravyn then pulled away, opening the door.

"*Buona notte, Luca*," she said softly.

"*Buona notte, Ravyn*," he said as he stroked her face before leaving.

Ravyn turned the lock and went back to the double bed, feeling the warmth where Luca had lain beginning to cool. She rolled toward the space where he had slept, wishing she could curl against him. She heard the motor of a distant vehicle start. "That's probably Luca's motorcycle," Ravyn thought as she drifted back to sleep.

When her alarm went off later that morning, Ravyn once again reached for Luca. When she remembered he wasn't there, she stretched, rolled over, and looked at her smartphone. She had a few minutes before she needed to get up and get ready, so she'd be able to have breakfast at the hotel before she left for class. She pulled the duvet up against her chin, wiggling down into the bed.

It was Thursday morning and Ravyn felt the week was flying by. She was very much enjoying Luca and his company. It was fun to have a handsome Italian man showering her with so much attention. She wondered how hard it would be to say goodbye for good in just a few days. She shook her head, trying to banish that thought from her mind. She would just enjoy it while it lasted.

Ravyn realized that with all the attention from Luca, she'd been neglecting her travel journal. She also needed to try to download a few of the photos from Gavin's camera and send a few to Chase so he could get an idea of what art he will have for the cover story. He might also suggest some photos for her to get for a sidebar story or anything else she might need.

Cooking Up Trouble

Ravyn blew out her breath and sat up, swinging her legs over and planting her bare feet on the cold floor. Her feet and back still ached from all the walking she had done around Rome. Truth be told, there were other parts of her body that were sore, too, but she smiled. Luca was responsible for that.

She picked up her neglected leather travel journal and began to write.

Rome is spectacular. Luca is the ultimate tour guide, too. We went to the Vatican yesterday. We toured the Vatican Museums first, then spent a few hours at Saint Peter's. I saw the Pieta for the first time and cried. The way the marble looks like flesh, the look on the Madonna's face, holding her son in her arms.

Luca is wonderful, too. He is so kind and thoughtful. God, he is handsome, and a really good lover. Should I even write that?! I worry since this will be a short-lived affair, but he really is wonderful. He makes me feel so alive. I miss that. I miss that in my life.

Ugh! I should be writing about the cooking school. That has been a lot of fun so far. I can't believe how fast the week has been going. We are making some incredible dishes. I think I'll be able to make some of the dishes when I get back to Atlanta. Most of them are pretty simple to make. A few are more challenging, and I'm not sure I'd eat some of the dishes again. We made a pasta and lentil dish last night, but it wasn't really for me. I'm not really a fan of lentils.

I am going to have to host some dinner parties when I get back to make the dishes I did like, though. If I don't invite people over, I'll be making way too much food and gain 100 pounds. Haha!

I'm headed to class now. I know the food will be good and I'm glad we will be done by early afternoon. I want to see the Colosseum today, as well as the Ancient Forum. Looks like it will be sunny, if a cool day, so that should be a good plan.

Ravyn looked up from her journal at the time and realized she didn't have time to send the preliminary photos to Chase. She'd have to do that later.

Ravyn got to class early and found India outside the cooking school, gazing into the jewelry store.

"Look at that!" India exclaimed, pointing to a sapphire necklace now on display in the store's front window.

"That's beautiful," Ravyn replied, peering through the glass.

"I want it," India stated flatly.

"Then you should buy it," Ravyn responded. "But I thought you got the amber necklace yesterday."

"I did. But it's because Stevie wouldn't let me buy that emerald one yesterday that I really wanted," India said, pointing to the sapphire necklace in the window case, her brows furrowed. "Now I want that one. He says we are on a budget since we got married. But I really want it and he's not here to stop me."

India began pacing in front of the store window, biting her thumb.

"Well, it certainly is beautiful," Ravyn said. Truthfully, Ravyn wished she could buy the necklace, set in what appeared to be white gold or platinum. Ravyn was fond of white gold or sterling silver against sapphires.

She owned a white gold sapphire ring that had belonged to her grandmother Margaret. Ravyn's sister Jane had their grandmother's ruby ring. That one was set in gold, with small diamonds ringing the center set ruby. Ravyn and Jane had spent their summers as children with their grandparents and Ravyn had fond memories of her time with them.

Ravyn looked down at her hand, twisting the sapphire ring on her finger, the same one her grandmother had given Ravyn upon Ravyn's graduation from the University of Missouri.

"Stevie will go mad if I buy it," India said, now looking sad.

"Well, it's a beautiful necklace, regardless," Ravyn said. "Is there a lottery here in Rome? Maybe we can win that and then buy all the beautiful things in the store we want."

India smiled ruefully. "That may be the only way I get that necklace. Take my advice, don't marry a poor man."

Ravyn tried not to look shocked. She smiled with what she hoped was a genuine smile. "Well, I guess you are right. But they say you can love a poor man as well as a rich man, right?"

"You may love a poor man, but you *marry* a rich man. Don't marry a poor man, Ravyn," India replied, turning her face and looking pained. "I'm sorry I did."

Cooking Up Trouble

Ravyn didn't know how to respond to India. She really hadn't thought about it. The guys she had dated in her life were, by and large, on her same economic scale.

Ravyn then thought about her dating life during what she considered her "lean years" when she was freelancing and trying — sometimes failing — to pay her bills. When it came to her dating life then, some men had been below her poverty line and some had been above it.

Her last boyfriend, Marc Linder, had been a former attorney turned technology entrepreneur who owned his own business. His business, LindMark Enterprises, had been successful on paper but was struggling financially. Still, she'd loved him and had hoped they'd make it as a couple. They had not.

Ravyn pulled herself out of her memories of Marc and turned toward India. "Well, we can still dream. That necklace is very beautiful."

"At this point, I'm going to have to burgle this place to get that necklace," India said, bending down to get a better look at the necklace in the window.

Ravyn threw her head back and barked out a laugh. "Good luck with that."

India stood up and laughed then, too. "Well, a girl can dream," she said, smiling coyly.

India and Ravyn took the elevator, then climbed the final stairs up to the landing of the cooking school.

"Where is Steve today?" Ravyn asked. "Isn't he coming?"

"Oh," India responded quickly. "He'll be here later. He was running late. He's a late sleeper."

Ravyn thought that would not go over well with Dolores, who appeared to like to run a tight ship in her cooking school. That was fine, Ravyn thought. It was her school and she should run it as she saw fit. But clients like Steven Prescott probably drove Dolores to a second or third glass of wine, or the whole bottle, when class was over for the day.

Ravyn pulled her blue canvas backpack off her shoulder and withdrew Gavin's Nikon camera, playing with the lens and settings, hoping she was remembering his instructions correctly. She began snapping a few photos before class, trying to get more casual photos, rather than some of her stiffly posed classmates.

People weren't always natural in front of a camera, she was discovering. She got photos of the day's ingredients lined up on the tile countertop, the white papery garlic, the soft green sage, the yellow bell peppers.

She then tried to get some candid photos of her classmates, shooting Amy Foster laughing but Carl and Clare Richards posing stiffly. Well, she had tried! She started to delete the photos of Carl and Clare but then stopped. She'd delete them when she got back to Atlanta.

Ravyn turned her camera to India Prescott, looking pensive by the round window that looked out onto Vittorio Emanuele II. Ravyn looked down at the digital photo. "That's a great shot of India," she thought. "I should be sure to give it to her."

Then Ravyn turned to Dolores, in her bright blue skirt and white top, capturing her laughing as she pulled a clean white apron around her ample middle.

Ravyn had fun in class that day. She and her classmates made another veal dish, saltimbocca alla Romana, the same dish she'd ordered in the restaurant on the night she had met Luca.

They also made yellow pepper soup and Ravyn realized she'd need to buy a food mill to make the soup and her own pasta sauce at home. Her own pasta sauce! "I'll be a real foodie if I could manage that," she thought.

Ravyn never really thought of herself as a "foodie," even though she lived in Atlanta and loved to dine out. She did attend a lot of restaurant openings as a freelancer and now as managing editor of a lifestyle magazine.

Her job did have some great perks. As a single woman living alone in a condo, dining out on someone else's dime, enjoying free food and drinks, was definitely a solid perk.

Earlier in the year, she'd attended the opening of Polaris, a revolving restaurant and bar atop Atlanta's downtown Hyatt Regency Hotel. The Polaris, 22 floors above street level, had been a hot spot in the late 1960s and

1970s in Atlanta. It shuttered in 2004. Now it was reopened, renewed, in 2014.

The opening events lasted a week, but Ravyn was there the night a wicked thunderstorm blew through. She watched out the Polaris's space-pod type windows as rain blew sideways and lightning struck close. She could see traffic at a standstill on the Downtown Connector. Then the storm passed and the sky was streaked purple, orange and pink. She had gotten some great shots of it with her smartphone.

Ravyn stepped out onto Via del Plebiscito, chatting excitedly with Amy Foster and India Prescott, the bright blue November afternoon sky above them. Ravyn marveled at how wonderful the weather had been all week. It was almost magical.

Almost as if on cue, Amy's friends pulled up in their car and Amy climbed in and waved goodbye. "See you mates tomorrow!" Amy called out.

India pulled Ravyn's arm. "Let's go back into the jewelry store. I want to look at more pretty things. I really want a bracelet to go with my amber necklace. Maybe I'll find one to match. Maybe some earrings, too."

Ravyn felt pulled along. Honestly, Ravyn didn't want to buy much more. She was sure her credit card was nearing its limit and she was almost out of euros. Any more expensive purchases and she'd have to find an ATM to get more cash.

She mentally calculated what was in her bank account back in Atlanta. Although she had a full-time job now, having scrimped and saved during her lean years made her very money cautious. Still, the jewelry in the shop window was so lovely. Ravyn looked through the window again at the sapphire necklace and sighed.

Ravyn still wanted to get something special for Julie. She missed her friend and she missed not talking to her every day. She realized she hadn't even texted or emailed her since she'd met Luca earlier in the week.

Ravyn had bought an international texting plan for her smartphone for the month, so she should text Julie today, even if it was just to say hello. Maybe she would even tell Julie about Luca. But what would she say?

"Julie, I've met a hunky Italian man and I'm screwing him day and night! Don't want to come back! Hope you are well!"

Well, maybe not that, Ravyn thought, smiling inwardly. No telling what Julie might think about that text. But she would have to text her something about Luca. Ravyn realized she didn't even have a photo of Luca to send Julie. She'd have to get a selfie with him when they got together later this evening.

Ravyn found India at the store counter, haggling with the saleswoman. At least she thought they were haggling. It sounded a bit more like an argument.

Three bracelets lie in a row on a black velvet jewelry display. Ravyn could see India's scowl and the saleswoman shaking her head, so the negotiations were not going in India's favor.

Ravyn heard a sharp clap as India slapped her hand on the countertop, turned and marched out of the store, uttering a few choice words as she rushed past Ravyn. The saleswoman was uttering some sharp Italian in reply and collecting the bracelets up in her hands.

"Well, I never!" India said when Ravyn stepped outside the store. "She was completely unreasonable! She wouldn't even bargain with me. Bloody bitch!"

"Maybe she's not allowed to bargain," Ravyn said, trying to soothe India.

"Everyone bargains, Ravyn! It's how it's done!" she retorted. "That bitch probably thought I was trying to steal something. Bloody racist bitch."

"I don't think she…"

"Oh, don't defend her! You probably thought the same thing."

"I most certainly did not," Ravyn started to defend herself, but India cut in.

"Just forget it! Forget it!"

India began walking quickly down Via del Plebiscito. Ravyn stood stock still in front of the jewelry store, shocked by what had just happened. "What is her problem?" she wondered. "Why the hell is India angry with me?"

Ravyn shook her head, slung her backpack over her shoulder and began to walk back to her hotel. She had the

Cooking Up Trouble

afternoon to herself and she wanted to see the Colosseum and the ancient Forum since the weather was so nice.

Ravyn sat on the end of her neatly made hotel bed, once again rubbing her feet. Her low back ached, too, from standing on the tile floors in Dolores's kitchen all morning. She flopped back onto the bed, stretching her arms over her head. "Ugh!" Ravyn thought. "If I don't get up right now I could close my eyes and nap for days."

She rolled over onto her stomach and pulled out her phone, mentally figuring out what the time was in Atlanta. Ravyn decided Julie would probably be up early getting her young daughters Lexie and Ashley ready for school, so it was safe to text her.

Hey Jules, how are you? I'm having fun in Rome! I met a hunky Italian man who is showing me lots of the city.

Ravyn hit send, then smiled slyly and began typing again.

And he's showing me lots of HIM.

Ravyn could see the bubbles of a forthcoming reply.

OMG! Dish! I want to know all!

Ravyn flipped over onto her back, continuing to text Julie.

His name is Luca and he is a fox. Tall, dark wavy hair to his shoulders. Dark smoldering eyes. Tattoos on his arm and hip. Maybe a bit of a bad boy.

Big feet and hands? Julie asked.

Ravyn snorted a laugh, almost dropping her phone. Why do you want to know his shoe size?

You know why. Dish!

More than adequate shoe size.

Good in bed?

Very good in bed. He knows all the right moves. And he murmurs sweet nothings to me in Italian.

You dirty girl. Putting a man on the menu. Cooking up trouble, I see. Jealous! I've got to get the girls off to school. Text me later.

TTYL

Ravyn sat up and put her phone back in her handbag, feeling a bit recharged and ready to take on the Roman ruins.

Ravyn wandered through the Ancient Forum, throngs of tourists milling along the dusty paths. She visited the Temple of Vesta, and the surrounding complex of the Vestal Virgins, although that was fenced off.

She visited the Shrine of Vulcan and the Temple of Saturn. She walked to the sidewalks on the outskirts of the Forum to buy a bottle of water, then wandered past the Temple of Castor and Pollux. She couldn't believe how old everything was. America's oldest buildings seemed new by comparison.

Finally, Ravyn headed toward the Colosseum, arriving just before the last admission for the day, giving her just over an hour to wander the iconic ruin.

As she stood in line to get in, men in gladiator and Roman centurion costumes walked up and down the queue, trying to get tourists to pay to take a photo with them. She'd been warned about the pickpockets around the Colosseum, so kept her handbag close.

"Oh, *signora*, please take your picture with me! You want a picture with a real man!" one man, with a shiny breastplate and sword, red and gold tunic and red-plumed helmet, pleaded with Ravyn. He beat his fist on his breastplate for emphasis. She smiled, but declined, holding her handbag tighter. The costumed man gave a brief frown then continued down the queue, making the same plea to the next woman he saw.

Children ran excitedly alongside him, trying to touch his sword, waving their arms as if to fight him with imaginary weapons, but he waved them away. He only seemed interested in pretty women.

Once through the turnstile entrance, Ravyn walked out along the boardwalk to the center of the amphitheater, looking down into the Colosseum's substructure. She'd heard about the tours given beneath the arena floor which allowed tourists to see where the gladiators and animals had waited before they battled. She was sorry she'd been too late for that.

Ravyn found a stairway to an upper level, running her hand along the travertine bricks as she climbed the narrow steps, awed by the thought that Romans nearly 2,000 years ago ran their hands along the same rough red building blocks.

Small yellow flowers poked out between bricks and dirt on areas that must have once been seats, Ravyn assumed. She raised Gavin's camera and took a few photos of that.

Some parts of the Colosseum had iron bars blocking entrance to some niches, but Ravyn could see broken marble and other broken bits there. She also found a stray gray and white kitten sound asleep on top of a broken column. There seemed to be lots of cats around the Colosseum, she noted.

Ravyn raised Gavin's camera hanging loose around her neck and took a couple of photos of the pink-nosed kitten. Not even the flash of the camera woke it.

Ravyn then got out her phone and got some selfies around the structure but also asked two fellow tourists to take her photo. She sent a text message of the photo to her parents and sister. "Having a wonderful time!" She sent another to Julie with the same message.

After she left the Colosseum, Ravyn crossed the street and found a gelateria, treating herself to *pinoli*, or pine nut, and Irish coffee flavors. She knew she probably shouldn't have gotten two scoops since she was planning to meet Luca for dinner, but she wanted to try more than one flavor.

Ravyn also spotted what she thought were food trucks, selling panini, on the sidewalks near the ruins. She saw from the signboard there were spinach and ricotta panini and mushroom and ham panini.

Even though the smells from the trucks made her mouth water, she dared not buy anything from them. She decided on another bottle of water, though, opting for the still mineral water, rather than the "gassata" carbonated water.

Ravyn wondered when she would see Luca. She was annoyed that she hadn't asked him what time they would meet that night and she didn't have his cell number, so she couldn't call or text him.

Clare had asked Ravyn in class earlier if she'd like to meet her and Carl for a drink before dinner. Ravyn had declined, but now she wished she had said yes. She didn't want to just go back to the hotel and wait on Luca. She had never been a woman to wait on a man, no matter how handsome he was. Was it too late to try to text Clare for that drink?

Ravyn got back to the hotel and the front desk clerk waved a little piece of white paper at her.

"Miss Shaw, I have a message for you," the woman said.

"Oh, thank you," Ravyn said, taking the slip of paper from her.

Meet me at Piazza Rotonda tonight at 20:00. Luca

Ravyn looked up at the desk clerk. "What is 20:00? Is that an address?"

"Eight o'clock this evening," she replied.

"Oh, right. Sorry. I wasn't thinking about military time."

"Military time?"

"The 24-hour clock," Ravyn replied, waving the paper at her. "Thank you. *Grazie.*"

"*Prego,*" the desk clerk nodded. "You are meeting your handsome Italian man?"

Ravyn smiled brightly. "Yes."

"I'd be careful with that one, Miss Shaw."

Ravyn looked surprised, then looked concerned. "Why? Do you know Luca Ricci?"

"No, Miss Shaw," she frowned, "but I know men like him. He may be taking advantage of you. Please be careful of that one."

"Yes, of course, I will. Thank you for your concern."

Ravyn hurried to her hotel room, shutting and locking the door behind her.

The conversation with the clerk had unnerved her. Perhaps it was because, in the back of her mind, she had some doubts about Luca as well.

"This is just a vacation fling," Ravyn thought. "What really do you need to know about a man you won't see again after this week? We've been careful with condoms. It's not like I'm having his baby or I'll get an STD."

Ravyn felt a cold sweat down her back. The condom had never slipped, had it? No. It hadn't. She was safe in that regard.

Cooking Up Trouble

But their fling had happened pretty quickly. Ravyn didn't really know much about Luca other than what he'd told her. She didn't have a way to reach him.

She tried to put those worries out of her mind. She was enjoying her time with Luca. He'd told her about himself. He wasn't being secretive. Even if there were gaps in what she knew of him. That's how an early romance worked, right?

Ravyn saw the wine bottle from the other night neatly placed on the small bedside table. There was just enough in the bottle for a glass, so Ravyn poured out some of the red elixir and stepped out onto the balcony. Green plants on pots crowded around her. It wouldn't be long before the plants would need to be taken in, or they'd be dead.

The sun had set and the streetlights were illuminated. Ravyn could see the church near the end of the street, which curved around to where she didn't know. She'd never walked down that way, always taking the steps down to the level below where Trajan's Column, Market, and Forum were located.

Ravyn felt the evening's cool air on her skin. She almost turned back into the room to get her jacket, but decided against it, taking a deep drink of red wine instead. She still had a couple of hours before she was to meet up with Luca.

Ravyn watched as cars drove past below her, and saw patrons spilling out of the trattoria across the way. She took a deep breath, enjoying the moment.

Ravyn finished her wine and stepped back into the hotel room. She decided to take a couple more ibuprofen for her aching feet and back since she would be walking back over to the Pantheon, which was at least a quarter- to half-mile away.

She looked at the pain reliever's bottle to see how many pills she should take, but the label was all in Italian. She had no idea if it was stronger than what she usually bought in the United States. "Oh well," Ravyn thought, as she popped two in her mouth.

She reached for her phone to try Julie again.

Hey Jules, you there? Have some time to chat before I have to meet lover boy tonight. Missing you.

Ravyn waited to see the bubbles of a text reply but saw nothing. She sighed. Now that she had that seed of doubt about Luca, she wanted to talk to Julie about it.

Julie was always a good sounding board for Ravyn. They'd known each other for years, meeting when they both had worked at the daily newspaper in Atlanta. They'd been hired on about the same time.

Since she couldn't reach Julie, Ravyn decided she would check in with her neighbor, Jack Parker, to see how her cat Felix was doing. Jack, who lived down the hall in Ravyn's condo complex, was feeding and watering her gray tomcat while she was away.

Hi Jack. Just checking to make sure everything is OK. How is Felix?

Ravyn waited just a moment, then saw Jack's reply: All is well here. Felix misses you. Condo is OK. Ur back Saturday, right?

Yes. I'll be back late on Saturday. Please feed and water Felix Saturday too.

OK

Thanks so much! What's new in Atlanta?

Not much. SSDD. TTYL

Ravyn laughed at Jack's response. "So, not much new going on in the ATL," she thought. "Typical Thursday." She put her phone down and picked up her brown leather travel journal.

"Day four of the cooking school. I can't believe there is just one more day of class. This week is just rushing by.

We made several dishes today, some of which I will try to make once I get home. I'm going to have to up my game with better knives and pots and pans. No more using my mismatched sets of pots from my college days and my 'one good knife' that is bent and dull.

I had a weird encounter with India Prescott this afternoon. She had a disagreement with the saleswoman at the jewelry store and then came out and yelled at me. I am not sure what I did to piss her off. I don't think I did anything. Up until then, I thought she was a pretty pleasant person, but I think she has a short temper.

Maybe she was upset because her husband Steve never showed up for class today. She said he was running late, but he never showed up at all. Strange. I still think they both are pretty odd. The odd couple. Haha! Steve would definitely be the neat one, with his "only burn a candle for three hours nonsense." I can't picture India as the messy Oscar Maddison type, though. She's always put together in the way she dresses. Of course, she could be a complete slob at home, but I bet not. Several times during the cooking classes I thought Dolores was going to brain Steve. And sometimes I thought India would run him through with a sharp knife. What a pair!

I'm about to get ready to meet Luca tonight for dinner back at Piazza della Rotonda. I wonder if we are going to his cousin's restaurant again. Or rather, where his cousin works. The desk clerk warned me today to be wary of Luca. I wonder if she knows him. She said she didn't, just knew men like him.

She said he might be taking advantage of me. It makes me wonder if he is. Or maybe all Italian men are that way? I don't know. It's all been so wonderful with him, but is it too wonderful? If so, what does he want with me, other than maybe sex? I'm sure he can get that from any number of Italian women. He's certainly no novice. He knows his way around the female body, that's for sure.

I hope the clerk is wrong about him and she's just concerned for me. I hope he's not just using me. I like him and I'd hate to think he doesn't have at least some feelings for me. Maybe I'll ask him about it tonight when I see him. Good grief, I sound like a middle school girl with her first crush!"

Saltimbocca alla Romana
(Veal With Prosciutto and Sage)

The literal translation of saltimbocca is "jump in the mouth," and that's what this tasty combination of veal, prosciutto, sage, and white wine will do.

8 small flat pieces of lean veal (about 1 1/2 pounds) I've also made this dish with thin slices of chicken breast
4 thin slices of prosciutto
8 fresh sage leaves
4 Tbsp. butter
4 Tbsp. dry white wine
Flour for dredging
Salt and pepper

Salt and pepper each veal slice. Place a sage leaf then half a slice of prosciutto on top of each seasoned veal slice, using a wooden toothpick to skewer them together. Dredge each seasoned slice in the flour on a plate.

Melt the butter and gently brown the veal, turning the slices over so the prosciutto side is briefly in contact with the hot butter. Transfer the veal to plates and tent to keep warm, if needed.

Add white wine to the pan, gently scraping up the brown bits. Simmer to reduce the sauce before spooning sauce over the veal. Serve veal over sautéed spinach or potatoes. Serves 4.

Buon appetito!

Chapter 6

POLLO

Ravyn walked into Piazza Rotunda shortly before 8 p.m., taking in the festive atmosphere of the square. She looked over at the Pantheon, dramatically lit by floodlights on the ground surrounding the front of the monument, shadows deep along its sides.

Street performers, hucksters, people selling flowers and tourists milled about. Ravyn looked at the throngs of people and wondered how she would find Luca. She crossed the square to the restaurant they had patronized just two days before. She stood outside the front door, scanning the crowd for his face.

By 8:15 p.m., Ravyn was walking down the side of the restaurant and back to its front, getting anxious. "Where was he?" she wondered. People crowded around her as she stood, then paced again. She didn't have a way to text him. She didn't have his number. "Why had I never gotten his number?" she asked herself.

Ravyn decided if Luca wasn't there by 8:30 p.m., she would head back to her hotel. Surely, he'd know to find her there. A few moments later she felt an arm wrap around her shoulder.

"There you are," Luca said, looking pleased. "I was waiting on the other side of the square, where you would come from the street. I must have missed you."

"Oh, I got here a bit early and looked for you, but thought maybe you'd be here," she replied, relief flooding through her.

Luca bent down and kissed Ravyn. "I missed you today, *cara*," he said. "How was your class?"

"It was good, we made this really good soup — *zuppa* — today with big yellow bell peppers."

"*Sembra delizioso*," Luca said. "*Ho fame*. Let's eat."

Luca led Ravyn into the restaurant, lifting his chin in greeting at the maître d' and speaking rapid and friendly Italian. "Probably another cousin," Ravyn thought, smiling.

The maître d' laughed, turned and gave Ravyn a big grin. Ravyn wished she understood more than just her tourist Italian so she'd know what Luca had just told him.

Despite people waiting for a table, Luca and Ravyn were seated immediately at a small table toward the back of the restaurant. A bottle of red wine was placed on the table shortly afterward and Luca's cousin Matteo came over to greet them.

"*Ciao*, Luca! *Come va*? How are you? How is your mother? Is she well?" Matteo asked.

Luca stood and grasped Matteo by the arms before bear-hugging him. They chatted for a while before Luca turned to introduce Ravyn.

"Ah, Ravyn, you are very beautiful," Matteo said, who took Ravyn's hand as she stood to be introduced. "Why are you with this dog, eh? You should go out with me."

Luca playfully punched Matteo on the arm.

"OK, OK," Matteo said, throwing up his hands in defeat. "*Basta*! Let me bring out the specials of the day. *Godere*!"

Luca held the chair out for Ravyn, who sat down again. She flicked the black cloth napkin onto her lap and looked around the restaurant. They had been outside on the patio the first time they had eaten here. Now they were in a cozy corner.

The walls of the restaurant were cream, with rust and brown accents. Ochre-colored wall sconces threw off a soft golden glow. It gave the restaurant a very romantic feel. Ravyn shifted in her chair, feeling flushed.

"What is it, *cara*?" Luca asked, pouring some wine in her glass.

"This restaurant is lovely. Very romantic."

Luca reached across the table and took Ravyn's hand, kissing her palm. "I will show you romantic, later."

Ravyn really felt a rush of desire, but she was still worried that she'd almost missed Luca and this moment.

She reached into her handbag and grabbed her phone.

"Listen, I nearly missed you tonight. Let me get your number so I can text you next time."

Luca looked surprised, then held his hand out for her phone. "I will put my number in your phone." He quickly took her phone and plugged in some digits, before handing it back to her.

"Did you put your name in?" she asked, not seeing the numbers and scrolling through to find his name.

"Yes, under Luca. Tell me about your day. Tell me about your classmates," he said, putting his hand over her phone and changing the subject. He then poured himself a glass of wine. "Who are they? From America, too?"

"Well, you've met Clare and Carl Richards. They were at dinner that night we met. They are from Chicago, in America. They told me they go to many cooking schools. They've been to ones in France and Spain."

"Spain?" Luca asked.

"Yes, why? That's what they told me."

"They must like to travel and cook a lot."

"I guess so. Steve and India Prescott are newlyweds from England. I think this is sort of their honeymoon. I got into a bit of an argument with India today. She was trying to haggle with the clerk at the jewelry store and…"

"At the jewelry store?"

"Yes, the one we were in the day before. The one right below the cooking school."

"What happened?"

"Well, I guess she was trying to haggle over some bracelets and they argued."

"Who? The clerk and India or the clerk and you?"

"No, the clerk and India. India stormed out of the store then got mad at me."

"Why you?"

"Yes, why me?" Ravyn took a big sip of her wine and sighed. "This is delicious. And Amy Foster is from Australia. You met her the other day outside of class."

"Ah, yes. The pretty blonde woman," Luca said, smiling.

Ravyn tore off a small piece of bread from the basket on the table and playfully threw it at Luca, hitting him in the shoulder. "Don't get any ideas, Luca!"

Luca laughed, his brown eyes bright. "What ideas could I possibly have? I only want to be with you, *cara*."

He shifted in his chair, then asked about the Prescotts.

"They seem, how do you say it? Uptight?"

"Yes. I can't quite figure them out. They are supposed to be on their honeymoon, but you should hear them argue with each other. He says he's in sales. I don't know what she does. I don't think she ever said when we were introducing ourselves that first day of class. He's kind of an odd man. Kind of fussy, yet messy at the same time. You should hear what he told us about burning candles!"

"Burning candles?" Luca gave her a quizzical look.

Just then Matteo arrived with plates of food. Ravyn's mouth began to water as she smelled the fresh scents.

"Never mind," she said, reaching for her fork. "It was really silly. I can't figure those two out either."

After a long, delicious dinner of Roman artichokes, a plate of carbonara and a shared panna cotta with lemons for dessert, Ravyn and Luca walked back to her hotel hand in hand. Ravyn again felt slightly tipsy with all the wine they had drunk, and Luca once again had a bottle of red wine tucked under his right arm.

She leaned into him as they walked along the sidewalk, taking in the Roman nightlife. The street was busy for a Thursday night, but Ravyn also recognized there were lots of tourists milling about.

She could see some tourists with selfie sticks taking their pictures with the Monument to Vittorio Emanuele II in the background. Ravyn took out her smartphone and stopped, attempting to get a selfie of her and Luca, but Luca pulled her along before she could get the photo. What she got was a blurry mess.

"Hey, I wanted to get a photo of us!" she protested, tucking her phone back in her handbag.

"I want to get back to the hotel," Luca answered huskily into her hair. "I want to get you in the bed."

Ravyn giggled and quickened her pace. "Can't argue with a horny man," she thought.

For the second time in the middle of the night, Ravyn awoke to Luca pulling on his pants, getting ready to leave.

"*Mi dispiace, cara,* I have to go," he said.

"But why?" Ravyn asked groggily, reaching for his arm. "Stay with me, *per favore.*"

It was not like Ravyn to beg, but she didn't like Luca leaving her in the middle of the night. She enjoyed his warm body next to hers. She missed having a man next to her, the connection she felt with another human being.

"I have to go. I have to work tomorrow," he replied.

Ravyn raised up on one arm on the bed. "But why can't you go later this morning? Come back to bed, Luca."

"I must go," he said, running a finger along her cheek before reaching down to kiss her deeply. "Lock the door when I leave."

Ravyn awoke with a start as her smartphone trilled the morning alarm. She reached over on the bed, wishing Luca was still there, then stretched and got up. At least she'd be ready for breakfast at the hotel's dining room and get to the cooking school on time. It was hard to believe the trip was almost over.

Ravyn got up, feeling a slight headache and spied a half a glass of red wine on the side table. "Screw it," she thought, as she gulped it down. "I'll have Italian coffee soon enough."

The air was crisp as she walked to the cooking school on Friday morning. She stood at the crosswalk in front of Vittorio Emanuele II and saw a hesitant tourist. "Follow me," she said as she strode confidently into the busy street. Vehicles and Vespas whizzed around her, but Ravyn kept her gaze straight ahead.

When she reached the other side, the timid tourist, somewhat shakily, thanked her. Ravyn gave her a curt nod. She was beginning to feel like a native Roman. She felt exhilarated.

Ravyn felt less exhilarated as she approached the cooking school, which was blocked by bright blue and white police, or *polizia*, vehicles. Ravyn wondered what was going on.

Dolores Reed was at the front door of the cooking school building, wringing her hands. "This is just awful," she said, gesturing to a shop window.

"What's happened?" Ravyn asked, seeing Amy Foster and Clare Richards standing next to Dolores, who looked flushed and distressed.

"The jewelry shop!" Dolores exclaimed. "It's been burgled! Sometime last night. This is just awful! What if they had come into my apartment!"

"Burgled?" Ravyn thought. "Robbed?"

She looked at the shop, her view partially blocked by policemen and women standing about. She didn't see any broken glass. She didn't hear a piercing alarm going off. How had it been robbed? she wondered.

But as she got a better look through the plate glass window she could see a blank space where the sapphire necklace she had admired yesterday had been.

"Oh!" Ravyn said. "The necklace is gone!"

A policeman, dressed in a navy blue uniform, heard her exclaim and approached.

"*Signora, hai informazioni?*" he asked.

Ravyn stared at him blankly. "I, I don't speak Italian." she stammered. "*Non parlo Italiano. Parla inglese?*"

The man waved over a nearby policewoman.

"*Sì?*" she asked.

"Do you speak English?" Ravyn asked. "*Parla inglese?*"

"*Sì.* Yes," she said. "Did you see what happened?"

"No. But I see the sapphire necklace in the shop window is gone." Ravyn said, pointing to the window.

"How do you know that?"

"I was here yesterday, and I admired it in the window," she said.

"You were here yesterday?" the policewoman asked, opening a small notebook and beginning to take notes.

"Well, I've been here all week. I'm attending the cooking school here," Ravyn said, sweeping her hand toward her fellow cooking school students. Amy, Clare and now Carl stood on the sidewalk next to Dolores, who still looked stricken.

Ravyn was sorry she had pointed them out to the police officer.

"Why were you here yesterday?" the policewoman asked skeptically.

"Oh, I was just admiring the jewelry with India," Ravyn said. "She's a fellow cooking school student."

Ravyn turned to see if India was standing at the door, but didn't see her or Steve.

"Well, India's not here," she said, turning back to the policewoman. "But we were just admiring the jewelry yesterday. And we both admired the sapphire necklace. It's not in the window now. Was it stolen?"

"I can't say," the policewoman said. "I need your name. Are you staying here in Rome? What hotel are you staying at?"

Ravyn gave her the information rather reluctantly before joining Dolores, Amy, Carl, and Clare on the sidewalk.

"May we go up to our class?" Dolores asked the policeman who seemed to be in charge. "We are already late!"

"Yes, but we may need to talk to you later," he said. "What is your phone number?"

Dolores gave him the information, then shepherded her students through the front door, up the elevator, and into the cooking school.

"Well, that was a bit of excitement," Dolores said as they got settled in the commercial kitchen.

Ravyn almost giggled thinking that was the British coming out in Dolores. "Stiff upper lip and all that," she thought.

Ravyn wondered if Dolores would nip a bit of sherry out of the cupboard to steady her nerves, then really had to stifle a giggle thinking of it. "I've been watching too much Downton Abbey."

Ravyn tried to put on a serious face and looked around, wondering where India and Steve Prescott were this morning. Maybe they were just running late. That seemed to be their habit.

"Well, I know this is unusual, but let's get started," Dolores said.

"What about India and Steve?" Ravyn asked.

"They sent an email that they would be late today," she answered, curtly. "We shan't wait on them. Today is our final day, so let's get started."

Ravyn looked over at the kitchen counter and saw a whole chicken, garlic and rosemary. She smiled thinking she and Amy would be chopping garlic again this morning and smelling garlic on their fingers later tonight.

The class was about an hour in, with the chicken roasting in the oven, when Steve and India arrived.

"Sorry we're late," Steve said brightly. "Just had to do a little shopping before we leave for Florence later today. We have to catch the train right after class."

Dolores gave the pair a shocked look of disbelief and Ravyn thought it was ballsy of Steve to admit they'd gone shopping rather than show up to class. Why not just say they overslept or something?

"Yes, well, we didn't wait," Dolores said coldly.

"Oh, we didn't expect you to wait," Steve said, oblivious to the chilly mood of the teacher. He hung his coat on the stand near the door. "I hope we didn't miss any of the good food or wine," he added, rubbing his hands together.

Steve was smiling broadly, but India was quiet and looking none too happy, Ravyn noticed. "And what happened downstairs? There were bobbies everywhere," he said. "They almost didn't want to let us pass."

"The jewelry store was robbed overnight," Amy answered.

"That necklace we both liked is gone, India," Ravyn added.

India didn't look surprised or sad, Ravyn thought.

"Just as well. I couldn't afford it anyway," was all India said with a shrug of her shoulders.

As Dolores pulled the roasted chicken out of the oven, Ravyn stood to her side, getting photos for the magazine.

Cooking Up Trouble

The chicken looked golden brown and Dolores's face looked flushed from the heat of the oven. Ravyn also got photos of the chicken by itself on the kitchen table, placing a bottle of white wine next to it with a stemmed wine glass and a place setting in front of it.

Dolores's plates were a colorful assortment, with bright yellow and blue flowers around the rims. Ravyn had seen similar plates in the shops. It might be fun to buy a plate or two as a reminder of the trip, she thought.

"Let's eat before it gets cold," Dolores said and Ravyn knew that was her cue to stop taking photos. She placed Gavin's camera on a side chair by the front door, near where she'd left her handbag.

The roasted chicken, made with onions, garlic, rosemary, fennel seeds, and black olives, was one of the best dishes she'd had all week, Ravyn thought. Simple ingredients, but so flavorful and wonderful. This was a dish she planned to make again when she got back to Atlanta.

Conversation around the table was light, considering the earlier drama of the robbery and the tension of Steve and India's arrival.

"What will you do when you get back to Atlanta?" Clare was asking Ravyn.

"Well, I'll go through all the photos and my notes and get started on the story for the magazine. What about you two? Are you already planning your next cooking adventure?"

"We'll head back to Chicago so we can spend the holidays with our children and grandchildren," Clare responded. "I'm thinking I'll make this chicken recipe over the Thanksgiving holiday. We'll travel to our daughter's house in Fort Wayne, Indiana, for the holiday, but I think we'll want a nice chicken like this for when we get back."

"I agree," Ravyn said. "I want to make this for my parents. Goodness knows if I made it for myself I'd have to eat chicken all week."

Ravyn was thinking it would be a nice dinner to make when she saw her parents in South Carolina. Maybe she could convince her mother to let her make the chicken for Thanksgiving instead of a turkey.

Suddenly, she was very homesick. She usually talked to her mother once or twice a week, but she hadn't called her mother at all this week and only texted a few photos. She'd been so busy with the class during the day and then so busy with Luca at night.

Ravyn felt herself flushing at the thought of Luca. She wondered if she'd see him later today. They hadn't really discussed their plans as he made his escape in the middle of the night.

Escape. Why had Ravyn thought of that word? Was Luca really escaping from her every night? He hadn't that first night they were together. Where did he work? Where did he live? Maybe he wasn't single. Maybe he had to get back to another woman.

Ravyn realized she knew very little about the man, other than he seemed to have cousins all over Rome and he was very proud of his motorcycle. Was that enough to know about a vacation lover? She frowned inwardly. "I guess it doesn't really matter since I leave the day after tomorrow," she thought glumly.

"Why the long face, Ravyn?" Amy asked.

"Oh, just thinking about leaving tomorrow morning," she sighed. "I've had such a good week here. I don't really want it to end."

"I bet not," Amy said, smiling broadly. "Do you think you'll see your man after you go?"

"I'm not sure," Ravyn answered truthfully. "We haven't talked about it."

"You haven't?" Amy asked, looking shocked. "Why not? I know I'd like a hot Italian man to show off to my mates back home."

"You're right," she said. "I can at least ask him."

"So, you'll see him again today?"

"I think so," Ravyn said, frowning. "He's been meeting me either here or at the hotel. But I can text him. I think I know how to do it. Is there a code I have to use?"

Amy looked doubtful. "Yeah, but you need to have a plan to do that. You have a plan on your phone?"

"Yes," Ravyn said. "I got it before I left."

"I'm sure your young man will show up to see you," Clare chimed in. "He seems very interested in you."

Ravyn knew their time was drawing to a close, but maybe he'd like to come visit her in Atlanta. Dreamily, she began to think of all the places she'd like to show him. She'd take him to some of her favorite places like Piedmont Park and Stone Mountain, and tourist attractions like the Georgia Aquarium and the World of Coca-Cola, a museum dedicated to the soft drink invented in Atlanta.

She almost always brought out-of-town guests to one or more of these places. She'd bring him to some of the new restaurants in town, as well. She could show him off to her best friend, Julie. It had been so long since she had been out on a double date with Julie and her husband, Rob. It would be fun.

Ravyn sighed, coming out of her reverie. She didn't have to think about leaving Rome for another day and she would ask Luca this evening if he'd like to visit her in Atlanta. She was excited just thinking about having him all to herself for a solid week. He wouldn't be getting up in the middle of the night to leave her then.

The group began cleaning up after class, everyone lingering, not really wanting to go. Once again, it was more the women of the class who were doing the actual cleaning, or rather, Amy, Clare, and Ravyn.

Carl and Steve chatted near the door as India sat nearby, texting into her phone.

Suddenly, Steve looked up. "Hey, let me get a photo of the washing wenches," he exclaimed, taking Ravyn's 35mm camera and pointing it at the working women.

"Steve, the lens cap is on, and please be careful with that," Ravyn said, a bit distressed. "It's not mine. The magazine's photographer would kill me if I let anything happen to it. It's his, and one of his favorites."

"Oh right," Steve said, plucking the lens cap off the camera and once again pointing it at the women. "There. Now you have some photos of the real work that went on."

India looked up, scowling, and Ravyn wasn't so sure she, Amy nor Clare had smiled after being called "washing wenches." Ravyn would certainly not miss Steve when class was over.

Steve continued to point and shoot with Ravyn's camera. When he turned toward Carl and India, both playfully turned their heads and put out hands, blocking the lens. "Oh, you two are no fun!" Steve exclaimed.

"Get that out of my face, Stevie," India said with venom. "I barely had time to put on mascara this morning. You were in such a rush to leave the hotel."

Steve looked sheepishly at India and then replaced the lens cap and put the camera back next to Ravyn's handbag. "Sorry love," he said, softly. "Don't be cross with me. You're the most beautiful woman with or without mascara."

India's face softened as she stood up and walked over to him, taking his hands. "Oh, Stevie. I can't stay cross with you for too long."

Everyone turned away as the couple went in for a long kiss.

"Get a room, you snoggers," Amy whispered under her breath and Ravyn had to swallow a snorting laugh. Now Amy was a classmate Ravyn would certainly miss.

Roasted Chicken With Black Olives
1 whole chicken, about 4 pounds
3 onions, chopped
3 cloves garlic, minced
1 8-ounce jar of kalamata olives in olive oil or brine
6 bay leaves
2 sprigs fresh rosemary or 2 Tbsp. dried rosemary
2 Tbsp. fennel seeds
2 Tbsp. olive oil
1 bottle dry white wine
Salt and pepper

Finely chop the onions and mix with half the fennel seeds, salt, pepper, rosemary, and one bay leaf. Rub the insides of the chicken with the mixture.

Brush a little olive oil on the chicken and sprinkle on the remaining fennel seeds, salt, and pepper.

Place the chicken in an oiled roasting pan surrounded by the chopped onions, minced garlic and bay leaves.

Roast at 350 degrees F for about 1 ½ hours, or until chicken reaches 165 degrees F internally, basting every 15 to

20 minutes with some of the white wine. Oven temps may vary, so check the chicken at about an hour.

Remove chicken, baste again and add olives. If packed in olive oil, you can add the entire jar, if desired. If using olives in brine, drain before adding olives. Return chicken with the olives to the oven for another 10 minutes.

Remove chicken and let stand 15 minutes before cutting and serving. Serves 4 to 6.

Buon   appetito!

Chapter 7

PECHE

Ravyn hugged Amy, Clare, and Dolores as she said good-bye at the end of class. They had exchanged phone numbers and emails and promised to stay in touch. She was going to miss them.

She hoped they would stay in touch but knew it may only be for a few weeks or months. Ravyn bid a polite good-bye to Carl, Steve, and India, knowing she'd never hear from the British couple again and wasn't all that unhappy about it.

Ravyn lingered just a bit to talk to Dolores at the top of the stairs, then gathered her handbag and the camera, walking out the door to head back to the Il Giardino hotel. Just as she exited, the policewoman Ravyn had seen earlier stopped her.

"*Mi scusi, signora,*" the policewoman said to Ravyn. "We'd like to ask you some more questions. Can you come with us to the *stazione?*"

The woman gripped Ravyn forcefully by the arm, walking her toward a police car. Ravyn was suddenly alarmed, trying to turn back to Dolores's door, but it was closed and all of her classmates were long gone. Ravyn saw several passers-by staring at her.

"Is this necessary?" Ravyn asked, feeling panic rising. "Can't you interview me here?"

"*Signora*, it will be more comfortable at the station," the policewoman said. "We can bring you back to your hotel once we finish the interview. No harm will come to you."

The policewoman, with her black hair pulled back into a neat bun, smiled at Ravyn, but it didn't look like a friendly smile, Ravyn thought. More like a crocodile smile you'd give just before something bad happened.

The woman wasn't releasing her grip and Ravyn soon found herself in the back of a police car, speeding down Roman streets with its lights flashing and siren blaring.

Ravyn felt sick and very alone.

"Please sit down," the policewoman said, pointing to a dull gray metal chair.

Ravyn, clutching her handbag and Gavin's camera, sat down with her back straight in a drab room inside the police station. The walls were a grayish green and a fluorescent light on the ceiling cast a stark light on the desk where the policewoman sat. Ravyn guessed the policewoman to be in her 40s. She was trim and appeared to be all business.

"Can I get you anything to drink? A coffee maybe? Some water?" the policewoman asked.

"Some water would be fine, thank you. *Grazie*," Ravyn replied, her voice shaky.

The policewoman stood up and removed her navy blue police jacket before she waved to a nearby officer, spoke brief Italian, then turned her attention back to Ravyn.

"Do you have your passport with you?" the policewoman asked, loosening her navy tie. Ravyn assumed it was part of her police uniform: a white dress shirt, a navy tie, a navy skirt. The policewoman had reached up to straighten her bun.

"No, it's at the hotel, why?"

"Do you have a driver's license with you?"

"Yes, I have that," Ravyn responded, reaching into her handbag for her wallet.

After Ravyn handed over her Georgia driver's license, the policewoman placed it on her computer keyboard and began typing something, glancing at the license frequently.

Ravyn looked at the officer. She wasn't wearing much makeup. Ravyn assumed the policewoman tried to make herself look older and more masculine because she was a woman doing what traditionally was a man's job. Ravyn cocked her head and looked at her, realizing that with her black hair let down, the policewoman would probably be a striking woman.

Almost sensing Ravyn was looking at her, the policewoman looked up, giving Ravyn a stern look.

"What is going on, officer?" Ravyn asked.

"We have some more questions about the robbery and what you know about it."

"But I don't know anything about the robbery," Ravyn said quickly. "I found out about it this morning when I walked over to class."

"Yes, you said that. But you knew the necklace was missing."

"Yes, I explained that. I had been admiring it with another classmate yesterday."

"Can you describe the necklace?"

"I'm sure the shop owner can describe it better than I can," Ravyn started to say.

"Please describe the necklace, Miss Shaw," the policewoman said bluntly.

Ravyn could feel tears starting to begin behind her eyes. She had visions of Amanda Knox, the American student who spent years in an Italian prison after being accused of murder. She'd been freed after four years and just earlier this year had been exonerated by Italian courts.

Knox's story had given Ravyn chills hearing about how she was treated. Ravyn now feared she might be falsely accused as well, and who would know she was here? Not her family, not her friends, not Luca. Luca. She wished she could call him right now or text him. Maybe he'd know what to do.

"Miss Shaw! Please describe the necklace!" the policewoman said, barking the command.

"It was a sapphire necklace, with a silver chain," Ravyn said meekly. "I think it had some diamonds as well, but the sapphire was the main gem, right in the center." Ravyn pointed to her chest, about where the necklace would have hung on her.

"Did you go in to see how much the necklace cost?" the policewoman asked.

"No, we never went into the shop to see the price," Ravyn answered.

"We?"

"I was with my classmate India Prescott. We were both admiring it."

"And where is India Prescott now?"

"Our class ended today. She and her husband are probably heading to Florence. They are on their honeymoon. I think they said they were going to Florence after the cooking school, but I'm not sure. They are both from England."

"And what is her husband's name?"

"Steve, or Stephen, I think, but he goes by Steve."

"And when are you leaving Rome, now that your class is over? What kind of class was this? There are no universities near *la gioielleria*."

"*La gioielleria?*" Ravyn asked, not understanding the policewoman.

"*Mi scusi.* I forgot you don't speak Italian, no?"

"No, I only know a few words."

"The jewelry store. Where is the university near the jewelry store?"

"It was a cooking school, in a space above the store. I was taking classes on Italian cooking. But I'm leaving tomorrow," Ravyn replied, wiping her sweaty palms on her pant legs. "The classes ended today. I'm heading back to the United States."

The policewoman raised an eyebrow at Ravyn. "Can you delay your trip home if you need to?"

Now Ravyn really felt panicked. Were they arresting her? What was going on? Why were they asking her all these questions, when the shop owner would know more about the necklace?

"I, ah, I don't have a refundable plane ticket. I need to leave tomorrow to get home and back to work," she said, feeling herself near tears again.

Another police officer entered the room with two bottles of water, carefully placing them on a side table before quietly leaving.

"Your water, Miss Shaw," the policewoman said, waving her hand at the bottles. Ravyn glanced at them and realized one was still water and the other was seltzer water. She thought she ought to drink the still water since her stomach was now in knots. She didn't think fizzy water would stay down.

"Why are you asking me all these questions?" Ravyn asked. "Surely the shop owner…"

"We have talked to the shop owner," the policewoman cut in. "But you are seen on the security camera several times in the store, Miss Shaw. Perhaps you were there to see the layout of the store, no?"

Ravyn's eyes grew wide. "No!" she said. "I was there admiring the jewelry, but that's it. India went in thinking she would buy something. She did buy one necklace. She almost bought a different necklace but didn't, saying it was too expensive. I couldn't afford anything in there, either."

"So, you thought you might steal the necklace?"

"No!" Ravyn nearly shouted and stood up, spilling some of the water. "I am not a thief!"

"Sit down, Miss Shaw," the policewoman said, calmly.

Ravyn still stood, shaking. The room seemed to be too cold. Ravyn was sweating but felt like she was freezing.

"Please, Miss Shaw, sit down," the woman said, gesturing toward the metal chair once again.

Ravyn slowly sat down, but still felt shaky. Thoughts whirled through her mind. Should she ask for an attorney? Was that how it worked in Italy as well? But wasn't that part of Amanda Knox's story? She'd been held for months, years, without representation. Should she call the American Embassy? What would she even say?

"Why don't you tell me again what you are doing in Rome, Miss Shaw," the policewoman said.

"I told you. I'm here for a cooking class," Ravyn said, now with tears running down her cheeks. "I came here for a week of cooking classes at Dolores Reed's school. That's all."

"Did you come alone or with a boyfriend, perhaps?"

"I don't have a boyfriend. I came alone."

"No boyfriend? As pretty as you are?" the woman asked. "Then who is the man in the jewelry shop with you, Miss Shaw?"

Ravyn stared at the woman, not understanding her. What man in the jewelry shop? They'd all gone in at one point. Carl and Steve. Then Ravyn remembered Luca had met her at the school earlier in the week and they had gone in the stores. It's where she bought the handbag she was now holding so tightly in the police station.

The policewoman rotated her computer screen toward Ravyn. A grainy security camera showed Ravyn and India in the store, with Luca in the doorway.

"Do you recognize this man?" the woman asked.

"That's Luca. He's my…" Ravyn's voice fell off.

"He's your what, Miss Shaw?"

"He's my friend. My friend. I met him earlier this week and he's been showing me around Rome. We went to the Vatican on Wednesday."

"And what is this man Luca's last name?"

Ravyn looked at the policewoman blankly. What was Luca's last name? Did he ever tell her what it was? Of course, he did. She was panicked and couldn't recall his name. "I can't remember."

The policewoman smirked. "Can't remember? Come now, Miss Shaw. Surely you can do better than that?"

"I can't remember!" Ravyn cried. "I really can't. You are making me nervous!"

"And why am I making you nervous? What is there to be nervous about?" the woman asked calmly.

"Ricci!" Ravyn blurted. "His name is Luca Ricci."

"Ah, so now you can remember," the policewoman said.

Ravyn felt like she had just thrown Luca to the police wolves. He hadn't done anything wrong. He'd just followed her into the jewelry shop that day and now the police would track him down, maybe at his office.

Maybe it would embarrass him or make him look bad at work. He'd told her he worked in the financial services, didn't he? Probably an uptight office. He wouldn't be too happy she'd gotten him mixed up with the police.

Or what if he really had a girlfriend or wife and that's why he kept leaving in the night. The police would confront him and his girlfriend or wife would find out about her.

Ravyn felt another tear fall down her cheek. She just wanted to go home. The whole day was ruined and she was beginning to feel like the whole trip was ruined. It would be if the police didn't let her go.

Could they keep her in jail? Even if she wasn't guilty of anything? It happened all the time, didn't it? They could keep her a few days even if she hadn't been charged with anything, right? Ravyn felt another wave of anxiety and nausea washing over her. She took another sip of the bottled water, trying to calm down.

"Do you know where we can contact Luca Ricci?" the policewoman asked.

"Yes, yes," she said, reaching into her handbag and grabbing at her phone. "I have his number right here. He can clear this up. He usually meets me after class and we walk around the city, seeing the sites."

Ravyn looked through her phone, finally finding the number Luca had put in. She called out the number to the policewoman. Then Ravyn reached for a tissue on the policewoman's desk and wiped her eyes.

The officer typed some more into her computer, then said, "But your man, ah, your friend, he was not there today, no?"

"No."

"So, you will not see him today?"

"I guess not. He wasn't there after class. I can try to call or text him."

"You realize this number is fake?"

Ravyn was shocked. "No. He put it in my phone. It's his number."

"Miss Shaw, this telephone number is for a restaurant."

"It can't be," Ravyn said. "Let me give it to you again."

Ravyn called out the numbers once more. "Can you dial it?"

The policewoman did some more typing on her computer.

"I used the police computer. It comes out as a phone number for a restaurant in San Lorenzo, just outside the city."

"Maybe one of his cousins works there. He said he's got family all over."

"Why did he give you a bad number? He is your friend, you say?"

"I thought that was his number," Ravyn said, feeling another tear roll down her face.

"Men are not always honest, are they, Miss Shaw?"

The policewoman waved at the male officer to come into the room. Ravyn didn't understand their conversation but could hear Luca Ricci's name spoken. The man left and the policewoman turned back to Ravyn.

"We will want to talk to your boyfriend," she said.

"He's not my boyfriend. Just a friend."

Again, the policewoman raised an eyebrow at Ravyn. "Just a friend? Not a, what do you call it, sex friend?"

Sex friend? It made Luca sound like a gigolo. Did she mean "friends with benefits?" She and Luca really weren't that either, or maybe they were. Ravyn felt herself blushing. "We've spent a lot of time together this week, but we are not boyfriend and girlfriend. We're just friends."

The policewoman gave Ravyn that crocodile smile again. "Very well, Miss Shaw. Just friends."

The policewoman stood up from the desk and moved toward the door. Ravyn stood up, too, thinking maybe this questioning was over at last, but the policewoman turned and motioned for Ravyn to sit back down.

"You stay here," she said. "I'll be back *in un minuto*."

Ravyn slowly sat back down and covered her face with her hands. "This isn't happening," she told herself. "There is some horrible mistake."

She took out her phone and tried texting the number Luca gave her, but the message said it couldn't be delivered. She then called the number but got a voice mail in Italian. From what she could understand, the voice mail gave the hours the restaurant was open. She stared at her phone trying to understand.

Ravyn put her hands back in her lap and began to look around the room for any signs of warmth. There didn't seem to be any.

The walls were painted a dull gray-green, with no adornments. A small dead plant sat in one corner in a purple pot. The walls held no paintings, plaques or certificates, as one might expect in an office, but there was a small window with yellowing and dusty old metal window blinds. Ravyn got up and walked over to the window, but the view was of a back alley with a dumpster.

She walked around the room a bit to stretch and looked at the policewoman's computer screen, which revealed nothing but a starburst screen saver. The desk held no photos or other mementos.

Ravyn sat back down and looked up at the ceiling, where she saw what she assumed was a security camera. She was being watched, even when no one was in the room with her.

After about 20 minutes, the policewoman re-entered the room holding a manila folder, which she placed on the desk in front of Ravyn.

"Please open the folder," the woman commanded.

Ravyn did as she was told, looking down on grainy photos from security cameras on the street near the cooking school and jewelry shop. She could see a figure that looked like her, so she assumed it was. She could also see a man that appeared to be Luca.

"Do you recognize anyone in the first photo?" the policewoman asked.

"May I touch the photo?"

The woman nodded.

Ravyn gingerly picked up the black and white photo and peered at it. "I think this is me," she said, pointing to one figure. "And I think this is Luca. When was this taken?"

"I'll ask the questions, Miss Shaw," the policewoman replied. "Please look at the next photo."

Ravyn picked up the second photo and could see a grainier close-up photo of her and Luca kissing. Ravyn flushed. "That looks like me and Luca again."

"Still just friends, Miss Shaw?"

"What was this woman getting at?" Ravyn wondered. "Is she the morality police?" The thought almost made her giggle with nervous laughter. Almost.

"Yes. Just friends. We are not boyfriend and girlfriend." Ravyn was getting tired and annoyed.

"But you don't have a phone number for your friend?" she asked.

"As you well know, I do not. He didn't give me a real number, according to you. I wish I did have his real number, so I could ask if this kind of questioning is typical of Italian jurisprudence."

Ravyn immediately regretted her snark. "I'm sorry. I'm tired and I don't understand why I am here. I did not break into the jewelry shop. I did not steal the necklace. I am just here in Rome for vacation and cooking school."

"Your friend, Miss Shaw, is not who he appears to be," the policewoman said.

Ravyn stared at the woman, shocked. It is almost exactly what the desk clerk had said to her about Luca. "What are you saying? That Luca broke into the jewelry store? He couldn't have."

"And why not, Miss Shaw?"

Ravyn realized her mistake immediately. She knew why Luca couldn't have broken into the shop. Because he was with her the night before. At least some of the night.

"He was with me most of the evening before," Ravyn replied, trying to stay as close to the truth as she could. "He walked me back to my hotel. It was later when he left."

"And what time did he leave your company, Miss Shaw?"

"I'm not sure what time it was. I didn't look at my watch."

"Was it before midnight? After midnight?"

"I'm really not sure."

The policewoman sighed deeply. "This is not a game, Miss Shaw."

"I don't believe that it is. What do you mean Luca isn't who he appears to be?"

"We haven't been able to establish that Luca Ricci is his real name."

Now Ravyn looked at the woman with shock. "What?"

"It may be that it is, but we don't find a record of a Luca Ricci in our driving license records," the policewoman said. "And we don't find a record of that name in our arrest files."

Ravyn felt a small bit of relief at that.

"Maybe I got his last name wrong. I thought he told me it was Ricci, but maybe I misunderstood him."

"We are running him through our facial recognition software. We will find out who he is."

Ravyn felt sick again. Had Luca given her a false name? No. That couldn't be right. Surely, she just heard him wrong. And she had never asked to see his driver's license or any identification. He'd always paid cash for their meals when they'd had to pay for a meal. She'd never seen him use a credit card, and therefore, no name.

"Maybe Luca is his middle name?" Ravyn asked, trying to be helpful.

"Perhaps."

"Should I be talking to an attorney?" Ravyn asked, trying to figure out if she was a suspect.

"I don't know, Miss Shaw. Should you?"

"I have nothing to do with the robbery. And how did someone break-in? I didn't see any broken glass on the street."

"You are very observant, Miss Shaw."

"Well, I am a reporter. Or I was. I used to be a reporter at a newspaper in Atlanta, where I live. I've covered police cases, too."

"A reporter?" the policewoman asked, appearing to be surprised.

"Yes, but I work at a magazine now. That's why I'm here in Rome. I'm here on vacation, but I'll be writing a story about the cooking school and my vacation for the magazine."

"Miss Shaw, if you have written stories about the police, then you understand we must ask a lot of questions."

"I understand asking questions. I don't understand interrogating me."

"Are you being interrogated? Are you in a jail cell or other uncomfortable room?"

Ravyn looked around the drab office. If she said what she thought about the comfort of the room she might insult the policewoman, especially if this was her actual office.

"I just don't understand why you are questioning me. I don't have any information other than what I've told you."

The policewoman pointed to Ravyn's camera. "Do you have a photo of your friend, Luca Ricci?"

Ravyn looked over at Gavin's camera. "Oh! The camera! Yes, but I don't have any photos of him. I tried to get one of us with my iPhone, but it was blurry."

"So, no photos of your good friend?" the policewoman asked, waving at Ravyn for the camera. "Do you mind if we have a look?"

Ravyn hesitated. She didn't want to hand over Gavin's camera. What if she never got it back?

"Please don't take the camera," Ravyn pleaded. "It's not mine. If you need the photos, can you make a copy of the photos from the memory card? I've got to have these photos for the story. I've been taking photos of the food and the people in the cooking school for the magazine story."

"I think we can do that," the policewoman said. Then she smiled what almost seemed a genuine smile. It unnerved Ravyn. "May I have the memory card?"

Ravyn turned the camera over and flipped the slot to eject the memory card. It was empty. Ravyn gasped. "Oh my God! It's gone!"

Ravyn looked up at the policewoman in horror, tears springing to her eyes. "Oh my God! Oh my God! It's gone! It's gone! Someone took it! I have no photos for the story! I have no photos!"

Ravyn tried turning the camera on, hoping she'd see some photos stored in the camera anyway, but a blank digital screen stared back at her. There were no photos left on the camera.

"Could it have fallen out?" the policewoman asked skeptically, watching Ravyn turn the camera upside down, right side up, then upside down again.

"No. No. You have to push this to take the memory card out. It's spring-loaded. See?" She pushed the camera toward the policewoman, showing her the empty memory card slot. "It's gone! What am I going to do?"

"You seem more upset by this than the robbery," the policewoman said flatly.

"You don't understand! If I go back to Atlanta with no photos for the cover story, you will have a homicide to investigate! Chase will kill me!"

"Who is Chase?" the woman asked.

"He's our art director at the magazine. He's going to kill me if I don't have any photos for the story. Oh my God! I had photos of our teacher, the students, the food we were preparing! All gone!" Ravyn said.

"You are very excited, Miss Shaw. Why don't you take a moment to collect yourself."

Ravyn felt like she'd been slapped. Did this woman not understand what had happened? Ravyn was devastated. All her hard work! The entire trip now seemed like a loss with no photos for the cover story.

What would they do now? Did someone truly intentionally take the memory card? Or had she somehow lost it? "Maybe it's back in the hotel room," she thought. "Maybe it fell out there. God, I hope so!"

"Maybe it fell out somewhere. At the school or my hotel." Ravyn said, saying what she was thinking, but knowing she was grasping at straws. It was highly unlikely the memory card fell out on its own. Not the way it had to be inserted and removed. Someone deliberately took it out. But why?

The policewoman walked Ravyn out of the police station to a waiting police car.

"Officer Russo will take you back to your hotel," she said, curtly, pointing to a young officer standing at attention by the car. "We have your identification number and your mobile number. We will contact you if we need more information."

Bewildered, Ravyn wondered what more information she could give, since she didn't know anything about the robbery to begin with.

"Please contact me if you have any other questions or information," the policewoman said, handing Ravyn a business card.

"I don't even know your name," Ravyn said, looking down at the card, which was written in Italian. "And I don't know Italian."

The policewoman took the card back and flipped it over, showing her name and information written in English. Angelica Bianchi. That was her name. For such a severe woman, Angelica was not a name Ravyn would have guessed for her.

"*Grazie*, Officer Bianchi," Ravyn said, grateful to be leaving the police station.

The policewoman gave a curt nod of her head, turned on her heel and walked back into the police station.

Ravyn climbed into the police car and felt a wave of relief. She was released. Soon she would be back at her hotel and she would be heading back to Atlanta the next day.

Ravyn climbed the stairs to the landing of the hotel's small lobby and saw the familiar female desk clerk.

"Any messages?" Ravyn asked hopefully.

"No, *signora*," she replied. "*Mi dispiace.* No messages for you."

Ravyn frowned. She continued down the hall, opened the door of her room, threw her handbag and Gavin's camera on the side chair and flopped down on the bed, feeling tears of relief fall into her pillow.

Ravyn woke up with a start, not realizing she had fallen asleep. It was nearing dusk, the evening beginning to fall on her last night in Rome. She hadn't gotten to visit any sites that afternoon since she had spent more than two hours at the police station.

And she'd had no word from Luca. She looked down at her phone, but the message she had tried to text him still read "undeliverable." Would she see him tonight? She didn't know, and now she realized she had no way to contact him.

She grabbed her smartphone and texted Clare. She went on to explain that she had been questioned by the police about the jewelry store robbery and asked if the police had questioned her and Carl as well. Ravyn waited for a reply and got none.

"Maybe they've already left for home," Ravyn thought. She'd be on her own tonight.

The questioning at the police station and the discovery of the missing memory card from the camera had unsettled her, but now she was starting to get hungry. She could still go out to dinner. Perhaps a small meal and a glass of wine would improve her mood and salvage what was left of the day.

Ravyn heard the engine of a motorcycle on the street and ran to the little balcony, opening the doors hoping to see Luca down below, but all she saw was the red taillight of a motorbike. Down the street, she noticed the trattoria, the one she and Luca had visited earlier in the week. She decided to eat there, not wanting to stray far from the hotel.

Ravyn entered the restaurant, finding it packed. She tried heading to the bar to eat there, but no bar stools were available. She caught a waiter's arm, asking when a table might be available.

"*Signora,* it is Friday night," he responded. "All of Rome is out to eat tonight. You won't get a table here for an hour, or more. *Mi dispiace.*"

Disappointed, Ravyn left, wandering toward the steep steps down to Trajan's Market. She'd walk a few blocks to see if there was anything open nearby. A cool wind blew. She wrapped her jacket tighter around her. It was turning colder. The balmy weather she'd enjoyed all week was starting to shift.

Ravyn sat down heavily into a chair at a table near the back of a small restaurant not too far from Vittorio Emanuele II Monument, along a side street that ran perpendicular to the main road.

A waitress brought her a one-sheet menu and asked what she wanted to drink. "*Vino rosso della casa,*" Ravyn responded. "House red wine would be perfect to end this miserable day," she thought.

"*Prego,*" the waitress responded and disappeared.

Cooking Up Trouble

As soon as a glass with the deep ruby-colored liquid arrived, Ravyn took a long sip and felt the tension inside her begin to ease. She closed her eyes and let the warmth of the wine run through her. She looked at the menu, ordered a pasta dish and sat back again with her wine.

Ravyn was trying to make sense of the jewelry store robbery, the police interview and the missing memory card from her camera. If the police had security camera photos of her and Luca, didn't they have security photos of whoever broke into the store? "Maybe the robbers dismantled the camera, or blocked the lens," she thought. "Maybe I've been watching too many TV police shows."

And what had Officer Bianchi meant when she said the police had no record of Luca? No driver's license record? She'd ridden all over Rome with him on his motorcycle. Maybe he didn't have one if it had been suspended. But Officer Bianchi said he had no arrest record. It was all so strange.

"He has all those cousins here in Rome!" she thought. "He's native! He's got a big family. Didn't he say he worked in the financial services industry?"

Ravyn tried remembering everything Luca had told her about himself but realized he wasn't all that forthcoming. She knew very little about him, really. He probably knew more about her than she did about him.

Maybe she should walk back over to the restaurant at the Pantheon and talk to his cousin, Matteo was it? He'd have Luca's number. Or would that make her seem desperate?

Considering she was heading back to Atlanta tomorrow, maybe she should forget the whole thing. "Just remember this week with Luca for what it was," Ravyn thought. "A lusty little vacation fling with an Italian stallion."

She sighed and sipped more of her red wine and motioned for a second glass. "There are worse ways to spend a vacation than in bed with a hot man," she thought. And for the first time all evening, she smiled.

Ravyn ambled slowly back to her hotel, the cool breeze a bit stronger. She wanted to linger just a bit more on the streets now that she felt the rosy glow of the red wine in her.

The night sky was clear, although she couldn't see any stars as she looked skyward. There were too many streetlights for that. She shoved her hands deep into the pockets of her jacket as she turned toward Trajan's Column. She could see the Colosseum in the distance, a full yellow moon rising just to its left.

The sight caught her breath. It was so beautiful. A moon like that had risen for thousands of years over that ancient structure and she was in Rome to witness it happen once again.

Ravyn reached into her handbag for her iPhone to take a picture but knew it couldn't capture the natural beauty she was seeing. She didn't have Gavin's camera with her, either. She'd left it at the hotel. Then she grimaced. Without a memory card, Gavin's camera wouldn't have taken a photo to do that picturesque scene justice either. It couldn't have taken any photo.

Ravyn stood on the sidewalk a little longer gazing at the Colosseum and the full moon. She wanted this to be the final, beautiful reminder of her time in Rome.

Linguine With Tuna, Lemon and Arugula

This is one of my all-time favorite dishes in the summer. The peppery arugula plays well against the lemon juice and rich oil-packed tuna. It takes just about 20 minutes start to finish.

1 pound of linguine
2 6-ounce cans of tuna filet packed in olive oil
1 cup arugula, roughly chopped or torn
Juice of two lemons
2 garlic cloves, finely chopped
1 small red onion, chopped
1 dry red chili, crushed, or red pepper flakes, to taste
3 Tbsp. olive oil
Salt and pepper, to taste

Prepare linguine according to package directions.

Cooking Up Trouble

As pasta is cooking, heat olive oil and sauté garlic, red onion, and red pepper flakes or chili, taking care not to burn the garlic. As the garlic begins to change color, add the tuna, including its olive oil for extra flavor, to pan. Warm through.

Drain pasta and place in large pasta bowl. Add arugula and tuna mixture. Squeeze lemon juice into mixture.

Using wooden spoons or other utensils, stir the hot pasta and tuna until the arugula wilts and the dish is mixed thoroughly. Salt and pepper to taste.

Serve immediately. Serves 4.

Buon   appetito!

Chapter 8

CONTORNO

Ravyn took a cab to Termini Station before catching a train out to Rome-Fiumicino International Airport. She was grateful she had a direct flight back to Atlanta. No connection through Paris's Charles de Gaulle Airport this time.

She was tired, not having slept well the night before. She had dreamed of Luca and she had dreamed of the police station. Sometimes the two dreams had intertwined. She had dreamed Luca had come to her rescue at the police station, but then the dream shifted and he arrived at the station in handcuffs, cursing her for turning him in.

That had been more like a nightmare and she'd woken with a start, then had trouble falling back asleep. She had listened in the night for the sound of Luca's motorcycle, hoping against hope he'd still try to see her before she left. She had wanted him to comfort her.

Strong Italian coffee was going to be Ravyn's only comfort this morning. She'd had a quick breakfast at the hotel before checking out.

As she stood in the security line at the airport, she hoped she'd have time to grab another cup of coffee and do a little shopping in the duty-free shops. She hadn't had time to find a gift for her friend Julie since she spent most of Friday afternoon at the police station.

What a disaster that had been! Ravyn hadn't had the courage to email Chase to tell him she had no photos for the cover story. She felt sick. "At least whoever took the memory card hadn't taken the entire camera," she thought. "I'd never hear the end of it if Gavin's camera had been stolen."

Ravyn cleared security and headed toward her gate, found a coffee stand and a shop with some colorful scarves along the way. She picked out a red and black one for Julie. The scarf's colors were that of the University of Georgia, where Julie had gone to college. She'd like that, Ravyn knew.

She also bought a small wine stopper made with Murano glass for Jack, her neighbor who was feeding her cat, Felix. She liked the stopper so much, she bought two more, one for herself and one for her sister, Jane. She'd see Jane in South Carolina at the upcoming Thanksgiving holiday and could give it to her then.

An hour later, Ravyn boarded her plane, got as comfortable as she could in an economy seat, and closed her eyes, trying not to think of the catastrophe she would face at work without photos for the March cover story. Ravyn knew they could use stock photos of brightly colored vegetables and of models cooking in a generic kitchen, but it wouldn't be the same.

The faces of Amy, Carl, Clare, Dolores, Steve, and India swam through her mind. Then Luca's face came into her memory. She had no photos of him either. He would eventually fade from her mind, just as this vacation would without pictures to remind her of what she had seen and done.

A light snack was served shortly after the flight began, then Ravyn pulled from her blue backpack her travel journal, which had remained untouched for the past few days. She wasn't even sure where to begin to write down her feelings and experiences about the end of the trip.

"Where do I even begin to describe the past three days? I've been inside an Italian police station, questioned by the police about a crime I know nothing about, and ghosted by Luca. I'm not sure which makes me more upset. I thought he really liked me and I never heard from him after Thursday night, or rather early Friday morning. I thought we'd meet up Friday after class, but that morning when I got to class the jewelry store below had been robbed.

After class, a policewoman dragged me down to the station to question me. As if I knew anything! And she asked me all kinds of questions about Luca, too. They had security camera photos of us together at the jewelry store. She said they didn't have his name on record. It was weird. Could he have had something to do with it? I don't think so. I hope not anyway! But it was weird how he kept leaving in the middle of the night those last few days. Maybe he really did have to be at work early. Or had to get home to a wife or girlfriend, more likely, now that I think about it. But what if he was planning the robbery? I'm letting my imagination get away with me. Still…

I don't know what I'm going to tell Chase. In all the crazy of the police station questioning I found out the memory card from Gavin's camera is gone. All my photos are gone! I have no idea what we are going to do for the March issue now. God, I hope they don't fire me for this. It wasn't my fault! Someone had to deliberately take the memory card. It couldn't just have fallen out.

I don't know where or when that could have happened. Did Luca take it while we were at the hotel? Did someone take it while we were at the cooking school? Why would anyone take it anyway? It just had pictures of the cooking class, lots of ingredients and of us cooking things. OMG! What if it was someone in the cooking class that did the robbery and I had a photo of him — or her, I guess. OK, now I really am letting my imagination run wild. I can't see Amy or Clare or Carl being the robbers. I can't even see Steve or India, although with what India said, they did have some money problems. But who doesn't?

God, I don't know what to think and I'm getting sleepy. Maybe a nice nap on this flight will set me right."

Ravyn awoke with an ache in her neck and the lunch service just starting. The travel pillow she'd brought had come off as she slept and her shoulder and neck hurt. She got up quickly to stretch, use the restroom and walk around a little bit before the large silver airline food cart blocked her seat row.

She returned to her seat just as her meal arrived, a beef and pasta dish that didn't look all that appetizing, but she was hungry and only had a granola bar and some chocolates she'd bought at the Rome airport as snacks. "Oh, to still be at the cooking school making culinary delights!" she thought.

Her seatmates had been relatively quiet on the flight, which was fine by Ravyn. She wasn't in the mood to talk to anyone. She watched an in-flight movie before dozing off again, this time making sure her travel pillow was firmly around her neck.

A coffee service woke her up later, about an hour before the flight was scheduled to land in Atlanta. Ravyn was tired and restless at the same time. It was too late to start another in-flight movie, and she wasn't interested in the book she had downloaded on her e-reader. The woman next to her was reading the bestseller "Gone Girl" in paperback. The book had recently been made into a movie, but Ravyn hadn't seen it and hadn't read the book either.

She tried to stretch in her seat.

"Do you want to get out?" the woman next to Ravyn asked.

"I think so," she replied. "I'm stiff from sleeping upright."

"That's why I never sleep on an airplane," the woman responded. "I just get a good book and keep going."

"I haven't read 'Gone Girl.' Is it any good?"

"Oh yes. Lots of twists and turns. If you like a good thriller, you should read it."

"I might have to give it a try then when I get back to Atlanta."

The woman let Ravyn out of the seat row and she headed back down the aisle to the restroom. A line had formed, but Ravyn didn't mind since it let her stand and stretch a bit longer.

The rest of the flight was uneventful, with a near-perfect touchdown. Another hour through customs and Ravyn was on her way back to her Midtown condo.

Ravyn rented the condo and hoped that now that she was employed full time she could think about buying a place of her own. She wasn't sure how much longer she could continue to rent as the economy got stronger and so did the housing market.

She'd rented the condo for almost a song when the original owner lost it to foreclosure. An investor had purchased it and allowed her to stay in it.

But 2014 was turning out to be a lot different than 2009 and she wasn't sure how much longer she'd be able to rent the one-bedroom condo with great views of downtown Atlanta for as little as she did. Lots of the condos in her building were starting to flip to new owners, sometimes twice already this year.

Ravyn took Atlanta's train from the airport to the Midtown station, which was a short walk to her condo. She'd thought about taking an Uber from the station, but the fall evening was balmy and it felt good to walk a bit after the long flight.

She threw her keys on the breakfast bar in her kitchen and was greeted by a yowl from her tomcat Felix.

Ravyn reached down to scratch the top of his head as Felix wound around her legs, purring loudly. "Did you miss me, Felix? I sure did miss you!"

Ravyn threw her suitcase on the bed and emptied its clothing contents into the washing machine. Even though it was Saturday night and she was exhausted from the flight, she wanted to try to get herself sorted before going into work Monday morning. She knew she could call in an extra day, but wasn't sure she wanted to delay the inevitable when she saw Gavin and Chase.

As she transferred the clothes from the washer to the dryer, she laid down in her bed, expecting to hear the buzzer when the machine finished. Instead, she awoke late Sunday morning to a hungry tomcat yowling for attention and food.

Ravyn rushed into *Cleopatra*'s offices in downtown Atlanta, spilling some of the coffee out of her travel mug. "Shit!" she muttered, shaking her wet and burned hand. She dropped three manila folders onto her desk and tossed her new Italian handbag onto a side chair. She carefully placed Gavin's camera on her desk.

"Welcome back!" Gavin said as he stood in her doorway.

"Thanks, but I need to talk to you and Chase about photos. There was a big problem."

"Oh no! What happened?" Gavin said, alarmed, looking at his camera on her desk. "Did the camera not work? Did you forget the settings?"

"No, I got photos. I remembered the settings. Someone stole the memory card out of the camera. I have no photos for the cover piece!"

Gavin's brown eyes grew wide, grabbing up the camera and flipping it over to check the memory card slot. "What?! Someone stole the memory card? Who the hell would do that? And why?"

"I'm not sure. I just know the memory card is gone and so are the photos."

Chase came into the room holding a Starbucks cup.

"Welcome back! I can't wait to hear about your trip and see what you've got," he said, nodding toward the camera.

"She's got nothing," Gavin said, showing Chase the slot where the memory card should have been. "The memory card is gone."

"What?!" Chase said, almost dropping his coffee. "What are you talking about?"

"I took photos all week long and on the last day, someone took the memory card out of the camera. I don't know who, I don't know why and I don't know when. I know the camera was working on Thursday, maybe even Friday morning, but later Friday afternoon I noticed it missing when I was at the police station."

"The police station? Why were you at the police station?" Gavin asked, removing Ravyn's handbag and sitting down in the side chair.

"I was being questioned by the police about a robbery at the jewelry store below the cooking school. We were up on the third or fourth floor, I think, and the store was on the street level. Someone robbed the place and we were questioned to see if we saw anything or knew anything. Or, at least, I was. I'm not sure if anyone else was questioned. It all happened kind of fast on the last day I was there."

"So, no photos?" Chase asked angrily. "What the hell am I supposed to do now?"

"I don't know, Chase. I really don't know. I'm sick about it. I had photos of all of us at the school, cooking. I had photos of the teacher, the ingredients, everything. What can we do? Can we use some stock art? I can email Dolores Reed and see if she can send some photos. I think she has some on her website."

"They'll need to be high resolution or we can't use them," Chase said. "Dammit! I knew I shouldn't have trusted you."

Ravyn was shocked. "What do you mean, you knew you shouldn't have trusted me? Are you saying I'm no good at my job?!"

"No, no," Chase said, backing off. "I don't mean it like that. I shouldn't have relied on you for the photos, too. I should have hired a freelance photographer."

"Why? I had everything. It's not my fault the memory card was stolen!" Ravyn said, her voice becoming louder. "I didn't know I was going to be robbed!"

"You weren't robbed," Chase said, exasperated. "No one held a gun to you, did they?"

"No. No one held a gun to me, but the memory card was taken nonetheless," Ravyn said, feeling tears start to well in her eyes. She did not want to cry at work in front of her co-workers.

"Don't get upset, Ravyn," Gavin said, putting his hand on her arm. "Chill out, Chase! We'll figure something out. Maybe I can go to one of the Italian restaurants in town and shoot some background stuff with vegetables and pots and things like that."

"I'm sorry. It's just this is such a big story. But Gavin's idea sounds like a good one," Chase said, pointing his coffee cup at Gavin. "Let's start there. Ravyn, you email the teacher and see if you can get some photos of former classes and students. Maybe the other students took photos? Can you email them?"

"Yes, I have their emails. Let me try that, too," Ravyn said. She was starting to feel better. Maybe this would come together.

Ravyn spent the rest of the day catching up on emails, checking up on stories that were out to freelancers and editing stories that had come in for the January/February issue. She began to feel tired by early afternoon when it was evening in Rome. Ravyn wasn't yet back on East Coast time and decided to leave work early.

She was just shutting down her desktop computer when her boss, Samantha Hunt called.

"Ravyn, welcome home!" Samantha said.

Cleopatra magazine was a lifestyle magazine with sister magazines in several cities, including Los Angeles, Boston, Phoenix, Chicago, Miami, Dallas, and other major U.S. cities. The magazine focused on the home, dining, and fashion in each city.

The cover story on a destination vacation to Rome for a cooking school was a bit of a stretch, but not unheard of for a lifestyle magazine. The editor, Samantha Hunt, was based in New York, where Horizon Publishing, the parent company was located.

"Samantha, hello. Good to hear from you. What can I do for you?"

"I'm just calling to let you know I've turned in my notice, Ravyn," Samantha said.

Ravyn was shocked. Samantha had worked at Horizon Publishing, overseeing all of the magazines, for years. She couldn't believe Samantha was leaving. She was such a good sounding board for Ravyn, and someone she looked up to.

"Samantha, I don't know what to say," Ravyn said. "You will be terribly missed, especially by me. May I ask why you are leaving?"

"I can't disclose where I'm going just yet, but I've gotten an opportunity I can't pass up," Samantha replied. "But my leaving certainly affects all of the magazines and we are hiring a new editor to replace me who will continue to oversee the magazines. We've got a couple of candidates in mind and we should make a hire within the month. When that happens, we'll bring the managing editors up to New York to meet him or her. I just wanted you to know and to hear this news from me."

"Thank you," Ravyn said. "I appreciate that. And congratulations, although I really will miss you and all you have done for me and *Cleopatra*."

"I think this will be a great opportunity for growth," Samantha said. "Change is always hard, but the new editor will come in with new ideas and new energy. I expect great things from *Cleopatra* and you, too."

"I certainly want to grow the magazine and grow with the company," Ravyn said, surprising herself. She'd never really thought about where her work at *Cleopatra* might take her, but if there were opportunities to grow with Horizon Publishing, she might not always stay in Atlanta.

"Well, I'll be in touch and let you know when we hire the new editor and when you might come up to New York," Samantha said. "With the holidays coming up, it might be right after the new year, realistically."

"Of course," Ravyn said. "Thank you for letting me know and congratulations again."

The pair hung up and Ravyn sat back down at her desk, feeling like the wind had been knocked out of her.

Samantha was leaving. She'd be getting a new boss. Just when Ravyn felt like she was hitting her stride at *Cleopatra*, understanding the magazine's operations, deadlines, quirks. She had also begun to understand what Samantha Hunt expected of her and how she operated.

Now a new boss would come in and could change things around. Ravyn wondered if the new boss would want to make changes to management and if her job was in jeopardy. Ravyn would have to ask Samantha. She felt sure Samantha would be straight with her.

Ravyn stood up again, collected the keys to her Honda Civic and headed for the elevator banks.

"Ravyn, glad I caught you," said Joel Greenberg, the magazine's advertising director. Joel, wearing his usual brown sweater vest over a dress shirt and khaki pants, was an older man who recently went through a messy divorce from his wife. His marital woes had been office gossip ever since she'd started at the magazine.

Now that Joel was single again and dating, he bragged about the "hot young women" he went out with. One was a flight attendant for Delta, another was an Asian woman in real estate. Ravyn often felt uncomfortable being alone with him. Joel, although he appeared harmless, just gave her the creeps.

"Joel, I was just leaving," she said. "Can it wait until tomorrow?"

"I'll only take a minute of your time," he said, walking back toward her office.

Ravyn turned and followed Joel into her office, putting her bag down once again on her desk. Joel closed the door.

"I just wanted to say welcome back," he said.

Ravyn eyed the closed door, wondering what he was doing.

"Thank you, Joel," she responded, beginning to feel a little uneasy.

"I've got preliminary ad stacks for the next issue and we're a little off on our numbers," he said. "Can you give me a couple more days to beat the bushes and get some more ad revenue?"

"How far off are we?" Ravyn asked, pulling over a legal notepad to take some notes. She'd need to know if she'd have to hold some stories if there wasn't enough ad revenue for a full magazine.

"Oh, we're not that far off, but I could use a couple of days," Joel said, placing his hand on top of Ravyn's. Ravyn pulled her hand away as if she'd been stung.

"Did you talk to production about this?" Ravyn asked. Joel and production director Eric Duke usually hammered these issues out. And Samantha Hunt was the one to give the final say on any delay. Why was Joel asking her permission?

"Yes, Eric said he was OK with it as long as you were OK with it."

"Fine, Joel," she said, standing and moving toward her closed door. "I can give you a couple of days, but we can't be late to press next week. I'm sure Eric told you with the Thanksgiving holiday coming up, the press will be down for the long holiday weekend and if we miss our press run, we'll be screwed."

"We wouldn't want that," Joel said with a leer.

"No, and I'll let Samantha know I've given you an extension," Ravyn replied, opening the door.

Joel's grin faded, a deep scowl appearing on his face. "You don't have to tell that bitch anything," he barked.

"I beg your pardon?" Ravyn shot back, shocked at her co-worker's outburst.

"Sorry, sorry," Joel said, trying to make his face neutral. "I know you won't tell Mrs. Hunt what I said. I'm in enough hot water with her."

Ravyn drove to her condo feeling uneasy about her conversation with Joel. She began to worry that he had used her to get an extension without really going through the proper channels. She would have to check with Eric to be sure he had.

She didn't really have to deal with Joel that much. Craig, the graphic designer who had helped Ravyn get the job at *Cleopatra*, dealt with him more when it came to designing ads. Maybe she should ask Craig about Joel. Was he always like this or was he just having a bad time because of his recent divorce?

Ravyn dropped her keys and mail on the kitchen bar before walking into her bedroom and taking off her shoes. She laid down, feeling the effects of jet lag. She looked at her phone and realized it was about 9 p.m. in Rome. She missed the city already. She missed Luca, feeling the strength and warmth of him.

Her phone pinged an incoming text from her neighbor Jack Parker.

Hey, I saw your car in the lot. You're back

Yes. Thanks for watching Felix

He was no trouble. He wanted a lot of attention and treats by the end of the week. He missed you. I'll bring your key down later tonight

Great. thx.

Ravyn felt lucky to have a neighbor who was willing to feed and water her cat for the week. To hire a pet sitter meant having to get an access card for the condo from the management company, as well as giving out a door key. With Jack just down the hall, Ravyn just had to give him a spare key and remind him of the dates she was gone.

Since she planned to go to South Carolina to see her parents and sister Jane for Thanksgiving, she'd ask Jack if he would keep the spare key and check on Felix while she was away for the long holiday weekend. Ravyn didn't even want to think about packing another suitcase. She just wanted to stay home for a bit, get her bearings and get back in her normal routine.

Ravyn's phone pinged again, this time it was a text message from Julie Montgomery.

Ravyn immediately dialed her friend's number.

"Hey, you are back! And awake!" Julie teased. "I didn't want to call in case you were asleep."

"Not asleep yet, but I'm pretty wiped out. It will take me a couple of days to get back to East Coast time."

"So, how was the Italian man? Did you have one last night of mad passionate sex before you left?"

"Well, no. I ended my final day in Rome in a police station getting grilled by a very severe policewoman about a jewelry store robbery," Ravyn said with a sigh.

"What?! Where was your Italian stallion in all of this?" Julie asked. "Wasn't he in the cell next to you?"

"He ghosted me. Luca left in the middle of the night Thursday and I haven't seen nor heard from him since. I have no way of reaching him, either. I don't have his phone number or email or anything."

"Why not?"

"Julie, he gave me a fake number. It was a number to a restaurant. I tried to call him when I was at the police station. Some things are making me wonder about Luca. He never let me take his photo. I don't have his number. What if he was one of the robbers?"

"Ravyn, you can't be serious."

"Not really. It's probably just my wild imagination, but some things just aren't adding up."

"What do you mean?"

"Oh, just some of his behavior. How weird it was when the policewoman said they had no record of him in their files. I mean, if you've never been in trouble with the law would you even be in a police record system?"

"I have no idea. You were the police reporter back in the day, remember? I just wrote fluffy feature stories at the paper."

Ravyn laughed. "That's not really true. You did some great stories, too."

Ravyn and Julie met when both worked at Atlanta's daily newspaper. Julie ended up meeting and marrying a man she had interviewed for a story, leaving the paper years before Ravyn. Ravyn stayed at the paper longer as a general assignment and police reporter, until she was laid off.

"Hey, do you want to come over tonight for dinner? Lexie and Ashley don't have piano lessons or soccer practice tonight, so we are actually home this evening. You are welcome to come over and join us for dinner. Just relax and let me take care of you."

Julie lived in upscale Buckhead, which was not too far from Ravyn's condo in Midtown Atlanta. Even so, Atlanta's notorious rush-hour traffic meant it could take Ravyn 45 minutes to get to Julie's home less than five miles away.

"Can I take a rain check? I'm probably headed for bed early tonight to try to get back on track," she said. "I'll probably just have cereal for dinner or order delivery."

"OK, but I want to hear all about Luca and this police station stuff. You weren't arrested were you?"

"No, I wasn't arrested, but I wasn't free to go, either, until the policewoman said I could. Her name was Angelica, but she was more like something from your worst nightmare, or rather, *my* worst nightmare. It was awful."

Ravyn could feel tears running down her face again. Julie could hear Ravyn's hitch in her voice.

"Oh, honey," Julie said softly. "I'm so sorry. That sounds terrible."

"It was, Julie. I was scared. I was afraid they would arrest me and no one would know where I was, or how I would contact anyone. I was afraid I would be the next Amanda Knox. I'm glad I'm home. There's more to it than that, but it would take me too long to explain."

"I'm glad you are home, too. I missed you. Sounds like we have a lot to catch up on. What about lunch this weekend at Twist?"

"That sounds great," Ravyn said wiping her eyes. She was looking forward to meeting Julie at their favorite sushi restaurant in Buckhead and getting back into a routine. "Everything OK with you?"

Julie and her husband Rob had had a rough patch last year and Rob had ended up having an affair, but the couple had gone to therapy and seemed to have worked out their problems. Ravyn hoped nothing had happened to derail that progress.

"Everything is great with me. I'll see you at Twist on Saturday. Should we make it around noon?"

"Sounds fine. See you then."

Potatoes with Garlic and Rosemary

A contorno is a side dish and this dish goes wonderfully with roasted chicken or beef. Not only can you eat the potatoes, but you can also peel and eat the softened garlic. It's especially good smeared on bread instead of butter. If eating the softened garlic sounds overwhelming, just pick the garlic out. The potatoes will still retain the delicious garlic flavor.

4 medium potatoes, diced

1 medium head of garlic. Separate the cloves, but do not peel

2 sprigs fresh rosemary, removed from the woody stalk and roughly chopped

Olive oil

Salt

Fry the diced potatoes and unpeeled garlic cloves in a little olive oil over medium heat.

When the potatoes are brown and cooked through, about 25 minutes, add the chopped rosemary.

Season with salt and serve immediately. Serves 4

Buon   appetito!

Chapter 9

INSALATA

Ravyn set the cruise control on her Honda Civic and drove north on Interstate 85 toward her parents' home in Clemson, South Carolina, for the Thanksgiving holiday. She opened the sunroof and turned up the music for the less-than-two-hour drive, letting the sunshine and rock beat wash over her.

It had been a busy few days leading up to the holiday break, with the magazine's January/February issue making it to production just in the nick of time. Joel Greenberg had just eked out enough advertising sales for a full issue, much to Ravyn's relief.

She hadn't heard back from Samantha Hunt, so Ravyn didn't know how the process of hiring a new editor was coming along. She hoped she'd have a good relationship with whomever got hired. She was sorry to see Samantha leave.

Ravyn had also had time to think about her trip and the way it had ended. She tried to remember more of the wonderful times she'd had and the experiences at the cooking school and with Luca, rather than focusing on what happened at the police station.

Ravyn was looking forward to the holiday. Her mother had agreed to let her make a few of the dishes she'd learned in Italy. The Shaw family would be enjoying the roasted chicken with olives for Thanksgiving instead of the traditional turkey.

Ravyn's sister Jane was also bringing her new boyfriend Nick with her. The family was going to meet him. "Must be getting serious," Ravyn thought.

Ravyn sighed. She would turn 34 in a few weeks and she was once again single. "I'm really ready to meet someone and settle down," she thought. "I'm tired of being alone."

"Ravyn, that chicken was absolutely delicious!" Nick said, wiping his mouth with his napkin. Her family nodded in agreement as she grinned. Her culinary skills had been a hit, and she liked her sister's boyfriend. Nick was very attentive to Jane and polite and respectful to her family. Everything she would want for her sister.

"I'm glad you liked it," she replied. "I had a great time in Rome and I learned a lot. I'm just glad I could fix this for the family. It would be a little too much food just for me."

"You can come up to Clemson any time to fix this for me, honey," her father said. "I even liked that fancy rice stuff you made."

"Dad, that's risotto, and I'm glad you liked it. I know you don't like asparagus much," Ravyn said.

"Oh, honey, I like it well enough," he said, smiling. "I just don't like what it does to me afterward."

Ravyn looked at her father quizzically, then laughed, realizing he meant the strong urine smell that came from eating the vegetable.

Ravyn, Jane and their mother Kaye began to clear the table.

"Let me help with that," Nick offered, stacking a couple of dishes, the clanking of the plates making Kaye cringe. She'd brought out her good china for Thanksgiving. She didn't want Nick to chip her grandmother's china.

"No, no," Kaye said, hurriedly, taking the plates from his hands. She smiled at him. "We've got it. Why don't you boys watch the game on TV? I know John wants to see the Dallas Cowboys game."

John Shaw, a professor at Clemson University, had played a little football in his high school and college days and always enjoyed the sport. Nick was quick to disappear into the living room where Ravyn could hear the sports announcers chattering as the game started.

"Do you think they are getting along out there?" Jane whispered to her sister, glancing back toward the living room.

"As long as Nick says he's a Cowboys fan, they will get along fine," Ravyn said. "You did warn him about which teams Dad likes best? Better not say you are an Eagles fan in this house!"

Jane laughed. "Oh, I warned him!"

"He seems really nice," Ravyn said, starting the sink to begin the task of washing the china by hand. She tossed a towel to Jane, who would dry the dishes. "Nick, I mean. Where did you two meet?"

"I sort of met him through mutual friends. Nick works with a guy who is friends with a woman I work with."

"Huh?"

"Yeah, that is a little hard to follow," Jane said. "Anyway, we all met up for drinks after work at this new place in Greenville, right downtown, and that's how we met."

"Sounds good. Is it getting serious?"

"Maybe. We've kind of been talking about moving in together when the lease is up on my apartment."

"Wow! That sounds serious to me," Ravyn said. "I'm really happy for you, Jane. You both look happy together."

Jane hugged her sister from behind, since Ravyn's hands were in the soapy water. "Thank you. I think he's really special. I think he could be The One," she whispered excitedly.

The One. Ravyn tried not to feel or look surprised, nor disappointed. As the older sister, Ravyn had always thought she might be the one to meet and marry first, even though she and Jane were just three years apart. Now it seemed Jane was very serious about Nick and Ravyn didn't have a serious boyfriend in sight.

"What are you two whispering about?" Kaye asked her daughters as she entered the kitchen, stacking more dirty dishes next to the sink.

"Nothing much," Ravyn said. "I just wanted to know how Nick and Jane met. I like 'How we met stories.' I love the one of how you met Dad."

Kaye laughed. The story was practically a legend now. Kaye had been an elementary school teacher, barely able to scrape by on her first salary. When her car got a flat, she couldn't afford a new tire, but fellow teachers had directed her to a place where she could buy a used tire, far cheaper.

Kaye, with the small spare on her car, had driven across town to the little garage and passed it by. It looked filthy, and the men hanging outside looked rough. She wasn't sure this was the place for her.

Kaye drove around the block twice, trying to shore up her courage to enter the garage to buy the tire. In the end, she had.

As she sat on a dirty and worn chair in the customer service area, she noticed a young man staring at her. He had come in with a friend, who also needed tires.

"Ah, hello," the young man said.

Kaye looked at him, unsure if she should start a conversation. She felt vulnerable being the only woman in the shop.

"Hello," she finally said.

"What are you reading?" the young man asked, pointing to the paperback in Kaye's lap.

Kaye looked down at the tome that was Colleen McCullough's "The Thorn Birds." She had been trying to read the book for weeks but kept picking it up and putting it down. All of her friends had raved about it though.

"The Thorn Birds," she replied. "Have you read it?"

"I don't have much time to read," the young man replied. "I'm in grad school. I only have time for textbooks, I'm afraid."

Kaye was impressed. Grad school.

"What are you studying?" she asked.

"Business management," he replied. "I'm going to take over my father's business one day."

"And what does he do?" Kaye asked.

"He owns this tire store," the young man replied.

Kaye blinked. This store? This tire store? Was there a future in that?

"I'd like to expand the business, open more stores," said the young man, who began to tell Kaye excitedly of his plans and dreams. He explained how with careful planning he could open at least one store a year for the next three years once he graduated the next year.

Kaye fell in love with John about 20 minutes into the conversation.

"Your father was so passionate about growing that business," Kaye said with a sigh. "It was awful when his father died suddenly and we found out how in debt he was. There was no way John could keep the business going, let alone expand. He had to sell everything off just to clear the slate."

Kaye looked wistful, then brightened. "But I am forever grateful for that flat tire! It's how I met your father!"

Ravyn loved the time between Thanksgiving and Christmas in Atlanta. She just didn't love the traffic. She shook her head in disgust as she sat in bumper to bumper traffic on Peachtree Road on a Saturday, trying to get to Phipps Plaza shopping mall to meet Julie.

"I have to be out of my head to get anywhere near the malls at Christmas!" Ravyn muttered to herself.

Trying to find a parking space at the mall was even more of a chore. Ravyn circled the large lot three times before stalking a shopper coming out of the mall to her parked car. Ravyn put the car blinker on and waited for several minutes as the shopper put her bags in the trunk of her black Lexus sedan.

Ravyn watched as the woman then reapplied her makeup in the driver's mirror before finally pulling out of the parking space. Ravyn's jaw dropped when the shopper then flipped Ravyn the bird as she drove off.

"Bah, humbug, to you, too, bitch!" Ravyn scowled.

She locked her car door and stomped toward the entrance to Twist, a favorite restaurant of hers and Julie's.

Just walking in, Ravyn texted Julie. Traffic was awful and some bitch just flipped me off as I parked.

Girl, you are lucky you didn't get shot. Ppl are crazy for a parking spot this time of year. Why didn't u valet? I'm at a table in the back.

Ravyn rolled her eyes at the text. Only in Atlanta did shoppers valet their cars at the Buckhead malls. Ravyn had never done it. She'd never had the funds to spare. Plus, she just found it dumb. She prided herself on good parking karma.

Julie looked up from her phone and waved at Ravyn. "I hope you are hungry. I ordered us a couple of sushi rolls and some seaweed salad."

"I'm famished," Ravyn said. "I didn't eat anything before I went out for my run. I had just enough time to get cleaned up before I hopped in the car to get here. My God, Julie! Buckhead traffic is terrible. How do you stand it?"

"I guess I'm used to it," Julie said. "But traffic in Midtown isn't any different."

"No, but it's only really bad when there is a show at the Fox or game day at Georgia Tech," Ravyn said, referring to the Fox Theater in Atlanta and the Yellow Jackets home football games. "Then I just walk everywhere or just stay at home!"

Their lunch arrived and they made a game plan for the afternoon shopping.

"What's on your list?" Ravyn asked.

"I need to start at Nordstrom to see if I can find holiday dresses for Lexie and Ashley," Julie said. "They both have Christmas concerts at school. And I've been told that the dresses can't match each other this year. I've always gotten them cute matching dresses."

"Well, they are tweens now," Ravyn said. "They want to be their own selves."

"Ugh," Julie grunted. "Don't remind me! I'm getting more sass and lip from them than ever. I want my little girls back!"

"I can't help you there," Ravyn said.

"What are you shopping for today?" Julie asked.

"Oh, I'll tag along with you. Jane's got a new boyfriend, Nick, and it seems pretty serious. I'll need to find something for him this year."

"Really? How serious?"

"Jane said they are planning to move in together," Ravyn said, dipping her sushi in some soy sauce before popping it in her mouth.

"That's a big step for Jane."

Ravyn nodded and chewed at the same time.

"I know," she said, finally. "She's always broken up with her beaus before we got to meet them. She introduced us to Nick at Thanksgiving. We were all a little nervous that we'd meet him and it would be over. But this looks pretty serious."

"Well, good for her. Now, what are we going to do about you?" Julie asked before biting into a piece of the rainbow roll.

"We aren't going to do anything about me," she said, reaching for another bite of the colorful sushi roll. "I've got a lot to do in the next few weeks for the March issue and I don't have time to devote to dating right now."

"Ravyn Shaw, that is the biggest bunch of bullshit I've ever heard you say, and I've heard you say some bullshit," Julie admonished her friend, pointing at her with her chopsticks.

"It's true, Julie," Ravyn said, defensively. "I have got to write the story up. I've tried organizing my thoughts and I just can't. I don't know if it is because of the bad experience I had in the police station, but it's like I'm blocked when it comes to trying to write the story. I want to do it justice. The cooking school was wonderful and the people I met were wonderful. I just need to knuckle down and do it. Maybe I can really get on it tonight."

"It's Saturday night tonight. You are telling me you are going to write your work story tonight? That's what Mondays are for, girlfriend."

"Well, as Sam Cooke once sang, 'Another Saturday night and I ain't got nobody,'" Ravyn warbled off-key.

"Do not quit your day job and go on 'America's Got Talent,'" Julie said. "You have none."

They both laughed and finished up the rolls.

"Come on. Let's get the check and go shopping!" Julie said, her eyes excited. Julie's superpower was shopping and Ravyn was more than willing to be her sidekick.

A few minutes later they walked the corridor of the luxury shopping mall, headed toward Nordstrom when Ravyn heard a male voice call her name.

She turned and saw Marc Linder coming toward her.

"Marc!" she exclaimed, surprised to see her ex-boyfriend.

"I thought it was you," he said, reaching for her arm. "How are you? Doing some holiday shopping?"

"Yes. You remember Julie?" Ravyn turned to introduce her friend, but Julie waved and began inching away to give the pair some privacy.

Ravyn and Marc had dated for several months the year before. Ravyn had thought she was in love with him, but Marc's ex-girlfriend had sabotaged some financial figures and Marc blamed the mistake on Ravyn.

By the time they realized what Laura Lucas had done, Marc and Ravyn had split. They had reconciled for a few brief weeks earlier this year, but it hadn't worked out. Or rather, Ravyn had a hard time forgetting how he'd treated her.

"I've missed you," Marc said, reaching down to take Ravyn's hand, surprising her.

"I, ah, I've missed you, too," Ravyn stammered, looking into his soft hazel eyes. The memories of him flooded her. She looked away, over his shoulder into the distance. "I hope your company is doing well. You got that funding for it, right?"

"Yeah, I got two rounds of funding, as a matter of fact," he said. "LindMark Enterprises is doing well."

Ravyn could smell his familiar spicy cologne, saw how the green in his jacket brought out the gold flecks in his hazel eyes. She did not want to fall for him all over again.

"That's great. I'm happy for you," Ravyn said, pulling away. "I'd better get a move on. Julie's waiting for me, and…"

"Sure. It was great seeing you, Ravyn," Marc said, squeezing her hand before letting it go. "Maybe we can have lunch together soon. May I call you?"

"Sure, lunch would be great. Great to see you, Marc. Good luck with your shopping," she said, as she turned to walk toward Julie.

"What is the matter with you?" Julie snapped at Ravyn when Marc was out of earshot. "He clearly wanted to spend time talking to you and you acted like he had the cooties."

"Had the cooties?" Ravyn laughed. "What are we, in middle school?"

"I spend way too much time around my daughters!" Julie said. "Seriously, Ravyn, he wanted to talk to you. I think he's still interested."

Ravyn shook her head as they walked on. "I'm not so sure. I'm not sure I want him to be interested, frankly."

Julie looked at her friend. That was probably the closest Ravyn had been honest about how Marc had treated her.

Ravyn couldn't get Marc or what Julie had said about him being still interested in her out of her head as they walked back to Julie's SUV loaded down with shopping bags.

"Here, hold my bag while I load the back," Julie said.

Ravyn took Julie's handbag as Julie began stuffing her shopping bags into black trash bags. "I don't want the girls to see these Nordstrom bags or they'll start snooping for gifts."

"Wonder where they learned to do that?" Ravyn asked, knowing Julie had often snooped for gifts from her husband Rob, then telling Ravyn weeks before Christmas what she was getting from him.

"Don't start," Julie said.

Distracted, Ravyn then put Julie's handbag in a black trash bag just before Julie closed the SUV's back hatch door.

"Where's my handbag?" Julie asked, searching for her hot pink Louis Vuitton handbag. "Didn't I give it to you?"

"Oh my God! I put it in the bag, in the trunk."

"My car keys were in it!" Julie said.

"Oh, shit! Oh my God, Julie. I'm so sorry. Do you have a spare key?"

"Rob's got it, but he's at the aquarium today with the girls."

"I've got AAA. I'll call them to come open the car. Shit, I am so sorry!"

Ravyn called the roadside service to come unlock Julie's SUV and was told the wait time was over an hour.

"Ma'am, it's the holidays," the customer service rep said, flatly. "Everyone's locking their keys in the car or getting a flat. It will be a while. We'll call you when we get close. Please be by your vehicle."

Ravyn hung up and sighed. It was chilly and she didn't want to wait outside.

"Let's go back in the mall and get a glass of wine," Ravyn said. "I owe you at least that. They'll call me when they get close to the mall."

"You'll have to buy. My money is in the trunk!" Julie laughed.

"I'm glad you have a sense of humor about this. I can't believe I did that."

"You were distracted. You were too busy thinking about Marc," Julie teased.

The pair headed back to the mall and just as they entered, Marc Linder stepped out.

"Back so soon? Did you forget to buy something?" he asked, smiling, clearly happy to see Ravyn again.

"No. I just accidentally locked Julie's car keys in her trunk. We're waiting on AAA and I'm buying her a glass of wine until they get here. I think I need a glass of wine, too."

"Is there anything I can do?" Marc asked, stepping in closer. "I can drive you somewhere if you need me to."

"No, we'll be fine, but thanks for asking," Ravyn said. She could smell his cologne again. She could feel dampness begin between her legs.

"Sure, well, Ravyn, if I don't see you before the holiday, Merry Christmas," Marc said as he bent over and kissed her cheek.

Stunned, Ravyn watched him walk out to the parking lot, one small shopping bag in his hand.

"Deny it all you want, Ravyn, that man is still interested in you. Now buy me a big glass of red wine," Julie said, taking her friend's arm and leading her back to Twist.

Wearing men's red plaid pajama bottoms and a light pink soft cotton T-shirt, Ravyn stared at her laptop, trying to summon inspiration for her cooking school article. She uncrossed her legs at the kitchen bar. No inspiration was forthcoming and she began to wonder again about her encounter with Marc.

She switched over to email and saw she had a few online bills that needed to be paid. She quickly went to her bank's website and input the bills for her cell phone and cable TV.

"That's odd," Ravyn thought, looking at her cable bill. It was slightly higher than last month's bill.

She opened the PDF of the bill and skimmed down, wondering if a rate increase had occurred and she didn't realize it.

"What is this?" Ravyn wondered, then her eyes got wide.

A $20 charge for an adult movie caught her eye. Ravyn looked at the date, November 10, when she was still in Italy.

"Felix, did you order up some kitty porn while I was away?" she asked, glancing over at her tomcat, who was busy cleaning the gray fur down his side.

She looked at the date again and she growled. "Dammit, Jack!"

She printed out the cable bill and padded down the hallway, knocking on Jack Parker's door.

"Hey, neighbor," he said, seeing it was Ravyn.

"Would you mind explaining this?" she said, angrily, shoving the print out in his face.

"What's that?"

"It's my cable bill, Jack. There seems to be an extra charge on there for some porn you watched while I was away."

Jack took the bill, then looked back into his condo, then stepped out in the hall, closing the door behind him. Ravyn stood in the hall with arms crossed, realizing she was in her pajamas.

"Hey, hey, I'm sorry about that. I meant to tell you I'd pay you back for that."

"Jack, who watches porn at someone else's place?" Ravyn asked, then shuddered, realizing Jack probably had done more than just watch porn on her couch. She might have to burn her furniture. Steam clean it at least.

"I didn't want Liz to know I watched it," Jack said, referring to his girlfriend.

"Jack, *I* didn't want to know you watched it," Ravyn replied. "At my condo! On my couch! And poor Liz!"

"Look, I'm really sorry. It won't happen again. Please don't tell Liz about this. I'll pay you for it. Let me get my wallet," he said, re-entering his condo and coming back out with a $20 bill.

Ravyn walked back to her condo, feeling like she needed another shower.

Caprese salad

Perhaps there is no salad that tastes more like summer than the classic Caprese salad. Made with ripe tomatoes, fresh basil, mozzarella cheese, and a little olive oil and balsamic vinegar, Caprese salad is a favorite in summer when basil and tomatoes are at their peak. It is quick and easy to make as an appetizer, salad or a meal.

Balsamic vinegar
3 ripe tomatoes
12 ounces fresh mozzarella, sliced thick
Large bunch of fresh basil leaves
Olive oil
Kosher salt and freshly ground black pepper, to taste

Slice the tomatoes into thick slices, arranging them on a platter, alternating with the mozzarella slices. Tuck whole basil leaves in between the tomato and cheese slices.

Drizzle the balsamic vinegar over the slices, then drizzle olive oil lightly over the top. Salt and pepper to taste. Serves about 8.

Buon   appetito!

Chapter 10

DOLCE

Her Christmas shopping nearly complete, Ravyn's social life began to pick up, with parties and get-togethers planned as the end of 2014 drew to a close.

She began to enjoy the slower time at work, too, as the January/February issue was out to be published and the March issue of *Cleopatra* was in the beginning stages. She and Chase had come up with a game plan for photos. Ravyn had emailed Dolores Reed, who was very sympathetic that all of the photos had been lost.

Dolores had emailed some photos of previous classes and some photos of garlic, onions, tomatoes, and basil on her countertop, similar to the photos Ravyn had taken. They'd be able to use some of the contributed photos inside the issue. Ravyn was relieved.

Ravyn planned to take several days off at Christmas to be with her parents. Jane would join them earlier on Christmas Day, but would then go to visit Nick at his parents' house. She knew Jane and Nick were spending a lot of time together and Jane could not stop talking about him. Ravyn was a little jealous of her sister.

She was hesitant to ask Jack Parker to feed and water Felix again. After finding out he'd ordered an adult movie on her cable service, she'd added parental controls to her

158

TV remote, which she found ridiculous since she lived alone with a cat.

She'd also been avoiding Jack and his girlfriend Liz. It was awkward when she saw them together. She didn't like knowing a secret about Jack. She wondered if he had an addiction or if he'd just been bored and ordered up porn. She tried to shake the thought from her head.

It was Jack who finally approached Ravyn in the tiny fitness center of their condo building. Rain and colder weather had kept Ravyn from her usual run over to Piedmont Park and she'd opted for the treadmill that morning. She hated the "dreadmill," but she wanted to get a few miles in before she started the errands she needed to do that day.

Jack, in jeans and a hoodie, walked by the fitness center and spied her, turned and walked in.

"Hey, Ravyn," Jack said, looking around to see if anyone else was in the fitness center.

"Hey, Jack." She took her headphones off and slowed the treadmill so she could talk.

"Listen, I know it has been weird between us. I don't want it to be that way."

"Me neither. It's just… Porn at my home?"

"I really am sorry," Jack said, shoving his hands in his pockets.

"OK. I don't want to grind on it," Ravyn said, stopping the treadmill and getting off. "And I still want us to be friends. I like you and Liz."

"We like you, too," Jack said. "And I can totally take care of Felix if you need me to. I will not touch the cable TV, I promise." He put up his hand in a Boy Scout salute.

"Well, I am going up to South Carolina for Christmas and I do need someone to watch him for the few days I'm gone," Ravyn said.

"I'd be happy to watch him for you. Or I can ask Liz to do it if that would make you feel better."

"No, Jack, I know she's allergic to cats. And I need to be able to trust you, so if you could do it I'd appreciate that. I'll come by later and drop off my spare key,"

"See you later then. Have a good run."

Later that day, Ravyn was busy getting her condo cleaned and ready for the girlfriends she had invited over for a holiday celebration. She was excited to make some of the dishes she'd learned at cooking school.

Her friends Tanya, Danica, Julie, and Lynne were coming over.

Danica Martinez was a single mother of three who worked at the veterinary clinic where Ravyn took Felix. The two women had met when Ravyn first adopted Felix from a local rescue shelter and they had hit it off.

Tanya Frasier worked at The Weather Channel, which was based in Atlanta. She worked in the IT department but had stories to tell of the TV personalities who always seemed to be in the danger zone of hurricanes and tornadoes.

Lynne Parsons was a friend of Julie Montgomery's that Ravyn had met the year before when Julie, Lynne and Lynne's sister Celia all enjoyed a girls' weekend at Lake Lanier, about an hour north of Atlanta.

They had done a lot of jet skiing, drinking, swimming and laughing, not necessarily in that order, that weekend. Ravyn was glad Lynne was able to come to the holiday gathering, even if her sister Celia had a prior commitment.

"It's just as well," Ravyn thought, pulling over her desk chair to add a fifth chair to her small IKEA dining table. "I don't have a whole lot of room in this condo."

Ravyn had lived in her one-bedroom condo for a few years, renting it after the owner had lost it to foreclosure. It was small but had a great view of downtown Atlanta from her balcony.

She'd gotten some white string lights to put around the balcony and a small Christmas tree that Felix couldn't knock over or climb as decorations. Felix did, however, like to take the little ornaments off the tree. She'd found several broken already, clearly used as cat toys.

The women arrived and Ravyn poured everyone a glass of prosecco before she pulled the eggplant rolls she had made out of the oven. A tray of meats and cheeses was already on the table and she'd have more goodies to pull out of the oven soon, including lasagna. It wasn't a dish she'd learned at cooking school, but it would be a good meal to serve to her guests.

"I can't believe how good these are," Lynne said, taking another bite of the eggplant rolls. "I normally don't like eggplant, but these are very good."

"Don't fill up on those," Ravyn said. "I've got panna cotta with raspberry sauce for dessert in the fridge."

"Oh, I won't! I love dessert."

"How long were you over in Italy?" Tanya asked.

"I was there a whole week," Ravyn said. "It was great. I got a paid vacation thanks to the magazine."

"How is it going at the magazine? Do you still like it?" Tanya asked.

"I love it," she replied. "I feel like I've found my calling."

"That's great," Tanya said.

"What about you, Danica?" Ravyn asked. "How are you doing?"

The last time the women had been together, Danica had shared her financial worries, thanks to an ex-husband not paying his child support on time.

"I'm doing great thanks to Tanya's brother," she said, smiling.

Tanya had offered to have Danica talk to her brother Adam, an attorney, and clearly that had been the right move.

"Adam took my ex to the cleaners, that piece of shit! He's paying what he should for his kids now, and on time!" Danica said, triumphantly.

"I'm glad to hear that," Ravyn said. "I know that was a big worry."

"And I've met someone that I've been dating pretty steady," she said. "He wasn't even scared off by my kids. He's got two of his own, although they mostly live with his ex-wife. But when we are together, we're one big happy family. Or mostly. My kids can fight. But no broken bones yet!"

Ravyn laughed. "Well, it was just me and my sister Jane but we could get into some knockdown fights when we were younger. That girl could pull some hair!"

"Hey, are you still seeing that guy, Marc?" Tanya asked.

"No, we broke up a while ago," she replied.

"You should ask her about the Italian stallion that she met over in Rome!" Julie interrupted. "Luca."

"Ooh! Tell us about Luca," Lynne chimed in, reaching for another bottle of prosecco and topping off everyone's glass.

"He certainly was handsome. Dark hair, dark eyes," Ravyn said. "I met him the second day I was there and he showed me all around the city that week."

"He showed her a very good time, I'm given to understand," Julie said, slyly.

The women cackled and clinked their glasses. "Here's to Italian stallions!"

"Did you keep in touch with him? Is he coming to visit you here in Atlanta?" Lynne asked. "Maybe we can all meet this gorgeous Italian man."

"No, we just parted ways at the end of the trip," Ravyn said, vaguely. She didn't want to explain the way the trip had ended, with her down at a police station and Luca nowhere to be found.

"No drama in the goodbyes?" Lynne asked.

"No drama," Ravyn lied. "Just a parting of ways."

"Well, that makes for a very wonderful memory, then," Lynne said. "To wonderful memories!"

And the women clinked glasses again.

Ravyn woke up early New Year's Day for the Resolution Run. In years past, this race had been held up in Kennesaw, a suburb several miles to the north of Atlanta, and was a 5K or a double loop 10K. It had always meant getting up early and driving up Interstate 75.

But this year the race was being held in Brookhaven, which was closer to Ravyn's condo, and was a 4-mile race. It was a straight shot up Peachtree Road. She smiled wanly as she passed the street where she had often turned to go to Marc's house.

The day was cold but sunny, and Ravyn was pleased with her running performance, considering she hadn't run much over the holidays and had not denied herself any of the holiday goodies that had been delivered to the office.

She'd forgotten what it had been like to work in an office during the Christmas holidays. When she had worked at the daily newspaper years ago, treats and goodies arrived from advertisers or PR agencies and would be left in the break room for all employees to enjoy.

When she was freelancing, Ravyn's only treats were a check that came in on time from a client. There were no goodies during those lean years.

Now at *Cleopatra*, Ravyn had been pleasantly surprised when cookies, peanut brittle, gourmet popcorn and even a nice bottle of wine had arrived. The small break room seemed to be overflowing some days. She'd laughed with co-workers the day they'd eaten the cheddar-flavored popcorn and washed it down with a small glass of the white wine.

With Jan. 1, 2015 falling on a Thursday, Ravyn didn't see any point in going into the office on Friday, so she gave herself the day off, but was sitting at her desk early on Monday.

She was getting organized and marking down upcoming magazine deadlines when her cell phone rang. It was an Atlanta number she didn't recognize and almost sent it to voicemail, but then thought better of it and answered.

"Hello, this is Ravyn Shaw."

"Miss Shaw, this is Agent Davis with the FBI's Atlanta Field Office. Do you have a moment to talk?"

Ravyn was surprised. Why was the FBI calling her? How did they get her cell number?

"Of course, what can I do for you?"

"I'm just following up on behalf of the Italian police about a jewelry shop robbery back in November 2014," he said. "I believe you are familiar with it?"

"I know that it happened," Ravyn said, feeling her pulse quicken. "I was questioned by the Italian police, but I couldn't tell them much. I didn't see it happen and I don't know who is responsible. I only walked up on the crime scene that morning."

"Would you mind coming over to our office? There are a few follow-up questions we'd like to ask," Agent Davis said.

"Do I need to bring an attorney with me?" Ravyn asked, now feeling panicked again.

"Oh, no, nothing like that," he said, trying to reassure her. "I'm just being asked to help the Italian police tie up some loose threads. There is nothing to worry about, I assure you. Do you have any photos of the cooking school you attended? Some that you may have come across since your return to the United States?"

Ravyn was startled. How did he know about that?

"I don't have any photos. The memory card was taken from my camera, and all of the photos that I had for the cooking school story went with it."

"And you don't have any other photos of the people you took the classes with?" he asked. "Even outside of class? Maybe from a cell phone? Did you go sightseeing with them or take photos at the hotel or anything like that?"

"No, I told you the photos were taken with the memory card," she said. "I only ever used our photographer's camera for the photos I'd need for the magazine article. I think the only photos I shot with my iPhone were of some of the ruins, like Trajan's Market and things like that, when I was by myself walking and wasn't carrying the camera with me. I took a few selfies, but that's about it."

"Ah, OK. I was just checking. Would it be possible for you to come to our office tomorrow morning?"

"Well, I work in downtown Atlanta. Where are the FBI offices?" Ravyn asked.

"We're up near the Atlanta campus of Mercer University, a little bit off Interstate 85," Agent Davis said, referring to an area just north of the city. "Do you have a pen? I'll give you the address."

Ravyn wrote the address down and agreed to meet with Agent Davis at 9 a.m. the next day. When she hung up her phone, her hands felt clammy and she wiped them on her pants. "Not again," she thought. "I do not want to go through this again!"

Ravyn drove down Flowers Road near Mercer University's Atlanta campus, following her phone's map app, but could have picked out the FBI's Atlanta Field Office building right away.

Fenced off behind black gates, the building had the hallmarks of a government office in the post-9/11 era. A beige and brown exterior was fortressed behind gates and barricades. Agent Davis had said Ravyn would have to check-in, and her name was on the list to be let in that morning.

The gate agent must have let Agent Davis know Ravyn was coming because he was there to greet her in the lobby. He shook her hand and led her back to his small office.

Ravyn had dressed a little more conservatively for the meeting, rather than her usual office attire, which was very casual. At the magazine's office, she'd often wear nice jeans and a casual top or sweater and sandals or cute boots, depending on how cold or hot it was in the office.

She was always perplexed at how it could be freezing in her office in the summer and sweltering in the winter. Altering the thermostat down the hall never seemed to help.

Today she was wearing a favorite navy pinstripe business jacket and matching skirt. A light blue dress blouse with stockings and navy dress pumps rounded out her attire. It was the most dressed up she'd been since she first started working at the magazine when she realized how relaxed the dress code was.

"Can I get you a cup of coffee or some water?" he asked, opening his office door and waving her in.

"No thanks, I had coffee at home," Ravyn said. "I'm fine."

"It's probably just as well," Agent Davis said. "The coffee here is terrible. I usually grab a Starbucks on the way in." He pointed to the ubiquitous white and green coffee cup sitting on the corner of his wooden desk and smiled.

Agent Davis was much younger than what Ravyn had expected. She'd expected an older man, one who was slightly overweight and sat at a desk all day, the stereotypical federal agent played by older character actors she'd seen on television or in the movies.

The man before her was just under six feet tall, with sandy brown hair, neatly trimmed. Not a military buzz cut, but a style that would be seen in any corporate office. He wore khakis and a pale blue golf shirt under his tan sports jacket.

Ravyn could see a handgun holstered just under his jacket and she shuddered inwardly. It reminded her of her questioning back in Italy.

Agent Davis gestured and said, "Please, sit down, Miss Shaw. Do you mind if I record this interview?"

Ravyn sat in the chair opposite his desk, unsure about what would happen next. "I guess that's fine," she said, as Agent Davis took out an old-fashioned tape recorder and placed it on the desk. He pushed the record buttons and began talking, announcing the date, time, where they were and Ravyn's full name.

"Let's begin, shall we? I know the Italian police have questioned you," Agent Davis said. "They sent over a transcript of your interview, so I know what you told them at the time of the robbery."

"I don't understand why I'm being questioned again," Ravyn said. "I told them then and I'll tell you now. I didn't see the robbery and I don't know who did it."

"I think the Italian police were interested in you because there was a chance you had photographs that might have helped them," the agent said. "The Italian police believe the robbery was actually the work of international jewel thieves, perhaps part of a larger organized crime ring. There appears to be a ring of robbers, albeit a small ring, that has been hitting smaller stores in and around Rome that don't have sophisticated security systems. There were some robberies in Spain, too, and they might be connected."

That was news to Ravyn.

"Is that why there weren't any security photos of the robbery? But the Italian police showed me photos of me in the shop from a few days before the robbery. Weren't there any more security photos? Other people must have gone in and out of that store that day."

"Yes, I know there are some security photos, but it seems the perpetrators disabled the cameras, so there's nothing from just before the time of the robbery."

"And you suspect what? That someone in the cooking school is the robber? I find that hard to believe," Ravyn said, exasperated.

"We're not sure that anyone connected with your class is involved," the agent said, trying to sound casual. "We're just trying to assist with the Italian police. The FBI does assist other agencies internationally, particularly with things like art crime and jewelry and gem theft. I think the Italian police have some suspicions about who may be involved, but I can't tell you more than that. We were just hoping that in the time since you've been back, you were able to come up with some photos, or remember anything suspicious."

"No, in fact having that memory card stolen put me in a real bind for work," Ravyn said. "I was counting on having photos from the cooking school for the article I'm writing."

"And you suspect someone deliberately took the memory card?" he asked.

"I do. There's no other explanation. The memory card is spring-loaded and you have to push on it to remove it. It wouldn't just fall out."

"When was the last time you remember having the memory card in the camera?" he asked.

"Ah, let me think," Ravyn said, looking toward the ceiling, trying to remember when she'd last taken photos on that trip. "I think the last time I took photos was the day of the robbery. I had the camera with me that morning when I walked up and saw all of the police around the store."

"And did you take photos in the class that day?"

"Yes, I did. Oh! One of my classmates also took my camera and took some photos of several of us. I was a little nervous when he handled it because it's not my camera and I didn't want it damaged in any way."

"And who was the classmate who used the camera?" Agent Davis asked.

"That was Steve Prescott," she replied.

"And do you have any reason to believe Steve Prescott took the memory card?"

"I don't think so, but I really don't know. I didn't have the camera the whole time in class. I took some photos and then put the camera down near my handbag so I could chop and cook and things like that. I didn't want the camera to get messy. I did that almost every day. I'd take some photos, then put it out of the way."

"So, the camera wasn't in your possession the entire time you were in class that morning?"

"No, it wasn't. There were times it was by itself by my handbag," Ravyn replied.

"And you didn't see anyone go near your camera or pick it up, other than Mr. Prescott?" Agent Davis asked.

"I didn't, but quite honestly, I wasn't paying that much attention to it," she said. "No one had bothered it all week. I trusted my classmates. None of them made me believe they would do something like that."

"I understand, Miss Shaw, and I'm not suggesting that anyone is a suspect, I'm just trying to understand the sequence of events on that day," he said.

Ravyn took a deep breath. Agent Davis wasn't questioning her in the stern way Angelica Bianchi had at the Rome police station. Ravyn smiled at the recollection of the policewoman's name. In the days after her return to Atlanta, Ravyn had tried so hard to forget that woman and that experience, yet she easily remembered her name now.

"Is something amusing, Miss Shaw?" Agent Davis asked, staring at Ravyn.

Ravyn jumped out of her reverie. "No, sorry. I was just thinking your questioning is much calmer than the one I got in Rome. You are a much nicer interrogator than Officer Bianchi."

Ravyn suddenly realized what she had said. "I'm sorry. I didn't mean to imply that you aren't thorough. I just meant you are nicer, friendlier."

Ravyn realized she was digging herself into a hole and stopped talking, blushing.

"I understand, Miss Shaw," Agent Davis said, smiling warmly. "I hope you don't think I'm interrogating you harshly."

Agent Davis ran his hand through his short-cropped hair giving it a slightly rumpled look, then began typing notes into the laptop that also sat on his desk. He looked up at Ravyn and smiled. "Just let me input a few notes if you don't mind."

"That's fine," she said. "He has a nice smile," Ravyn thought. "And with his hair slightly mussed…" Ravyn shook her head, banishing any further thoughts.

She looked around the room. Unlike the policewoman's office in Rome, which was devoid of mementos, Agent

Davis had a framed certificate on the wall behind him and what looked like a sports team photo, as well. Ravyn couldn't tell if Agent Davis was in the photo or not. The photo was too small and she was too far away. A small set of flags, one American and one the state flag of Georgia, sat in a stand on a side table. Some manila folders were neatly stacked on the far corner of his desk. She tried to read the label on the folder, but couldn't. She then looked away. She didn't want to appear too nosy to the FBI agent.

As if realizing he was being stared at, Agent Davis stopped typing and looked up.

"Was there anyone else who might have been able to remove the memory card?" he asked. "The Italian police file says you had a boyfriend, a Luca Ricci. Could he have removed it?"

Ravyn could feel herself flush. "Luca was a friend," she said. "He was not my boyfriend. And he couldn't have taken the memory card. I took photos in class after the police found the robbery."

"You are absolutely sure the memory card was in the camera when you took photos that day?" Agent Davis asked.

"Ah, actually, I'm not sure," Ravyn said, realizing she never checked the photos as she shot them that morning. "I guess I never looked. Maybe the memory card could have been taken earlier, like the day before, but I'm not sure."

Ravyn felt sick. Could Luca have taken the memory card the previous night? But why?

"Do you have any way of reaching Luca Ricci?" Agent Davis asked.

"No. I told Officer Bianchi the same thing. He gave me his number, but I don't think it worked. I mean, I think he gave me a fake number. And I don't have his email or anything."

Agent Davis looked up at Ravyn, puzzled.

"Yes, I know. It's weird. He kind of ghosted me," she said, exasperated. "Some friend! I went over this with Officer Bianchi."

"Sure, that's fine, Miss Shaw," he said, standing up. "I think we are done for today. Thank you for coming in."

The FBI agent walked around the desk and stuck his hand out to shake Ravyn's hand. Ravyn felt a little jolt of electricity as they touched.

"Oh, sorry," Agent Davis said, smiling. "Static electricity. It's these carpets. I'm always shocking myself on the doorknob."

"Oh, yeah," Ravyn said, nodding. "Electric heat during the winter doesn't help."

But was it static electricity, or was there some chemistry between them? Ravyn wondered. "This is nuts," she thought. "He's just questioning me. It's his job. I'll never see him again."

Agent Davis walked Ravyn back to the lobby. They didn't speak until she was near the front door.

"Miss Shaw, if I have any follow up questions, may I call you on your cell phone?" he asked, opening the door for her.

"Of course," she said, suddenly hoping she would hear from him again. "Good luck with the investigation."

"Thanks," he called out as Ravyn walked out. "I think I'm going to need it."

"So how was the meeting with the FBI?" Julie asked. "I can't believe I know someone now who has been questioned by the FBI!"

"It didn't go as badly as I thought," Ravyn said, shutting her office door so her co-workers couldn't hear her phone conversation. "And Agent Davis was a lot younger than I thought he'd be. He was a lot easier on the eyes than that Italian policewoman."

"Oh really? Just how young? How handsome? Was he wearing a wedding ring?" Julie asked. "Maybe this is how you meet the man of your dreams."

"Oh, Julie, you are too much! Why are you trying to play matchmaker all of a sudden? He was cute, though. Maybe a little younger than us. It was hard to tell. He had a bit of a boyish face. Sandy blond hair, nice build. A little taller than me, but not by much. And he was slightly tanned, you know, like he worked outside a lot."

"Maybe he golfs, or plays tennis."

"Maybe. I didn't ask any of that. It wasn't exactly a social meeting. I was there to be questioned, remember? He just went over the same questions the Italian police asked, but he did tell me they suspect someone from our cooking class might be involved in the robbery. Or he sort of suggested it, anyway."

"Really!? Who do you think did it?" Julie wanted to know.

"I can't really see any of my classmates being robbers, but I guess that would be the point, right? If they are true international jewelry thieves they aren't going to announce it. They'd be good at covering up what they were doing. At least, until they get caught."

"Do you think it was that weird couple from England?"

"Gosh, they were odd, but I'm not sure I can see Steve and India Prescott as jewelry thieves, although India did go on about money and their lack of it. She confided in me how she wished she'd married a rich man and not a poor man. And she did drag me into the jewelry shop several times."

"Maybe they were casing the joint," Julie exclaimed.

"Julie, I think you've been watching far too many police procedurals on TV," Ravyn laughed. "Who says 'casing the joint' anymore?"

"Well, you know what I mean," Julie said. "Sounds like they were trying to see the layout of the shop and were using you as an excuse."

"I just have a hard time picturing them as organized thieves," Ravyn said, thinking back on Steve and India. "They didn't seem all that organized! Half the time they were late for class."

"Oh, maybe that's when they were casing the shop!"

"Julie, it's not the Prescotts! I can't see Clare and Carl or Amy as thieves either. Gosh, Amy was always out clubbing with her friends. There were a couple of times she came to class hungover. Hardly good jewel thief material. Clare and Carl are retirees! They're too old to be thieves. They were probably in bed by 9 p.m. every night."

"No, maybe it *was* them! They just wanted you to *think* they were old farts. That was their perfect cover and they were actually cat burglars by night," Julie laughed.

Ravyn laughed now, too. "It's a good thing we're not on the case. We're pathetic detectives," she said.

"I won't quit my day job," Julie said, who was a stay-at-home mother. "Now, getting back to this Agent Davis. What is his first name?"

"I don't know," Ravyn said. "He actually never told me. He was pretty formal throughout our interview. He even recorded it. I did see the nameplate on his desk said L. Davis. His first name is probably Larry or Leonard or something."

"Maybe it's Lance, like Lance Bass, or Lorenzo," Julie chimed in, rolling her Rs as she said Lorenzo. "That would be romantic. *Lorenzo*. You'd go from one Italian man to another."

"I don't think Agent Davis is Italian," Ravyn said. "He didn't look like it. He was fair. Luca was the handsome dark Italian type."

"That doesn't mean anything," Julie said. "I took one of those ancestry DNA tests a few months ago and I have some Greek in me. I don't look Greek at all! Although I do love good spanakopita."

"That's true," Ravyn said. "I have some Irish in me and I don't have a single red hair or freckles."

"Not all Irish people have red hair or freckles," Julie said. "You can't go by that. Now, back to *Lorenzo*..."

"Don't call him that!" Ravyn cut in. "He's going to call me back for more questioning and I'm going to call him Lorenzo by accident and be embarrassed."

"Is he calling you back for more questioning? You didn't tell me that."

"Oh, well, I'm not sure he will. He asked if my cell was a good way to reach me."

"So, he wants to reach you again," Julie said brightly. "That's a good sign."

"Hey, he's an officer of the law," Ravyn said, trying to put a stop to her friend's suggestion that she and Agent Davis were going to be an item. "He's just doing his job. I have no idea if he'll call me back."

"For your sake, I hope he does," Julie said. "And if he does, be sure to meet him for coffee or something. Tell him it's too far to go to his office and meet him somewhere in the middle. Better yet, ask him to meet you for lunch."

"I think we are getting way ahead of ourselves, Julie. He is probably not really going to call me back. We are not going to have lunch or coffee or make beautiful babies together," Ravyn said.

"But you are thinking about it!" Julie said. "I know you! You've already thought of what your kids would look like!"

"Yes, but I just bet his name is Larry, and I don't think I can shout out the name 'Larry' during sex," Ravyn said.

"'Oh, Larry! Oh, Larry!'" Ravyn moaned into the phone, doing her best impersonation of Meg Ryan from the movie "When Harry Met Sally…" "That's not a good sex name," she said, returning to her normal voice.

Julie barked out a laugh. "You got that right! Larry's not going to cut it when you reach orgasm. That's when you have to yell, 'Oh, baby! Oh, baby!'"

Now Ravyn was laughing out loud. She looked up and realized she was getting a few stares through her office's glass window. "Hey, I'd better go. I think my co-workers could hear my part of the conversation and I'm getting funny looks."

"I bet you are! Everyone will wonder who you are talking to! Tell them it was your secret agent lover *Lorenzo*. Talk to you later," Julie said, as she hung up.

Ravyn looked up to see Joel Greenberg now standing in front of her window, giving her a big grin. His sweater vest today was red, black and white plaid, the colors of his beloved University of Georgia Bulldogs.

"Ugh! That's not what I need," Ravyn thought, as she walked over and opened her office door.

"Productive meeting?" Joel asked, wiggling his eyebrows at her.

Ravyn turned beet red and shut her door again.

Panna Cotta With Raspberry Sauce

Panna cotta literally means "cooked cream" and is a favorite dessert, whether you are Italian or not. This sweet creamy dessert is delicious topped with fresh seasonal fruit, such as raspberries, blackberries, blueberries or strawberries.

No berries? Panna cotta can also be made with or topped with other additives, such as lemon, coffee or caramel.

1 ¾ cup fresh cream
3 ½ Tbsp. sugar
Grated peel of 1 lemon
2 leaves of gelatin or about 2 tsp. of granulated plain gelatin (6 grams)
8 ounces, raspberries
1 Tbsp. sugar

Soak the gelatin leaves in cold water. Heat the cream, 3 ½ Tbsp. of sugar and lemon peel and boil gently for 1 minute. Take care that the cream does not boil over. Gently squeeze out the gelatin leaves and add to cream. Stir until gelatin is dissolved. Pour cream mixture into molds, such as ramekin cups or small dessert cups. Chill in refrigerator to set, about 4 hours.

Leave a few whole raspberries for decoration. Puree the remaining raspberries with the remaining sugar. Just before serving, turn out the set dessert and pour the raspberry sauce. Top with whole fruit. If not turning out the dessert, top it with sauce and whole fruit. Serves about 4.

Buon appetito!

Chapter 11

CAFFE

Ravyn could hear the phone ringing on her desk and rushed into her office. Samantha Hunt was calling.

"Hello, Samantha," Ravyn said, slightly out of breath.

"Ravyn, hello! I just wanted to call you personally to let you know we've hired a new editor, Jennifer Bagley. She comes highly recommended and plans to fly down to Atlanta later this week to meet the staff down there."

"Oh, that's great! I look forward to meeting her," Ravyn said, trying to sound excited, but really wishing Samantha was not leaving the company.

"And I'd like to invite you up for my farewell party here in New York," Samantha said. "I'm not sure what your schedule is, but we're having it on Thursday, January 22. I hope you can make it."

Ravyn looked quickly at her calendar. That might be cutting it close with the March issue beginning production in just a couple of weeks, but she'd like to say goodbye to Samantha personally.

"Let me check on flights and a hotel. I'd love to try to make it if I can."

"Wonderful. I'll send you the details in the invite and can recommend a couple of hotels near the restaurant where we are having the party. And Jennifer should be reaching out to you this week as well."

"Sounds great. I'm really going to miss you, Samantha," Ravyn said, starting to feel choked up. "Thank you for

175

believing in me and for giving me this job. I love it and I appreciate your taking a chance on me."

"You are a wonderful managing editor, and I have a feeling you will go far in this company," Samantha replied. "I'll see you on January 22 then."

Ravyn hung up and began checking on flights. Nothing was going to be all that cheap, but she really wanted to go. She found a flight she could swing, leaving early Thursday morning and returning to Atlanta early Saturday morning. She'd only have to get a hotel room for two nights.

Ravyn then checked her weather app to see what the temperature was in New York City. She gasped.

The city was experiencing a brutal cold snap, with overnight lows in the single digits. Ravyn didn't even own a heavy coat since winters in the South were fairly mild.

"I'm going to have to find a coat I can wear, too! This trip is costing more and more," she thought. "Maybe Julie will have something I can borrow."

She quickly called her friend.

"What's up?" Julie asked.

"I'm heading up for a quick trip to New York and the weather there is frigid. Do you have a coat I can borrow? I don't have anything warm enough. I'm already spending more than I want on the flight and I haven't booked my hotel yet. I'm hoping I don't have to buy a coat, too."

"You probably won't even find a coat now," Julie said. "It's January in Atlanta. The swimsuits are being put out on the shelves."

Ravyn laughed but knew it was probably true. Only in Atlanta did spring and summer clothes start arriving in stores in February.

"What am I going to do? I'll freeze to death. The high was 21 degrees today!"

"Crap that's cold. Let me see what's in my closet. I think I still have a jacket I bought when Rob and I went skiing two years ago."

"That would be awesome. I'd appreciate it."

"Do you have anything warm enough for your feet? Like boots?"

"I have dress boots," Ravyn said. "If I wear those up I won't have to try to pack them in a small carryon and can wear them to the party."

"That won't do. You'll need real boots, ugly little things with a warm lining so your toes won't fall off."

"I don't have anything like that. Where would I buy those?"

"Let me see if I have a pair that might fit you. Otherwise, go online and buy something now. If it is 21 degrees outside you will need to look like a polar bear when you get up there. Fashion kind of goes out the window in New York in the winter."

"Sounds like it."

"Hey, the girls are about to get off the bus," Julie said, referring to her daughters. "Let me call you back later tonight after I've checked on the coat and boots."

"Great. Thanks again. You are the best friend ever."

"Got that right," Julie said.

Ravyn had offered to pick Jennifer Bagley up at Hartsfield-Jackson Atlanta International Airport, but the new editor said she'd take a cab to the magazine's office before checking into her hotel.

Ravyn was nervous to meet the woman. They'd spoken briefly on the phone and Jennifer Bagley was all business. She didn't come off as warm and personable the way Samantha had been. Ravyn was hoping she'd just gotten the wrong impression of Jennifer. After all, it was a conversation over the phone. Maybe she was warmer in person.

Ravyn was walking to the break room for more coffee when an auburn-haired woman in a pale green sweater and green and tan plaid skirt stepped off the elevator into the magazine's lobby. She pulled a small wheeled suitcase behind her.

"Jennifer?" Ravyn asked, walking over and extending her hand, then realized Jennifer Bagley didn't have a free hand to shake.

"Yes. You are Ravyn, I presume," Jennifer said, looking Ravyn up and down.

Ravyn had dressed a little more formally today, knowing she was going to meet her new editor, but the look she got from Jennifer made her feel like she was dressed in rags.

"Yes," Ravyn replied. "Would you like to put your things in my office?"

"I think I'd rather put them in my office," Jennifer said.

Ravyn tried not to look shocked. "Her office?" she wondered. "Is she going to make Atlanta her home base and not New York?"

"Oh, do you need to work out of an office while you are here?" Ravyn asked.

"Yes, until I can get set up permanently."

"I didn't realize you'd be moving to Atlanta," Ravyn said. "I thought you'd be in New York."

"New York is lovely, but a bit expensive," Jennifer said, wheeling her suitcase down a row of offices, stopping to the left of Joel Greenberg's office. "Is this office empty?"

"Yes. And it's right next to our ad director. I'm sure you would be working closely with him," Ravyn said, trying to be helpful.

"And where is your office? I'm sure I will be working more closely with you," Jennifer said, turning to look at Ravyn.

"My office is just down the way, on the other side," she said, pointing. Ravyn's office wasn't a corner office by any means. She was stationed closer to the production side of the team, which worked well when the magazine was nearing completion of an issue. Chase Riley and Gavin Owens' offices were next to hers. Craig Taylor, the graphic designer who had put in a good word for her to help her get the job at *Cleopatra*, was in a cubicle close by as well.

"Oh," Jennifer said. "I assumed your office would be next to mine. Well, we can move you later."

Jennifer opened the office door and wheeled her bag inside.

"This will need some work," she said, putting her hands on her hips. "This is as dirty as can be. Can you call the cleaning service for me and get them up here to dust and mop this place?"

"Ah, sure," Ravyn said, alarmed that she was being bossed around like hired help and not a colleague. "I'll make that call shortly. Would you like me to show you around and introduce you to everyone?"

"I'd like you to do it now, please," Jennifer said, turning to Ravyn. "I need to get started right away here. There are a lot of problems that need to be worked out."

Problems? What problems? Ravyn wondered. Samantha Hunt had never expressed any concern over problems at the magazine.

"Of course, I'll just step down to my office," Ravyn said, anxious to get away from Jennifer. "If you need water or coffee or anything, the break room is down the hall to your right."

Ravyn practically sprinted to her office, closing the door behind her. She took a deep breath, trying to tamp down the anxiety she was starting to feel. She knew without a doubt she and Jennifer Bagley were not going to be friends.

"I really don't understand why this is the cover story for March," Jennifer Bagley said, looking at the spreadsheet for the upcoming magazine's issue. "Who authorized this? And why did you go? We could have hired a freelancer to write this up for much cheaper. And where are the photos? Why are we using so much stock art?"

Ravyn tried to calmly explain the trip and the fiasco with the memory card, leaving out how she had been questioned by the police.

"This will never happen again," Jennifer said, forcefully. "I will not authorize these personal junkets, Ravyn, so don't get any ideas that a perk like this will come your way again."

"No, ma'am," was all Ravyn could say.

Jennifer Bagley was slightly older than Ravyn, but not by much. Ravyn thought she was probably in her late 30s or early 40s, but she looked and acted older than that.

Ravyn had pieced together that Jennifer had come from California where she had worked on various lifestyle magazines there. She had decided to make Atlanta her home base because she had an aunt and uncle nearby. In fact, Jennifer was living with them temporarily while she looked at houses in the area.

Jennifer also had a cat and Ravyn, at first, thought that commonality would foster a better friendship. But no.

Jennifer Bagley was going to run a tight ship and that ship was a U-boat, Ravyn surmised.

"I think we should come up with a different cover story for March," Jennifer was saying, poring over the rough outline of all of the stories for the issue. "Without solid photos, this cooking school story just won't do."

Ravyn felt crestfallen. She'd worked so hard on the article! She had laid it out over a four-page spread, with the contributed photos from Dolores and the stock art she and Chase had found. And now it was going to be relegated to the back of the magazine and likely trimmed to one page. It wasn't fair!

"I disagree," Ravyn said, trying to keep the emotion out of her voice. "Many people take destination vacations now like they do with destination weddings. I think this will get a lot of interest. Plus, it's late in the production cycle for me to assign out another story."

"Well, I'm sure you can whip up another article on a different topic in time," Jennifer said, dismissing Ravyn's input and turning back to her computer. "Please send me three ideas by the end of today."

"I'll email them to you today," she said. "And I'm out of the office tomorrow and Friday. I'm flying up for Samantha Hunt's going away party."

"Can you afford the time?" Jennifer asked, looking up from her computer at Ravyn. "You just told me we are late in the production cycle."

"Well, I already have my plane ticket and hotel booked," Ravyn started to stammer.

"Very well then," Jennifer said, waving her hand dismissively. "Go play while we all stay here and work."

Ravyn got back to her office near tears. Who was this witch and how on earth was Ravyn going to work with her?

"Julie, I don't know what I'm going to do!" Ravyn said, sobbing to her friend. "She expects me to come up with three story ideas for the cover and write one of them! Like I can just pull a great story out of my ass!"

Ravyn was in her car in the office parking garage. She hadn't wanted anyone to hear how upset her conversation with Jennifer had made her.

"Oh, honey. I don't know what to say. She sounds like a complete bitch!" Julie was saying, trying to be sympathetic.

"She treats me like I'm a 3-year-old, or worse, the hired help," Ravyn cried. "I've been a reporter, editor, and writer for years, and yet she micromanages my every move. She makes me feel like I have no news sense. Said she couldn't understand why the cooking school feature was even a cover story idea! She's treating me like I don't have a brain in my head!"

"Sweetie, maybe it will get better," Julie tried to reassure her friend. "Maybe she's being all alpha male because she's so new and insecure."

"No, she's 100 percent a control freak," Ravyn shot back. "I haven't even worked with her for two weeks and I'm wondering if I can hold on."

"Ravyn, you don't mean that. You love this job," Julie said, alarmed.

"I do love this job," Ravyn said, beginning to cry again. "Or I did. I just don't know, Julie. She's awful."

"Well, go to New York," Julie said. "It will be a little break from her and maybe when you come back she'll be calmer and you'll have a better perspective. Don't do anything crazy, OK? Like, don't go back to the office and quit. You love this job and we need to figure out how to make it better."

"I know you are right," Ravyn said, wiping her tears with the back of her hand. "I do love this job. I need to put my big girl panties on and go back up to the office. I just hope I don't burst into tears in front of anyone!"

"That's my girl," Julie said. "I believe in you."

Ravyn landed in New York City early Thursday afternoon, glad she had missed the big rainstorm that had hit the city earlier in the week. She was a little nervous that a winter storm was predicted for the next day when she was supposed to leave Saturday. She checked into her hotel, changed and hailed a taxi to the restaurant where the festivities had already begun.

"Ravyn! I'm so glad you could make it!" Samantha said, greeting her near the bar. "We're in the room in the back and we have a small bar set up there. Wine, beer and a few cocktails that are free. If you want something else, you'll have to come up here and buy it."

"I'm sure a glass of red wine will be perfect. It's freezing out there!" Rayvn said, stamping her feet and pulling off the parka Julie had found for her to wear.

"The coat check is over there," Samantha pointed. "Then come back and fill me in on Jennifer Bagley."

"Oh, God!" Ravyn exclaimed, rolling her eyes, then realized she had done it in front of Samantha. "Sorry! Let me put my things in the coat closet."

Ravyn hurried off. She dropped off her coat and made a beeline for the free bar in the back of the room, getting a big glass of red wine and taking a few gulps before returning to talk to Samantha.

"So, I take it you are not a fan of Jennifer Bagley," said Samantha, who was wearing a long cream-colored knit dress with a wide gold belt around her waist. Her makeup was flawless and Samantha looked like she should be in a fashion magazine, Ravyn thought.

"It's early days, I guess, but she's rubbing me the wrong way," Ravyn said, honestly. "She's a bit of a micromanager and I'm not one to be micromanaged."

"Ah, I was a bit afraid of that," Samantha said, pulling Ravyn over to a quieter corner of the room. "She wasn't my first choice, to be honest, but the company liked her a lot. She's good on paper. I was a bit surprised that she wanted to work out of the Atlanta office. Most people who take jobs with us want to be in New York. It's usually always seen as a step up. But that's fine. She can work out of Atlanta and get up to meetings here easily."

"Why are you leaving, Samantha? I really liked working with you. I thought we worked well together," Ravyn said, almost pleading.

"We did. An opportunity arose that I just couldn't say no to," she replied. "I'm not at liberty to say where I am going just yet, but I will let you know. And Ravyn, try to give Jennifer a chance. I think you are a real asset to Horizon Publishing, and I can see you going further within the organization."

Ravyn was shocked. She had no idea Samantha had thought so highly of her.

"That's wonderful to hear," she replied. "I love working for *Cleopatra*. I feel like I've found my calling there."

"Do you think you'd always call Atlanta home? Would you consider moving to one of our other cities if an opportunity came up?" Samantha asked.

"I hadn't really thought about it since I'm still so new to the company. I'll have been with Horizon for a whole year in a couple of months. But I can see myself growing with the company. I'd never say never to a good opportunity, Samantha."

"Good. I'm glad to hear it," she answered. "I'll let the powers that be know that. Even if I'm not with the company for much longer, I still want to show them I know how to groom talent. Now, go get some food. I've got to talk to the CEO over there."

Samantha pointed to a tall gray-haired man in a dark gray business suit. He looked very handsome and very happy to see Samantha, Ravyn thought.

Ravyn awoke Friday morning in her hotel bed and stretched. She'd stayed at the party longer than she had expected, rolling in after midnight. More people from the corporate office had arrived and Ravyn had chatted with the chief financial officer and his wife and the director of human resources and her wife for a good part of the evening.

She'd reintroduced herself to Josie, the managing editor of *Athena*, the name of the New York magazine, and *Calliope*'s managing editor Joyce. They had traded war stories about freelancers, tight deadlines, missed deadlines and advertising flubs. It was fun to talk shop with women who understood the job. There were a couple of men who were managing editors of some other magazines, but they hadn't been able to make it.

Ravyn stretched again and looked at her phone to see the time. Even though it was cold outside, she was hoping to take a walk in Central Park. She hadn't brought running clothes and didn't think she owned any athletic gear that would stand up to a New York January, but if she bundled up in those ugly boots and parka Julie had let her borrow, she would be alright for a stroll. "I really want to see

Strawberry Fields, the Dakota building and the Alice in Wonderland statue," Ravyn thought.

She pushed herself out of bed, showered and bundled up, prepared to find a coffee shop for a bagel and coffee. "You can't come to New York and not have a bagel for breakfast," Ravyn said to herself.

She was standing in line to order when her cell phone rang. It was her former boyfriend, Marc Linder.

"Hey, Marc," Ravyn said as a greeting.

"Hi, Ravyn. Happy New Year!"

"Happy New Year to you, too."

"Did you do your New Year's run this year?" he asked.

Ravyn was surprised he'd remembered, but then remembered last New Year's Eve she'd spent the night at Marc's and had almost missed the race the following morning. They were enjoying other athletic activities together.

"Yes, I did make the race this year," she said. "What's up?"

"I was just calling to see if you wanted to have that lunch we talked about," he said.

"Oh, Marc, I'm sorry that slipped my mind," she said. "I'm actually in New York this weekend."

"Oh. Are you there for work?" he asked.

"Not really. Well, sort of. My boss is leaving the company and they threw her a farewell party last night."

"Sounds nice."

"It was. I'm going to miss her. Listen, sorry to cut you off, but I'm in line to order coffee and I'm just about to the front. Can I call you back about lunch?"

"Sure. It was great talking to you, Ravyn."

"Nice to talk with you, too, Marc."

Ravyn hung up, ordered, and walked through Central Park, finding the iconic "Imagine" mosaic in Strawberry Fields, wondering if Marc Linder was indeed trying to rekindle their romance.

Tiramisu

Italians take their coffee seriously. They even put it in some of their best desserts. Tiramisu means "pick me up" or "cheer me up" and contains coffee to do just that. In Italy, coffee usually means espresso, and you can use espresso, if desired, in this dessert. I tend to use strong regular coffee. This recipe is from the kitchen of two women I met in Tuscany, Emma, and Martina. I always add Amaretto to the recipe, but you can leave that out if you choose. I've also substituted decaf coffee when needed.

3 pieces semi-sweet chocolate (finely grated with a zester/grater)
4 egg yolks
4 egg whites
4 Tbsp. sugar
2 packages of ladyfinger cookies or biscuits (the hard cookies or biscuits work best)
16 oz. mascarpone cheese (sweet Italian cream cheese)
About ½ pot of coffee (regular or decaf)
Amaretto (optional)

Brew about a half pot of coffee, then add amaretto (optional, and as much or little as desired) to the brewed coffee.

Beat egg whites with a mixer until light and fluffy and peaks form as if making meringue.

In a separate bowl, mix mascarpone cheese, egg yolks and sugar with a mixer.

Blend fluffy egg whites into mascarpone mixture with a wooden spoon. Mix should be light yellow and creamy.

Layer bottom of a 9 by 13 glass pan with ⅓ of the mascarpone mixture, then sprinkle with ⅓ of grated chocolate.

Next dip ladyfinger cookies in the coffee and layer on top of the mascarpone mix, filling the bottom of the pan. The cookies will soak up some of the moisture of the mixture, so don't be alarmed if the cookies are still a bit hard as you layer them in the pan.

Repeat for the second layer, starting with mascarpone, chocolate and the ladyfingers dipped in coffee. Top off with the last ⅓ of mascarpone mix and a final sprinkle of chocolate. There will likely be coffee left over.

Chill at least 1 hour until ready to serve. Serves about 12.

Buon appetito!

Lisa R. Schoolcraft

Chapter 12

Digestivo

Ravyn sat down at her desk and heard the ping of an incoming email on her cell phone. She looked down to see a message from Jennifer Bagley. *Please see me in my office as soon as you arrive,* it said.

"Good morning to you, too, bitch, I'll get there when I get there," Ravyn muttered, putting away her handbag and booting up her desktop.

Jennifer Bagley stuck her head in Ravyn's office. "There you are. I asked to see you in my office, please," she said.

"I just got in and got your message," Ravyn said, sharply. "I'll be right in."

Jennifer gave Ravyn a look, then turned on her heel and walked back to her own office.

"Shit," Ravyn thought. "Now I've probably pissed her off. Not a good way to start my day."

Ravyn knocked on the door jam and Jennifer looked up from her desk.

"Please come in and shut the door, Ravyn," she said.

Inwardly, Ravyn groaned. "I'm about to get chewed out."

"Ravyn, I think you and I may have gotten off on the wrong foot," Jennifer began.

"Ya think?" Ravyn said to herself.

"I don't want our relationship to be adversarial. We have to work together to make *Cleopatra* the best that it can be," Jennifer continued. "I've given this some consideration, and I've decided we should go ahead with the cooking school article on the cover."

Ravyn could feel relief wash over her.

"Thank God!" she blurted. "I mean, I had one interview set up for the 'Spring Fling' idea for the new cover, but it was going to be a tight squeeze to get everything done by the time we went to production next week."

"Well, I still want you to work on that story. Moving forward, I'll be assigning out all cover stories, but you will still be in charge of all interior content," Jennifer said.

Ravyn felt as if she'd been slapped. All editorial content had been her job, including the cover story. She'd only had to get the blessing of the story ideas from Samantha, who usually loved her ideas. What was going on? Was this a power grab?

"I don't understand," Ravyn stammered. "We already have the editorial calendar for this year. All of the cover story ideas are set. Are you telling me we're not going to do any of those?"

The entire staff, with input from art director Chase Riley, photographer Gavin Owens, advertising director Joel Greenberg and others, had agreed on the editorial calendar for 2015. The cover story ideas for each issue were published on the magazine's website so advertisers and others would know what editorial direction each month would take. The July/August issue, for example, was a back-to-school issue.

"Oh no. We will use some of those ideas," Jennifer said. "Some of them will do. But I'll be reworking the editorial calendar to better reflect some of the ideas I have for cover stories for the rest of the year."

Ravyn could not believe her ears. Silently she sat fuming.

"Is something the matter, Ravyn?" Jennifer asked.

"No. Nothing is wrong," she lied. Ravyn was not going to blow up at her new boss of three weeks. That wouldn't end well for anyone, least of all her.

"Very well," Jennifer said. "I'm sure I can count on your help to let the staff know of these changes. If you'd send an email out right away, I'd appreciate it."

Ravyn stood up and walked out of the office without another word.

"Oh sure, let me be the bad guy in all this!" Ravyn thought.

She typed out an email and sent it to the staff, then waited for the first person to storm into her office. It was Chase.

"What the hell is this all about?" he said, walking in and shutting the door.

"Jennifer wants to assign out all cover stories with her own ideas," Ravyn said, trying to keep her voice neutral.

"What the hell?" Chase said.

Joel Greenberg didn't bother to knock, he just walked into her office next. "What's the meaning of this email?" he said, shaking a print out at her.

"Listen, don't blame the messenger!" Ravyn said, defensively. "Jennifer wants to assign out and change the cover stories."

"But we have an editorial calendar! I am lining up advertisers based on that calendar," Greenberg said. "That little red-head is playing with fire!"

"Joel, calm down and shut the door. She'll hear you!" Ravyn said.

"I don't give a shit what she hears!" he said louder, but Ravyn was already up and shutting the door with Chase and Joel inside her office.

"Listen, I'm not happy about it either," Ravyn said.

"I bet! She just took away most of what you do!" Joel said.

Ravyn winced. That was a blow. She had liked having complete editorial control, within reason, of the magazine. With her former boss Samantha in New York, Ravyn realized she'd had a lot of responsibility. With Jennifer now in Atlanta, that seemed to be changing.

Ravyn took a deep breath. "Listen, you know we sometimes change the editorial calendar as we move through the year."

"Yes, but that's once, maybe twice a year!" Joel said. "We've never just completely changed it."

"I know, I know. She did say she would be changing some of it, so maybe not all of it gets changed," Ravyn said, not liking that she was having to defend a decision she didn't agree with.

"But we all agreed on the editorial calendar," Chase said. "We all had input."

"I know," Ravyn answered.

"She's like a dictator coming in," Joel said. "I don't like it."

"Well, join the club," Ravyn said. Ravyn realized she wasn't being very professional, but she was frustrated.

"Reminds me of when David Watson was editor," Chase said, turning to Joel. "Remember him? Jesus, we used to go out for drinks after we put every issue into production because it was a miracle we got to press. He always made changes at the last minute."

"Oh, yeah, I remember him. He came to the Atlanta office a few times and I had to go up to New York to meet with him more than once," Joel said, sitting on the corner of Ravyn's desk. "Always called me up to New York right before my vacation, that asshole. I'd come back to Atlanta, get home and turn right back around to the airport. He knew my vacation schedule because he had to clear it. Like I said, asshole."

"Why did he leave? Didn't he become a real estate agent up there?" Chase asked. "Probably making more money now than he did with Horizon."

"Don't bet on it," Joel said. "The rumor I heard is, he was a little sticky-fingered with his budget. Had some sort of slush fund in his budget that he somehow got past the corporate bigwigs. The fund was for staff to order dinner on the nights they went to production. Except no one at any of the magazines ever got dinner. But the budget was always empty at the end of the year."

"Yeah, and then there was Ryan."

"Oh yeah! He was managing editor when I got here," Chase said. "He'd stay late and go into the production department and watch porn."

Ravyn's eyebrows shot up in surprise. She'd never heard this kind of gossip. She'd only known Samantha. She didn't know about the prior staff. "In production? Why'd he go in production?"

"Didn't want anyone to know he was watching porn on a company computer, or at least not his. But one night the computer crashed and Ryan couldn't get it booted back up. The next day they got it up and running and there was full-blown porn on the screen." Chase was belly laughing remembering the shenanigans. Then he turned serious. "Jennifer," he said. "What are we going to do about her?"

"What *can* we do about her?" Ravyn asked.

"Well, we may have to start meeting up for drinks again if this keeps up," Chase said, shaking his head.

"I'll buy the first round," Joel said, as he stood up and left the office.

Ravyn's cell phone rang, but she didn't recognize the number. It was late afternoon on January 29 and she was busy trying to finish up some edits for the March issue.

Ravyn started to let the call go to voicemail when she thought better of it and answered.

"Hello, this is Ravyn."

"Miss Shaw, this is Agent Davis, with the FBI," said a familiar voice.

"Oh! Agent Davis, hello. I wasn't expecting to hear from you again. I guess I should say I was hoping I wouldn't hear from you again." Ravyn cringed. That wasn't exactly what she meant. "I mean, no news is good news, right?"

"Miss Shaw, am I disturbing you?"

"Oh, no, not at all. I'm just finishing up some of the articles for the magazine. We found some photos that would work for the cooking school story. You know, after I lost all my photos."

"Yes, I remember that. Would it be possible to meet me today? Say at the Starbucks on Georgia Tech's campus? I think that is kind of between both of our offices."

"Probably easier for me than for you, but I can meet you there. Does it have to be today?"

"I think you'll be happier if we meet today if that's possible," Agent Davis said.

"You are sounding very secret agent-y," Ravyn teased. "Can you tell me what this is about?"

"How about I meet you in an hour and then you'll see," he said.

"Sure. I'll meet you there."

Parking on the Georgia Tech campus was never easy, especially now that classes were back in session after the holiday break.

Ravyn eased her Honda Civic into a parking spot in a surface lot across from the coffee shop, trying not to feel excited about seeing the handsome FBI agent.

In the weeks since she had seen him, she'd thought about him a few times, thinking how much nicer he was than the Italian police and remembering his boyish smile. "He has a nice smile," she thought, smiling as she opened the door to Starbucks.

Agent Davis waved a hand as he stood up from a small table. The Starbucks was actually inside a Barnes & Noble bookstore on campus and was on the small side. Ravyn was glad to see he'd grabbed a table or they would have had to stand to talk.

"Why don't you sit at the table and I'll grab us a couple of coffees," he said. "What do you like?"

"I can get the coffee," Ravyn said.

"Sorry, I can't accept any gifts as an FBI agent," Agent Davis said.

"Not even coffee?" Ravyn asked, surprised.

"Not even coffee," he said.

"Well, I'll take a regular cup of coffee and I can fix it at the milk bar over there," Ravyn said, pointing to the stand where the creamer, sugar and stir sticks sat.

"Great. Be right back."

Soon Agent Davis returned with two coffee cups, placing them carefully down on the table. Ravyn doctored her coffee with half and half and a sugar packet and sat back down.

As she was blowing on her hot coffee, Agent Davis pulled a small flash drive from his jacket pocket and slid it across the table to her.

"What's this?" Ravyn asked, puzzled.

"Officer Conti wanted you to have this."

"Who's Officer Conti?" Ravyn asked.

Cooking Up Trouble

"I believe you knew him as Luca Ricci," Agent Davis said, holding her gaze.

"What?!" Ravyn almost shouted and got a few stares from the college students sitting around her.

"Officer Conti found a memory card on one of the jewel thieves when he was arrested in England," he said.

"Luca was arrested in England?" Ravyn said, shocked.

"No, no. Sorry. Officer Conti made the arrest. He found the memory card in the possession of one of the jewel thieves he arrested in England and he thought you would want the photos. Didn't you say you knew Officer Conti? He made it sound like you two knew each other well."

Ravyn blushed deeply. "Yes, I knew him, but I didn't know he was a police officer. He told me he was in finance or financial services. Something like that."

"It's my understanding Officer Conti was on the case of the international jewel thieves. I believe he was undercover."

"He was undercover alright," Ravyn blurted out, then blushed, even more, when Agent Davis laughed. "And this was found on one of the suspects?" she asked, trying to recover her composure.

"Yes, the two people arrested were at the cooking school with you," Agent Davis explained, casually blowing on his hot coffee.

"Steve and India?!"

"No, it was Robert Benedict and his wife Constance. I think you knew them as Carl and Clare Richards," the FBI agent said.

"WHAT?!" Ravyn nearly knocked her coffee over.

"They are part of a ring of international jewel thieves," he explained, leaning toward her. "Jewels and jewelry are very easy to smuggle and very hard to identify. Think about it. A gun has a serial number. Even if you take the serial number off, there are still identifying marks on a weapon that make it easier to trace. But jewels, well, they are harder. Is one diamond different from another? To a trained eye, yes, but it's much, much harder to identify once it is stolen. Jewels can be cut or shaped differently. Thieves can be very hard to catch. Officer Conti did a great job."

"And Carl and Clare, I mean, Robert and Constance were found in England?"

"New Scotland Yard and Officer Conti caught up with them in Bath, England," the agent said. "Mr. Benedict still had your memory card on his person. Officer Conti downloaded the files and sent them over to me. I put them on this flash drive for you. They have to keep the original memory card as evidence. But he said he thought you might want the photos. He included a note, as well."

Agent Davis reached into his jacket pocket and handed her a folded note.

"Don't worry," he said. "I didn't read it. It seemed personal."

Ravyn took the note with a trembling hand.

"Cara, Ravyn. I am sorry I had to be a bit deceitful with you. I was undercover in this big case. We were so close to solving it, and you had access to the school. Dennis said he could introduce us, but I never thought you would be so beautiful. So lovely. I never meant for you to get hurt. I have had words with Angelica Bianchi for how she treated you. I only hope you can forgive me. You are wonderful, bella. I will always keep you in my heart. Luca"

Ravyn could feel tears at the back of her eyes. Luca hadn't tried to ghost her. He had to catch the criminals!

She put the letter down, smiling and felt the flash drive in her other hand. The photos! Ravyn was so happy she reached over and grabbed Agent Davis's hand.

"Thank you, Agent Davis! You've just saved the March issue of *Cleopatra* — maybe even my job!"

"Happy to help," he said, not moving his hand away. "And please, call me Luke."

"Luke?" Ravyn asked.

"Yes, that's my first name. I thought you knew."

Ravyn shook her head. She remembered the initial L on the agent's nameplate and how she and Julie had made fun of what they thought it might stand for. Lorenzo, indeed. She never guessed it could be Luke.

"Thank God it's not Larry!" she thought. "Luke. Luca. What a coincidence."

Luca's odd behavior now began to make some sense: Why he didn't want his picture taken. Why he had never given her his phone number. Why he had left during the middle of the night. And why he had struck up a friendship with her in the first place. He had to keep an eye out for Carl and Clare. Or rather, Robert and Constance. He may not have meant for her to get hurt, but she did, she thought. She frowned. "Why the long face, Miss Shaw?" Luke asked. "I thought you'd be happy to have the photos."

"I am Agent Davis, I mean, Luke. And please, call me Ravyn. It's just," Ravyn let out a sigh. "Officer Conti's friendship with me was a lie? Or just part of his job? Part of his undercover work?"

"I wouldn't know about that, Ravyn," Luke said, shrugging. "I know the police suspected the Benedicts were part of the theft ring and they were at the cooking school with you. There have been been similar robberies of jewelry shops in Spain, apparently when they were there as well. Does it really matter now?"

"No," Ravyn shook her head. "Officer Conti and I were just friends, after all. He was a wonderful tour guide and no more."

"Ravyn, your trip to Rome sounds interesting. I've always wanted to go there. I have a little bit of Italian on my grandmother's side. She came over from somewhere in Tuscany, I think. I don't remember much of her. She died when I was young, but I do remember some of her cooking. I'd love to hear more about the cooking school. Did you really cook a lot there?"

"Yes. Cooked, ate and drank. I think we drank wine with every meal we cooked. I came back with lots of recipes," she said, glad to change the subject. "There's a roasted chicken dish I really like making. But when I do, I end up eating chicken all week."

"Sounds delicious," Luke said, leaning in toward her again.

"It is," Ravyn admitted. She looked down at his tanned hands and fingers and saw no trace of a wedding ring or tan line indicating where one should have been. "Luke, are you officially off of the case now?"

"This pretty much wraps it up for me. There will just be a little more paperwork on my end, but I'm done."

"Would you like to come over for dinner sometime? I can make that roasted chicken."

"I'd love to. We can go over your statements about the case again," he said, smiling.

"I thought you said you were off the case!" she said, surprised.

"I am. But I have some new interrogation techniques I need to try out. I've been told I wasn't harsh enough last time."

"Sounds like we might be cooking up trouble," Ravyn said, grinning back at him.

Limoncello

The digestivo is served after the coffee in Italy. It's the drink that concludes the meal. Grappa or limoncello are both common digestivos, meant to ease the digestion of a long meal. Limoncello is a wonderful after-dinner drink, usually served very cold. Keep it stored in the refrigerator or placed in the freezer for a short time before serving. Be warned, I've broken a bottle of limoncello keeping it in the freezer too long!

14 fluid oz. vodka
14 fluid oz. water
1 ½ cups of sugar
8 lemons without wax on the skin

If the lemons have wax on the skin, soak in warm water and scrub lightly to remove. Zest all eight lemons, taking care not to get any bitter white pith in the bowl.

Heat half the water to dissolve the sugar. Pour into the bowl containing the lemon zest and add vodka and remaining water. Stir to make sure all of the sugar is dissolved. Cover and leave at room temperature for 48 to 72 hours.

Strain the lemon zest out of the bowl and pour liquid into a bottle. Store in the refrigerator and serve cold.

Buon appetito!

Afterword

Other books by Lisa R. Schoolcraft

Smartphone, Dumb User

Made in United States
Troutdale, OR
08/04/2024

21759829R10125